Twelve optimistic MM stories, one for every month of the year.

How do men meet? Each story is connected to a holiday or event—Epiphany, Valentine's Day, Pi Day, Arbor Day, Mothers' Day, Fathers' Day, summer vacation, a rodeo, Labor Day, Columbus Day, Thanksgiving, and Hanukkah—but may not be quite the celebration you're expecting.

Neither may the men, and when these men meet, attraction does not always equal love—at least immediately—but chemistry finds a way.

GAY ALL YEAR

Richard May

A NineStar Press Publication

www.ninestarpress.com

Gay All Year

Printed in the USA

Print ISBN: 978-1-64890-075-4

First Edition, August, 2020

Also available in eBook, ISBN: 978-1-64890-074-7

WARNING:
This book contains sexually explicit content, which is only suitable for mature readers, depictions of racial prejudice, racist language, racial stereotypes, homophobic slurs, infidelity, puppy play, death of a partner, and abuse by a priest.

To my partner Wayne Goodman, first and always

January

Epiphany

I never meant to live in San Francisco again, but here I was. At first, it was just a visit but when I saw how advanced the effects of my mother's lung cancer were, I decided I couldn't leave her to institutional caregivers and fly back to Boston, so I took a leave of absence, and then I telecommuted, and finally, my company offered me a transfer to the office in Menlo Park.

I also never expected to be inside a Catholic church again, but here I was. I had successfully avoided them in Boston, which is no easy trick when you're Irish and raised Catholic. But now, I was back inside Saint Paul's, fulfilling a deathbed promise to my mother. "Don't blame God," she had advised between wheezes and made me agree to go to mass. I wanted to scream. Of course, I blamed God and every fucking priest and every fucking Catholic in the world, but I bit my tongue and said I'd go, thinking her funeral mass would fulfill the promise. "And my funeral mass doesn't count," she'd said with the remainder of a twinkle in her eye. Trapped—and I didn't even get to scream.

I had put it off for six months until I'd run into Mrs. Andreozzi on Tuesday past, and she'd mentioned Saint Paul's had a new priest. "Very handsome," she informed me as if that were enough of an inducement for a gay twentysomething male. And perhaps it was because the very next Sunday I entered the building, genuflected toward the altar, crossed myself, and took a seat in a pew.

There was an excellent turnout of ladies and gay men. And Mrs. Andreozzi was right: the new priest was very handsome. He was a tall man, with dark wavy hair combed straight back from his forehead, regular features, and noticeably wide shoulders. Nothing at all like Father Michael, with his thinning red hair, sallow complexion, and sagging jowls. I hoped he was different from Father Michael in other ways as well, for the altar boys' sakes.

After mass, I tried to slip past the line of parishioners telling the new priest how much they liked this or that, but he stepped away from an older woman in midsentence to intercept me.

"Thank you for coming," he said, barring my way with his conspicuous body and extended right hand. "Father Adrian Doyle." I shook the hand hesitantly. Touching a priest was, and probably always would be, disgusting to me. Father Adrian's hand was warm, but then so had been Father Michael's.

"Stephen Kinney," I said. The priest's bright-blue eyes momentarily ceased sparkling. Apparently, he'd heard the name before. *I'm sure he has*, I thought with satisfaction.

"Good to see you, Stephen. See you next Sunday," he said, his eyes recovering. He gave my hand a final shake and went back to his line of well-wishers. I walked outside without a commitment, continued down the steps to Church Street and around the second corner to my parents' house. The park across the street was full of dogs, kids, and adult supervision. I had been one of those kids once upon a time.

I had mostly happy childhood memories and was on quite a nostalgia trip, integrating my things with those of my parents and grandparents. The park was certainly convenient for walking Boris, my mother's old and needy dog. Why she wanted a Russian wolfhound neither my sister nor I quite understood. It had always been Irish setters while our father was alive. Still, after Mom passed, Anne Marie and I fought over who'd get custody of Boris. Nothing else in the estate mattered as much. I won because I was already walking the dog on a twice-daily basis, feeding him, and acting *in loco parentis*. My sister lived outside Chicago. If the trip east didn't kill Boris, the Midwestern winter would.

Monday's alarm woke me from disturbing dreams vaguely remembered. Men in black, oppressive shadows, Father Adrian naked. The latter image disturbed me most of all. I rushed to be vertical and tried to ignore my erection.

After struggling into jogging clothes, I opened the door for Boris's stroll to the dog run. Immediately, an unfamiliar tenor yelled "Stephen!" at me. One of a crowd of runners passing by was waving. "Father Adrian!" he shouted in explanation, pointing at his chest, which was already eye-catching enough, even in a baggy sweatshirt. I waved back in a jerky side to side motion and watched the healthy bodies disappear. The priest's butt was obvious in his skimpy running shorts, shifting left and right, left and right. Lustful thoughts came to mind. "Good God," I said out loud. Boris whined. "Yes," I agreed. "Let's have none of that. Come on, boy."

The old dog broke into an eager amble across the street. After a few minutes sniffing this fascinating scent, inhaling that arousing aroma, and doing his business, we recrossed the road. I let Boris in the front door and took off at a trot toward Sanchez. Of course, I ran into the Saint Paul's joggers on their return trip.

"Join us!" the priest yelled, his tousled hair and happy face strong inducements. I heard several other runners second his call, which surprised me, given what I'd cost them. Misery loves company, I suppose, or maybe just following the lead of their priest. Still.

I was about to ignore all of them when someone dropped out of the line and yanked me into it. "Tony!" I yelped. Tony Rodriguez, the boy I'd had a crush on in sixth grade. The man who'd stood by me during the lawsuit. I assumed he'd left town. He hadn't been at my mother's funeral, and I hadn't run into him at Safeway or Royal Cleaners.

"I've been in Iraq, and Marylee was at her mother's," he exclaimed as if he read minds. Oh, right. He was in the National Guard.

I took up the rhythm of the run, Tony's admirable thighs racing alongside mine.

"Aren't you almost done?" I asked, looking for an escape route.

"I wish," he said, flashing the ten-thousand-dollar smile Dr. Davis of Twenty-fourth Street had given to both of us.

I looked ahead at the priest. "What do you think of the new guy?"

"He's good," Tony said, between inhales and exhales. "Up on technology."

"I thought his Epiphany homily was good," I said. "Especially the part about everyday epiphanies."

Tony nearly stopped running. "You went to mass?" he said, looking at me as if I were lying.

"I promised my mother."

"Uh huh," Tony grunted. Then he gave me a grin. "And Father Adrian *is* a good-looking dude," he said. Just as quickly, his face collapsed in dismay. "I'm sorry, Steve."

I kept looking ahead, which is what I'd told myself to do after I stopped going to church. The priest's butt was obscured by those of less worthy men. "No worries," I told him, but it might not have been loud enough for Tony to hear. In any case, we talked of other things before he peeled off for home a few blocks later.

"Be sure to call me about that beer!" he yelled. I gave him a thumbs-up. *If only he were gay*, I thought for the thousandth time.

The rest of us finally reached the steps of Saint Paul's. No one else had spoken to me since Tony had left for home and a shower. At the church, I meant to follow his example, but Father Adrian held me back. "If you ever want to talk," he said. His fingers gripped my arm with familiar strength and uncomfortable insistence.

"I did my talking to the attorneys," I replied and pulled out of his grasp. His face was even more handsome when less under control.

"My offer stands," he said, his lovely mouth now grim. "Don't let the crimes of a few evil men get in the way of your relationship with God."

I laughed in his face. "A few? See you later, Father." I trotted south without looking back.

I had been a cute, blond-haired boy of nine when I came under Father Michael's auspices. I was twenty-four when I organized other boys who'd become his prey to sue the diocese. There had been a settlement; the church knew it couldn't win. I bought the condo in Boston with my portion of the proceeds.

However, later that day, Father Adrian's offer was codified in a text.

> *Good to see you at church, Stephen. Hope you'll be with us again next Sunday. And, if you want to talk, my door is always open.*

He gave me a phone number. The question was, how did he get mine?

I should have deleted the text but didn't. I was impressed he spelled my name correctly and by his follow-up. In fact, I kept rereading it until I finally called the number. Mary Flannery answered. She had been the parish secretary for decades. After I said my name, there was a pause before Mary responded.

"Is Father expecting your call?" she asked with an icy edge.

"Yes," I said.

"Is this still about—" she began but hushed herself. "Just a moment, Stephen." She put me on hold. I wondered how much it cost her to say my name.

"Stephen!" Father Adrian's happy voice shouted into the phone. Credit him for enthusiasm.

"I'd like to have that talk," I said.

"Good," he answered after taking a quick breath. "Good," he repeated more optimistically. "After mass? Which one do you—"

"I'll see you Sunday at noon," I told him. "On the steps."

"Better make it twelve thirty in my office."

"No!" I said, much too loudly. Mary Flannery might have heard me, if she were listening. I had no intention of being alone with a priest ever again.

"Where then?" he asked, sounding irritated.

"In the park. Twelve thirty is fine."

I took Boris, whether for comfort or protection, I wasn't sure.

I saw the priest turn the corner and walk the half block to us. I made myself not wave. He was dressed in civilian clothes: faded jeans snug in the crotch and thighs, a black turtleneck sweater, and a red jacket against the cold. I fiddled with Boris's leash.

"May I join you?" he asked on arrival. I looked up into his snug crotch.

"Yes," I agreed, sounding a little croaky.

We waited for each other to begin. Finally, I spoke up. "You know about my lawsuit?"

He nodded.

"Then, you know what happened to me. When I was a boy, I mean."

He nodded again. After a moment, he spoke, his voice gentle. "I know about the past, Stephen, and I regret it as much as anyone in the church."

I started to object.

"But what I don't know is the present."

I looked at him blankly.

"Is there something else you want to say to me?"

"I feel like you're hitting on me, and I want you to stop!" I blurted out. Too loud again. Heads turned. Children stopped bouncing balls. Dogs paused, legs still in the air.

Father Adrian looked shocked and then angry. "Stephen, I take my vows very, very seriously. I am not hitting on you. If anything, I thought you were hitting on me."

There it was again: blame the victim. I crossed my arms, slumped down on the bench, and refused to say another word. I also didn't leave. But then, neither did Father Adrian.

He waited a minute or two through a mutual silence before asking, "Are you okay?" His face was calm and concerned.

I didn't answer. I wished I could be calm. Years of therapy had brought only intermittent peace and—more frequently—rages. I hadn't looked for a new therapist yet. Why bother?

"What's your dog's name?" Father Adrian asked, trying another topic.

Sighing and sitting up, I answered. "Boris."

He reached over to the dog and found his sweet spot, behind the left ear. Boris closed his eyes and let out a sigh. Father Adrian laughed and kept scratching. His long fingers rubbed and rubbed. When he stopped, Boris left my side to sit in front of him. He put a paw on the priest's knee.

"Boris!" I said, but Father Adrian just took my dog's paw in his hand.

"He wants to shake," he said, and so shook Boris's paw.

Boris responded with an open mouth and lolling tongue.

"He likes you," I said automatically.

Father Adrian gave the usual response. "Dogs usually do." He stood, crotch in my face again. "Shall we walk? I'm sure Boris would like to."

I sighed again and stood beside him. We were both of a height.

It was just a stroll around the block, slow for Boris's sake, with nothing of consequence said. I could tell what the good father was doing, trying to be of comfort to a troubled parishioner. *But I'm not his parishioner*, I told myself. *I'm nothing to him. He's nothing to me.* Still, we walked and talked until we found ourselves outside the rectory. He didn't invite me in, and I certainly didn't ask him to. I did watch him climb the rectory steps because, well, it was a sight worth seeing. I even returned his wave before walking unmindfully home, trying not to admit to myself I enjoyed being in the priest's company.

The next Saturday, I was sitting at a table for two at Eat, a local breakfast-lunch place. I heard everyone say, "Hello, Father!" as he crossed the room, but I determinedly concentrated on my scramble and didn't look up until I heard him ask, "May I sit here, Stephen?"

I was ready to say no, but, when I raised my head, he had removed his navy pea coat and was arranging it over the back of the chair opposite mine. It would have been ruder than even I could muster to say no at that point. Besides, he was wearing a blue flannel shirt that accented his eyes to very good effect. It was open two intriguing buttons at the neck, disclosing pale skin and dark chest hair.

"My name is Steve, Father," I said, staring at the shirt's disclosure.

"Steve," he repeated, adding, "Please call me Adrian."

"I'd rather not."

He looked amused. "All right then...Mister Kinney."

I laughed in spite of myself. "All right...Adrian."

With that, he eased his body into place, corduroy pants sinking like a gray ship below the surface of the table. His knees bumped mine. "Excuse me," we both said, pulling away, like opposites not attracting. I watched him fold his hands on the tabletop. His fingers were long, thick, and heavily veined. Dark hairs partially filled the spaces between the knuckles. The nails were evenly but unprofessionally trimmed.

"What'll it be, Father?" the cacophonous voice of the waitress asked.

He smiled up at her, charmingly, and asked for eggs over easy with turkey bacon, wheat toast, and black coffee. The waitress smiled back at him but looked at me without expression. I'm sure everyone liked Father Adrian. Everyone had liked Father Michael too.

While we waited for his meal to arrive, I finished eating, and we talked of football, trash collection in the neighborhood, and who might be running for the Board of Supervisors, now our longtime representative had announced his retirement. The priest's food arrived, and he ate. His table manners were impeccable, something that could not be said for Father Michael. Our feet sometimes met under the table as we shifted in our seats, and, once, our fingers touched as I handed him the salt. I felt the eyes of his parishioners on us but tried to ignore them. They would have to deal with it, whatever it might be.

I asked the waitress for my bill.

"See you tomorrow?" Father Adrian asked.

I blinked. Oh, yes. Mass.

I smiled and shook my head. "Goodbye, Father," I said, opting to be polite. Not every priest was a pervert, just an inordinate number of them.

Sunday morning, I was up early with Boris and back in the house, considering coffee and the Sunday *Times* when the kitchen clock informed me there were thirty-seven minutes left before early mass. If I hurried... I laughed at my renewed religious interest and brewed the first cup of coffee. But when the warning bells for eleven o'clock mass rang, I roused myself, dressed quickly, and ran.

Tony greeted me when I entered the vestibule. "Hey, buddy!" he said with upraised eyebrows and a surprised grin as he handed me a missal insert for the mass. "What about that beer?" We made a date, and I walked into the nave, knowing my appearance that day had nothing to do with promises to my mother.

Afterward, I stood in line down the aisle and into the vestibule with the rest of the congregation. I took Father Adrian's hand when he offered it. He was undeniably fetching in his cassock. It fit well where it ought to and where, for chastity's sake, it shouldn't. Maybe I did have a thing for priests. Maybe it *was* my fault.

"Can we have coffee some morning?" I heard him ask in a whisper. I thought he must mean someone behind me, but his expectant eyes were on me, not the middle-aged woman next in line. I frowned and he asked, "Stay, will you?" So, I moved to the near side of the vestibule and watched him receive the firm handshakes and gushing gratitude of the faithful. Father Adrian was, as Tony had said, a good-looking dude. Actually, that was an understatement. He was movie-star gorgeous. But he was still a priest. Did it matter Father Adrian was young and handsome and Father Michael had been middle-aged and sometimes in need of a bath? The flesh is weak, as the Bible says.

People noticed me loitering nearby and some stopped to talk, mainly young men and women I had grown up with. Each "glad to see you at mass" and "how are you?" gave me a chance to escape, to walk outside with them, perhaps to rekindle friendships over brunch, but I kept my responses short. I was waiting for the priest.

He appeared in front of me after the last of my former friends had left. "You know a lot of people here," he said with an ironic smile on his face.

"Yes, well, I grew up in this parish."

He nodded and said in a more studied tone, "I think we need to talk some more. Can you wait while I change?"

The word *change* made me blush. I could too easily picture his body inside the black of his religious uniform.

"Don't you have to officiate at the next mass?" I asked.

"No," he answered, sounding a bit like a boy let out of school early. "Father James has the afternoon masses." He was quiet a moment, staring at me, his eyes cobalt and unblinking. "I'll meet you at the park," he said brusquely and left the building. I followed him outside, intrigued by the abruptness of his departure and the opportunity to watch as he hurried down the steps at a diagonal and then manfully up Church Street. The eyes of stragglers from the church drew my attention. I didn't look away.

Twenty minutes later, I was in the park with two cups of coffee, one in my hand and one on the bench. Father Adrian arrived wearing a black leather jacket, red shirt, black jeans, and black boots. He certainly paid attention to his clothing. I handed him the cup of coffee on the bench.

"Black," I said.

"You remembered," he replied, looking as if he were smiling in spite of himself. He mumbled thanks and sat on the bench as far from me as he could get. For a while, we merely drank. I snuck peeks at him. The third peek he caught me.

"Stephen..." he began.

"Steve," I corrected.

"Steve," he amended and then stopped. "It's difficult," he said when he began again, "to speak of this, given your history."

Oh, God, I thought, *not more about all that.* I started to rise, ready to run, but relented. I wasn't ten any longer, and Father Adrian wasn't Father Michael. Didn't my therapist in Boston say not to be reactive? "Yes, Adrian," I said, butt back on the bench. "I'm sure it is." Dr. Bijan would have been proud.

"I take my vows very seriously, Steve."

"So you said," I responded, trying to remain serene.

He looked offended. "I'm sorry to repeat myself," he said far too sarcastically for a priest. "But I wanted to make sure you know how strongly I feel. About my vows, I mean." It was his turn to blush, enough to silence him. I waited. "I don't have sex," he said abruptly, like a slash with a knife. He collapsed a bit into himself, looked into the distance at something I couldn't distinguish, and took a breath. "Now, although of course I'm very complimented and—" He stopped talking like he'd been choked. "Well, better not say anything along that line," he muttered more to himself than to me, took another breath, and looked me in the face. "You're an attractive, intelligent young man, Steve. I'm sure you'll find someone more appropriate than I." He sounded like Father Michael when he told me I had grown too old for him. "What?" Father Adrian asked, seeing the laughter begin on my face.

"Nothing," I answered. What use would it be to say anything? I focused on my hands and then reconsidered. He should know. The whole damn church should know.

"I've never had a relationship with a man," I said, spitting the words at him.

He looked at me disbelievingly.

"Never. I'm ruined for it."

"Therapy seems to be of benefit to some," he stated rather ponderously.

"Oh, yes! For some," was my retort. "For me, not so much."

"Have you tried praying?" he asked without any apparent irony.

I stared, trying not to yell fire and brimstone upon him. He clasped his hands as if he were going to pray for me. I remained silent. After a minute or two, he asked, "How old are you, Steve?"

"Twenty-six. How old are you?"

He ignored my question. "Maybe it will take more time," he said.

I snorted in response.

"What about Tony Rodriguez?" he asked. "I've seen the two of you talking."

"You're pretty observant, Father," I said, my curiosity piqued. "Only, Tony isn't gay." *He just looks gay*, I said to myself. But how would the priest know? Maybe he read a book.

"Oh," he said before maintaining a longer silence as if he'd run out of ideas from Psychology 101. I started to leave, but he stopped me before I could stand, his hand restraining my arm. "I'm twenty-eight. And I've never had a relationship either." He looked rueful. "In some ways, I wish I had. I'd be better prepared to counsel my parishioners."

This sad and inadequate confession made me momentarily forget my aversion to priestly contact. Adrian's grasp felt kind and not abhorrent. I was beginning to enjoy being physically connected to another human being when Adrian jumped to his feet, said a quick "I'm sorry", and very nearly ran away.

I imagined him heading for the church. The sanctuary would probably still be mostly empty before the two o'clock mass. *Of course, he wants to keep his vows,* I thought and laughed out loud to the consternation of young parents nearby. *I'm attracted to a priest, and this one has ethics. Oh well,* I told myself, *at least now I can go back to sleep again on Sunday mornings—after I walk the dog.*

I stared across the street at my parents' house, my home again. The week ahead loomed ominously. So much to do, so many people to deal with. At least, I worked at home on Mondays and Fridays. I would only have to face three-dimensional people on the days in between, and they didn't really know me. Except for one: Tony. Damn. Maybe I could cancel. Maybe seeing another highly attractive and completely unavailable man wasn't such a good idea right now, but I'd put him off longer than I should have already. A friendly beer or two might be a comfort, so he and I met as planned Friday night at Tunney's, the last remaining dive bar in our gentrifying business district. He was seated in the last booth in the back.

He handed me a Guinness with a perfect head, meaning none, upon my arrival. I accepted the pint and sat across from him. Our knees did not collide.

"Thanks," I said. "Good to see you."

"Good to see you, too, bro," he said before clinking my glass with his lager. "Cheers!"

"Cheers," I repeated.

We talked about his job as a teacher and mine in tech before he got to the real subject matter of our meeting.

"I wanted to let you know," he began. I knew whatever was coming next was not likely to be good. "I wanted to let you know," he repeated, looking like the possum I'd surprised one night in my garden.

"People are talking," I said for him.

His expansive body relaxed against the back of the booth. "Yes," he said.

"About what?" I asked. It was his nickel, not mine.

He looked surprised. "Well," he stammered. "About you and Father Adrian."

I rearranged myself with better posture. Tony followed my movements with what I'd ceased to hope were gay eyes.

"I figured it was about me being back."

He took a big gulp of his beer. "At first, yeah. But lately..."

"What exactly are they saying?"

He looked into me with those mahogany eyes and heavy brows. "You don't want to know." He was right—I didn't—but we were in the maws of it now.

"There's nothing going on," I promised. "Father Adrian is true to his vows, and I'm not interested in unavailable men." I could have added: *like you.*

He searched my face, but I could tell he was considering the truth of what he wanted to say next, not how much he disbelieved what I'd just said.

"I think Father Adrian may be interested in you."

"Fuck!" I said, dropping my jaw and very nearly my drink. "That is not what I expected you to say."

Tony leaned across the table, his full red lips and five-o'clock shadow too close for friendly comfort. "I know you, buddy," he said in his throaty baritone. "We've been friends a long time. I don't want you to get hurt again."

I clinked his pint glass a second time. "Amen to that, brother!"

He clasped the table edge with his wide fingers and angled his head at me, a concerned frown furrowing his forehead. "Come on. Be serious."

"Look," I said, struggling as always not to kiss him. "I appreciate your concern. I really, really do but don't worry. I'm not going to let myself be hurt again. At least, not by a priest. Now, you, you heartbreaker..."

He laughed and relaxed against the bench on his side of the table. "Marylee always said I passed up a good thing in sixth grade."

"How is Marylee? And the kids?" I asked, as my fantasies of me and Tony faded once again into history. That maneuvered us back into safer waters. We could finish our beer and have two more. We could leave the bar, staggering close, but not too close, down Sanchez. I could accept his goodbye hug at Clipper with only vestiges of ancient regret and walk on toward home. However, the effects of alcohol and low-level arousal took me by the rectory instead. A light shone in an upstairs room. *I could knock,* I told myself. *I bet he'd answer. He might even let me in.* I hesitated at the bottom of the steps. *He's a priest, God damn it. One of the good ones. Besides, Father James might answer, not Adrian.* I walked on to Day Street and Boris the dog.

Three weeks and as many Sundays passed with me not in church and not running into Adrian. I had dinner with Tony and Marylee and saw how much Tony, Jr., had grown and how pretty his little sister was going to be. Marylee's gay brother was there also. They had tried to fix him up with me before, but I had cited the distance between our abodes, and they withdrew the offer. Now, of course, distance wasn't an argument. He only lived over the hill in Glen Park.

Kevin was attractive, thirty-two, and newly available. He found a way to corner me out of ear range of the others and asked me out. I accepted. If I didn't, I knew Marylee would be after me with indignation.

We met for dinner at an Italian restaurant in the Castro the next Friday. He asked me to go home with him, but I said I had to walk my dog. He drove me to Day Street, which was kind. I let him kiss me good night, had second thoughts, and didn't get out of the car. In Kevin's bedroom, I managed to overcome a panic attack and stay the night, but it was not a match made in heaven. After that, we saw each other only socially at Tony and Marylee's. My new therapist congratulated me. I didn't confess to her I had imagined Father Adrian on top of me while Kevin and I did the deed.

Saturday morning came with a vengeance, the winter sun pummeling my hangover through Kevin's sheers. He offered coffee, but I used Boris as an excuse to leave as quickly as I could. Walking home, I wondered what I would do with myself—and not just on that particular day. Run, I considered. Boston seemed like a good destination. Instead, I walked Boris, drank several lattes, and read the *Boston Herald* and the *Chronicle* online. I looked at my living room ceiling. It could do with a paint job, but somehow, I didn't find the thought motivating. Running still seemed like a good idea, so I tromped upstairs, changed into shorts and a Red Sox T-shirt, and set out toward the hills on the western edge of the neighborhood.

I ran hard to keep the cold and the demons at bay. Pounding feet told me a faster runner was approaching from behind. I swerved to the right to get out of their way, but they didn't pass. I looked at my impromptu running partner. It was Father Adrian, tight shorts, baggy sweatshirt, and all the rest of him as well.

"I see we had the same idea," he said, trying to smile. I didn't try to smile back. "Haven't seen you in mass," he ventured next. I didn't answer. "Race you!" he cried and took off up Twenty-ninth Street, which had a mutha of a final block. I only ran it when I was feeling frisky. I wasn't feeling at all frisky right then, but I followed the priest gamely. A challenge to one's manhood cannot be ignored.

Whether he slowed down, or I am a better runner than I think, I found myself gaining on him before Castro Street. In a few seconds, I was next to him.

We ran side by side across Castro and up—way up— toward the summit at Diamond without speaking a word to each other. There was no one on the street, no one outside the houses. The only sound was our breathing, in unison at first and then separate, mine rasping, his heavier and deeper. At the crest, we stopped precipitously and bent over simultaneously, almost bumping heads. His sweating face looked up at me, brow crinkling, hair massively disarranged. His open mouth and white teeth grinned at me, and mine unavoidably grinned back.

"I've been thinking," he said. "About you."

"You have," I said, catching my breath for two reasons now.

"Yes," his mouth enunciated and moved toward mine. As they met, we stood, slowly coming together, body to body. The length of him felt so good against the length of me. His kisses were a revelation, but my thoughts slowly returned to the world around us.

"We better not," I said, trying to pull away. He pulled me back with strength and conviction. "People will see." He let me go.

"I don't know if I care," he said, looking sullen and irresistibly rumpled. If he didn't care, why did I?

We ran the short block downhill to Day Street and turned east. Outside my house, he stopped in thudding, skidding steps. "Can I come in?" he asked.

"Are you sure?"

"Are you?"

"No," I admitted.

"Me either. Get your key out."

We stood for a time in the foyer, body to body, kissing and caressing. I could see why Boris liked Father Adrian's fingers. They traveled down my back, massaging and exploring. The waistband of my shorts made them pause, but they dug resolutely beneath it, considered the underwear, and slid inside. His hands were soft from a life without manual labor, but the fingers held on with strength and patience until I slid his shorts and underwear down. He gasped and a hint of pink tongue showed itself in his mouth. My tongue found it, and we kissed in a way I wager he'd never done, even in France.

"Oh, God!" he said expressively.

"Shh," I admonished. I most definitely wanted to leave God out of this.

I knelt and pulled the rest of his clothing down his legs and off his feet, untied his shoes, and removed his socks. He had pretty toes. I'd have to pay some attention to them later. Right now, I was about to be busy with other body parts. I took Adrian in my mouth, trying to ignore the demons dancing on my head.

"Oh, God!" he said again and pulled me to my feet, looking desperate. "I'm sorry. I can't do this." He took in hurried gulps of air. I watched him pull his clothes back on and rush out of the door. I didn't try to stop him.

I didn't think I'd see him again. Yes, there might be unavoidable accidental sightings, but we would probably avoid any real contact, maybe any contact at all. One or the other of us might cross the street or turn around and go the way we'd just come. I wouldn't go to mass.

However, I received a text later that afternoon which changed all that before it happened.

See you tomorrow at 11 a.m. mass.

I debated the rest of the day and into the night, but when I woke up Sunday morning, it was with a clear head and a decision to go. If Adrian could face me, I could face him. He wasn't Father Michael.

I dressed carefully, laughing at myself for taking such pains with my appearance but not changing into something less flattering to my figure and coloring. Tony was not at the eleven o'clock but plenty of people I knew were, and they all seemed to be eyeing me with disdain, disbelief, and plain old dissing. I bore it all for the pleasure of watching Adrian—back in priestly garb—move about the altar, hold up the host and blood of Christ, and invite us each to eat and drink. I hadn't confessed recently, but I accepted his invitation anyway. He seemed to be restraining a smile as he dipped the wafer into the wine and placed it on my tongue. I was glad to see him too.

In the praise and pass line, we held hands for only the appropriate seconds, smiled, and I moved on. Me as reference book had been read and returned to the library. I wondered if the handsome priest would check out any other books. I hoped not, for the sake of his vocation and my ego.

Before I could head back to the condo, some friends who were not Tony and Marylee asked me to go to lunch. We had a good time, remembering the old days and confiding what we were "up to now." We promised to see each other again. I had a feeling our promises would be kept.

On the way back to Boris, who probably needed another amble in the park, I checked my text messages. There was a brief one from Father Adrian.

Want to take a drive? I'll be at your place at 2.

I checked my watch. It was nearly two now. My heart pounding from much more than the dash to my door, I raced home and found him sitting on the stoop.

"This will make tongues wag," I quipped. He laughed but didn't waste any time getting inside. I thought the door closing behind us would be followed by a kiss, but he just proceeded to the living room.

"I'll wait here while you change," he said. He didn't seem embarrassed by the word.

"You're welcome to come up."

"Thank you," he said without expression. "I'll wait here." He took up a copy of *Via Magazine*, the only print material available.

When I galumphed back downstairs, Adrian looked me over appreciatively, told me how nice I looked, and headed for the door. That didn't seem to augur guilt and recriminations. I felt confused, and besides, his blue jeans fit really well.

"You look nice too," I said.

He stopped, looked back at me, and grimaced. "I'm way too vain," he said.

"You aren't dressing to entice, then?"

He considered that. "Not intentionally but maybe I'll have to dress *not* to entice."

"That would be very disappointing to many members of your flock," I said, trying to be playful.

"Really?" he asked, looking grim. "Then, I'll have to do something about it for sure. You ready?" I nodded I was, and we left for the garage.

"Where to?" I asked, once we were mobile.

"How about the woods?" he suggested.

"Woods?" I echoed. "As in Muir?" Visions of me naked against a tree and Adrian pounding away at my backside came to mind.

He nodded, and I headed north.

"Reservation?" the fortyish ranger asked at the entrance. We shook our heads. He grinned. "You're in luck, boys. There's room in the parking lot and space on the shuttle." He accepted my credit card.

We parked the car, took the shuttle, and began to walk. It was more of a toddle than a rigorous hike. Boris would have been proud. We kept to well-established, well-populated paths, and there was no discussion of seeking privacy or what we might do there. Sometimes we talked; sometimes we didn't. When we did, it was about our lives, mine excluding Father Michael, Adrian's excluding Saint Paul's. I learned where he was from; he learned what I did. We both learned about schools attended, majors pursued, and something of our life philosophies. At the end of three hours, we returned to the car, had dinner in Sausalito, and a drink in a bar where no one knew us. I left him outside the rectory well before curfew.

And so began our relationship, the first for either of us. We saw each other Monday through Saturday with the jogging Catholics, at mass on Sunday, and on at least one outing a week. I stopped thinking of him as a priest, except at mass. Otherwise, he was Adrian, a man I knew who worked on Sundays. Father Michael was an increasingly less frequent, less vividly bad memory.

There was, I swear to God, no sex between Adrian and me. No hand-holding, no kissing (furtive or otherwise), and certainly no fucking. It seemed to me we were dating but only platonically. However, several of his parishioners thought otherwise and reported him to the bishop.

He mentioned that fact to me one day, very casually.

"You what?" I yelped.

"I had to see the bishop about us," he repeated, nearly word for word. "I was able to assure him we were not engaged in a relationship of a carnal kind." He laughed. I didn't, but I also didn't ask what kind of a relationship we *were* engaged in. For me, it was enough to have one, although my new therapist thought otherwise.

"Sex is normal, Steve," Dr. Palmer said more than once. I told her and myself that whatever I had with Adrian was better than sex, and usually myself and I agreed. But there were times we didn't. Adrian seemed to sense them.

"You can go out with other men," he assured me one night when we were parked, observing the moonlight on the ocean.

"I don't want to."

"But sex..." he began cautiously.

"I've given it up!"

"Be serious," he insisted. "It would be okay." I didn't believe him. His eyes shifted right as he said it.

"I have porno and deft fingers," I answered.

He sighed.

"What does that mean?" I asked.

"It means I have deft fingers too," he answered. I didn't ask if he thought of me while he used them. I certainly thought of him.

The subject of permissible extracurricular sex came up again every once in a while, but I continued to maintain I didn't need it, and we continued to maintain the status quo. Adrian wanted to fulfill his vows, and I didn't want to lose him. And maybe he didn't want to lose me either.

We went on week after week, month after month, enjoying each other's company fully clothed, for the most part. One time we went to Palm Springs over a long weekend, a minivacation never to be repeated. We discovered Speedos were not enough of a separation between us and carnal thoughts, although we did avoid penetration and managed to sleep the rest of the weekend in separate bedrooms.

December arrived and brought Christmas with it. Adrian and I exchanged gifts in the early a.m. after he served midnight mass, which I attended, all two hours of it. We had agreed on matching crosses, bought them together, and put them on for each other. I imagined Adrian's lying against his hairy chest and wished I could exchange places with it.

"Epiphany is coming up," he said after we had returned to opposite chairs. We always avoided couches in private.

"Our anniversary," I joked.

"I had one, you know," he said. My head jerked in his direction.

"You had what?"

"An epiphany," he clarified. I assumed he meant of the religious variety. He was a priest, after all.

"Was that why you became a priest?" I asked. He laughed.

"Well, yes, but I meant a more recent one—at the Mass of the Epiphany last year."

I blushed considerably.

"And I had another recently," he said. "I've decided to leave the priesthood."

"No!" I said.

He nodded solemnly.

"Don't do that for me."

"I'm not," he said. "I'm doing it for us."

"There's already an us," I said even though part of me was thinking *Shut up! Shut up! Shut up!*

"Not the way I want. Or the way you want," Adrian said, his voice soft and meaningful. He waited for me to agree, but all I had for him was silence. My thoughts bounced between what I wanted for him as a priest and what I needed for me as a person. "Let's sit on the couch." He stood up, reached for my hand, and led me to it.

Holding hands had never felt so exciting. "I love you," he said.

I ignored the argument in my head and said I loved him too. He traced one of my eyebrows and then the other, kissed me a long, intruding kiss, and asked with a sly smile, "Shall we go upstairs?"

I leaped the stairs two at a time. Adrian followed more sedately, laughing as he came. "Wait for me," he yelled after me.

I have, I thought.

February

Finding Good in Plenty

I hadn't been to Plenty since the funeral but now here I was in the graveyard where Jack's ashes had been laid to rest. His burial was one of the few compromises Jack's parents and I had made after his death.

"He wanted to be cremated," I insisted during our several contentious phone calls.

"He needs a Christian burial!" his mother repeated just as often. I wondered if I were the only one who found it absurd, my partner's cremains in a child-size casket sitting deep in an adult-size grave. I know Jack would have laughed.

I'd like to say I heard him laugh that day, somewhere in the ether beside me, but I didn't. I hadn't felt his presence since his heart stopped beating in the hospital room at the U.T. hospital. I even prayed, but why should God listen to me after all those years? Anyway, he didn't.

Back in the present, I walked between lines of headstones, careful not to step where a body was likely lying, although the person they had been wouldn't care. I laughed self-consciously at myself and then shut up. There were other people at other graves with their own memories. They deserved some silence.

One young man in particular caught my eye, which made me hush myself again, although I hadn't said a word out loud about him. *Jack not dead a month and already I'm looking*, I admonished.

The man I was trying not to ogle was in his early twenties, a dirty blond dressed in very faded jeans, which only fit because he was young. He wore a light-blue T-shirt that showed off his slender chest, and he held a straw cowboy hat reverently in one hand. The other hand was wiping tears from his eyes. I ducked my head. I had shed enough tears myself to know when to leave people alone.

I found Jack's stone at the edge of the Carlson family plot, neatly fenced off from its neighbors by twelve-inch-tall iron railings recently painted a sober dark gray. *John Clayton Carlson, Jr.*, the stone read. *Born January 17, 1969 Plenty, Texas. Died July 13, 2015 Austin, Texas. He is with the Angels.*

I wondered why the "a" in "angels" was capitalized but shrugged it off. I hadn't been in charge of the memorial stone. Mrs. Carlson wanted a grave and a headstone; she could have her way with the words as well.

I started to step over the inconsequential fence but paused in midstep. If any of the living Carlsons were here, they'd be scandalized for sure. Of course, none of them would be. I'd told them I was coming—warned is more like it. They wouldn't want to see me. But I put my foot down anyway and walked to the gap between the fancy iron scrollwork.

Jack's grave was nearly at the end of the third row, one empty gravesite in. *Space for me,* I thought bitterly. I read the words chiseled in the marble a second time. So few words for such a good life. Both the life and the epitaph were too short. "Healthy as a horse!" he'd always say when he came back from his annual physical. Why had he lied to me the last three years?

I knelt at the foot of Jack's grave even though Methodists aren't kneelers—especially lapsed ones—but I thought maybe I ought to give prayer another chance since I was there. The dry ground was cement hard on my knees. "Dear God," I started, coming to an immediate stop. What should I pray for? "Dear God," I started off again. "If there is a heaven, I pray Jack is in it." I tried again, hoping God didn't hear that one. "Dear Jack, I miss you so much. If there's a heaven, I know you're in it because you were the kindest, most loving person I ever knew. If heaven doesn't exist, well, then, like you always said, 'What's the problem?'"

I started chuckling and then crying. I wanted to throw myself across the grave and clutch the short grass covering it but managed to restrain myself. I did blubber loudly, though, and didn't care who heard me. I remembered a quote I'd read on a book jacket: "I watered the ground with my tears." *Purple*, I thought at the time, but now I understood.

Behind me, someone cleared their throat. I prayed for sure then. *Oh, God, please don't let it be his family!*

I looked around apprehensively and saw only the young man in the jeans. "I'm sorry for your loss, sir," he said in a West Texas twang, nodding his cowboy hat at me. I wiped my eyes as he walked away and tried not to notice how shapely his ass was.

Turning my attention back to Jack, I arranged the twelve yellow roses I'd brought at the base of his gravestone. Jack, for all that he laughed at his native state, was still a Texan. He also twanged in that discordant West Texas way, wore boots and cowboy hats, and still looked good in tight jeans until the last year at least. He could even ride a horse. Many gay men dream about having a cowboy to love. I hadn't, but I wound up with one anyway.

I got to my feet and dusted dirt and bone-dry grass off my legs and ass. After I don't know how many more minutes staring at the grave, thinking about Jack and unfortunately thinking once or twice about the polite young man who had shared my grief, I decided it was time to make the drive back to Austin. In a better life, I would have driven my car to the Carlson ranch, had dinner, stayed over, gone to church with them on Sunday, and talked for hours about Jack. We would have cried and cried and hugged until we couldn't breathe. We would have comforted each other by our presence, but my presence had never been welcome in the Carlson home. They tolerated me all those years but made it clear after the burial I wasn't expected to join them at their house then or ever.

If Jack had died of AIDS and I'd infected him, I could have seen their point, but their son/brother/uncle/cousin died of cancer. Anyway, the result was the same. They didn't have to put up with me anymore.

On the way back to Austin, I resolved to visit Jack's grave every month, not only to spite Ma and Pa Carlson and the rest of their devil brood, but also because the first visit had made me feel better. There was something left of Jack in Plenty, even if it was just five pounds of cinders.

*

The air was cooler in late September but not by much. There were only two vehicles in the parking area when I turned off the narrow county road onto the cemetery's gravel drive. I'd picked eleven o'clock on Sunday, thinking all the good people of Plenty would be in church. I parked my Prius between a newish Honda and a fairly beat-up, formerly red pickup, automatically checking to see whether it was a Dodge, Chevy, or Ford before heading into the graveyard. Jack always did. I guess I picked up the habit from him.

Two lone figures, widely separated by space and grief, bent over plots of their dearly departed. The grass and weeds were green now and carefully mown. I'd brought shears and a weeding tool to tidy up Jack's grave, but somebody had done the work for me. The Carlson family plot was perfect within an inch of life—or, more appropriately, death. I distributed the twelve yellow roses across Jack's portion and wondered if the Carlsons had seen the August ones. That must have given them something to talk about. I resolved again not to be bitter. The only Carlson I should concern myself with was Jack.

I knelt at his grave again and said a prayer. It came more naturally this time since I'd had some practice since August. I'd gone to church a couple of times. For some reason, after visiting Jack's grave, it was the thing I most wanted to do—besides a few stiff drinks in the privacy of my own home.

Just like last month, someone cleared their throat behind me. I swear a shiver of hope ran down my spine. As I stood, a strong arm reached out to steady me.

"I'm sorry to bother you, sir," a tenor voice said. "But I see you brung some tools."

It was the young man from August all right, still in jeans and beat-up old cowboy hat. He was wearing a long-sleeved shirt this time since it was only in the nineties, but the sleeves were rolled up, and the shirt was unbuttoned three buttons down his chest. I saw some surprising cleavage and a lot of dark-blond hairs.

I bent quickly to pick up the shears and weeder. The strong arm restrained me. "Ah ken waiht till you finish," the young man said in pure West Texas. I handed them to him.

"No need," I said, hearing my East Texas drawl intensify. "I'm done with them for now."

"Thank you kindly, sir," he said, his eyes smiling at me. They were deep brown, just like Jack's. This wasn't him, was it? I peered into the young man's eyes and shook myself as the feeling faded. The young man smiled at me winsomely and walked away. I watched him go, long legs kicking out, ass almost immobile, until I remembered with a start why I was back in Plenty.

I got back to business, telling Jack what I'd been up to in Austin, how Georgie our Irish setter was doing, what color our neighbors the Oswalds were painting their house. "Surely is a strange color of pink," I said out loud.

"Cuse me, sir. What did you say?" a now familiar voice said behind me. It was the polite young man, returning my tools.

"Nothing," I answered quickly, wishing he wouldn't keep calling me sir.

I hadn't gotten unused to talking to Jack. I did it at home a lot but there was only Georgie to hear, and he probably thought I was talking to him. Oh, well, this guy looked like the forgiving sort. I took the tools from him, brushing his stranger's skin with my fingertips in a drive-by handshake. "Paul Dantly," I said.

"Jordan Powers," the young man said in response. His hand was expectedly tough, a working man's hand. Mine were soft. Teaching college English wasn't exactly manual labor.

Jordan Powers looked at Jack's gravestone. Dantly. Carlson. I knew it didn't add up. I could see the question in his eyes. Should I answer it? What should I say? "This is my partner's grave. We were together nearly fourteen years. His family doesn't like me. He died of cancer. Only forty-seven. I'm thirty-three."

I didn't say any of that, of course. I didn't say anything. The young man nodded at me and advised, "You take care now."

I answered, "You do the same," and watched him walk away. He was like a tall cat, gliding across the dirt and scrubby grass. He got into the pickup and put her in reverse but before he drove away, he waved out of his window at me. I waved back and then sat on Jack's grave and asked him what he thought. He had no opinion, as far as I could tell.

*

I went back in October on Columbus Day Monday. It wasn't an official university holiday, but I didn't have any Monday classes that semester and decided to cancel my office hours. Several people were standing at gravesites but no Carlsons and no Jordan Powers either. I chided myself for both my relief and disappointment, mumbled my prayer, and spread the yellow roses over Jack's grave a little haphazardly. I rearranged them more decorously and sat by the grave. I tried to have a conversation with Jack, reporting on what I'd been up to, but it only came in fits and starts. After a few unsatisfactory minutes, I patted his headstone and left, feeling inexplicably grumpy.

*

At Thanksgiving, I went to Plenty before heading to Dallas for dinner with my family. Jack and I had alternated, going to his family—which was arduous—and then to mine. I wondered what the Carlsons thought about me visiting Jack's grave. Did his mother, such a stickler for propriety, see it as proper? What did they do with the roses? Maybe one of the gardeners gave them to his wife or girlfriend. Or boyfriend.

Someone was at Jack's grave as I approached. Oh, Lord, save me from his father, I prayed. Jack looked exactly like his dad. I had started putting away some of his photos back at home. But, when the figure stood, it wasn't Jack's father staring at me.

"Paul, right?" the young man said.

"Yes," I agreed, looking at the small pile of weeds and clipped grass to the side of Jack's grave. Jordan looked embarrassed. I hadn't recognized him at first in slacks and a sweater, even with the same ratty hat on.

"I was tending my grandpa's grave. Wasn't sure you'd be here. Didn't see you last month so I thought I'd take care of your friend's, too, while I was at it." He said *friend* as if it were just a regular word.

"Thank you for that, Jordan," I said, stumbling only slightly over his name. "I came Columbus Day last month."

He looked me in the eye as if I were lying. "I had to work that day."

I wondered what he did, farming or ranching. Or oil.

"We had a passel of cars and trucks come in."

"Oh, you work in a garage?" I asked.

"I own one," he said, with a mouth suddenly tight. West Texas mouths can turn quickly.

"Whereabouts?" I asked, trying to cover my faux pas.

"Downtown Plenty," he said, relaxing. "I took over this year from old man Davis." Like I would know who that was. He looked over at my car appraisingly. I looked at it too. It was in really good condition, thanks to Jack's regular visits to his favorite mechanic. That brought a picture to mind I didn't like.

"I thought I'd come tomorrow," I said hurriedly. "I have to be in Dallas for Thanksgiving supper with my family. But, well, I just had to be here today." I started choking up. "It's our first Thanksgiving apart," I blurted, and the tears and sobs came flooding out. *Damn, I thought, when am I going to stop crying?* I wondered how Jordan Powers would take the news Jack Carlson and I had been something more than just friends.

Like a dream, I found myself in someone's arms. For a crazy moment, I thought it was Jack comforting me but then the arms registered as not his. Too wiry. Jack had been very muscular, a faithful adherent to the church of bodily perfection. I thought the arms would let me go when I stopped crying, but they stayed tight around me. It felt so good to be held by a man again. Too good. I pulled away, thanking him.

"No problem, Paul. Like I told you, I was gonna do Grandpa's anyway," he said.

"That's not what I meant."

"I know," he said softly. I looked away first, and he bent from the waist to gather up the debris and his tools. I saw a glimpse of tan skin and white underwear.

"Will you be here at Christmas?" he asked when he straightened up. I said I would. "What day?" He took his hat off, like we were going to have a lengthy conversation.

I took a deep breath before I answered. "Christmas Eve, I guess," I said, letting the air out. "That's when we opened presents."

"I'll see you then," he said with a look in his eye I couldn't translate.

I agreed, and Jordan nodded, put his hat back on, and walked away. He looked over his shoulder, smiled, and waved. I waved back after he'd turned back around.

"I'm sorry," I whispered when I dropped the yellow roses in a bunch on Jack's very tidy grave.

*

Jordan wasn't in the graveyard when I arrived Christmas Eve. If I said I didn't really care, I'd be lying.

I left Jack his present. It wasn't much, but it was something I knew he'd like. I hoped whoever cleaned up the graveyard got the Hickory Farms sausage and cheese box before the dogs did. There were always a couple of them around, sniffing and looking for the main chance.

I zipped my leather jacket all the way up against the cold and told Jack about my plans to visit with my family in Dallas for a few days and then go on to New Orleans for New Year's with Ben and Brady, our best friends when Jack was alive and still mine now he was gone. They had been a comfort these months of bereavement, not letting me be by myself unless I needed to, bringing dinner by on many a self-pitying night. New Orleans was their idea. It would be my first trip without Jack, if you didn't count Dallas and Plenty.

"It's time you got out," Ben had said, with Brady nodding agreement. I didn't realize "getting out" meant going to New Orleans, not the Violet Crown Cinema, but I'd left it up to them, so it was my own fault. New Orleans at New Year's didn't seem like the best choice for a man in my situation, still mourning the loss of a longtime lover and all, but the two *B*'s thought it was a grand idea.

"What do you think?" I asked the cold, dying grass over Jack's ashes. "Should I go? They've already bought the tickets. Said they're treating me. I shouldn't have agreed to that, I know. Anyway…" I went on to other news, taking a sideways look every once in a while, to make sure no one else had driven up and come within hearing distance. I heard myself wish Jordan Powers had.

"He's too young for me anyway," I told Jack. "Maybe I've become a chicken hawk!" I laughed into the chilly afternoon with no one to join me in the joke.

After more one-way conversation, I got up, dusted off any possible dirt or mud, and looked across the graveyard toward the area Jordan had been visiting. I was still alone. I walked that way, looking for graves with his last name and found a bunch of them but figured his grandfather must be Samuel L. Powers, 1933-2017. No mention of angels or earthly locations. There were dead branches and fallen leaves on Samuel's grave, so I got down on all fours to brush them off. That just shooed them onto the next grave, so I trotted back to my car for a recyclable plastic bag. I always had a few for shopping so I didn't have to accept another.

I gathered compostable debris from the grave of Mildred and Ebenezer Jacobs, Samuel's neighbors on the right. *Now what,* I thought, almost hearing Jack laugh at me. I waved my hand in the air as if to shoo him off. "I'll take the bag back to Austin and put everything in our compost bin," I told the Jacobs.

"That sounds like a good idea," Jordan's voice answered. I whirled around.

"I really have to stop talking to myself," I said, so glad to see his rawboned face. His hair blew free in the cold wind sweeping over us. He held the straw cowboy hat in one hand and something small and rectangular in the other.

"I talk to Grandpa sometimes," he said, looking at my bag. "Thank you for looking after him."

"I took care of his neighbors too," I told him.

"I didn't know them," he said, looking at their marker. I looked at him. His Adam's apple jerked in rapid swallows. I tried to find something to say, but before I landed on a suitable topic, Jordan said, "Sorry I was late. Got ya somethin'. It ain't much but, well, it being Christmas and all..." He handed me a small package badly wrapped in black Christmas paper. Whoever thought of that one?

"Thank you!" I said. "I've got something for you too." I ran to my car and jogged back with the pictorial book on cowboys, wrapped in holiday-neutral by the harried clerk at Book People.

"Should I open it?" he asked, looking delighted, like the kid he still must be. Was he even twenty?

"Sure," I replied. "Let's open them together." The words seemed intimate as if we were about to have sex. *Not a bad idea,* a voice somewhere said.

After the unwrapping, Jordan looked at photos while I tried to set the clasp on the copper bracelet he'd bought me. How did he know I liked copper? Maybe it was my hair color.

"Here, let me do that," he said, stuffing the book, wrapping paper, and ribbon under his left armpit and fastening the clasp for me. The metal hung cold against my skin. Jordan looked at me with Jack's eyes. I leaned toward him, ready for a kiss.

"Would you like to go for coffee?" he asked, bringing me up short.

"Now?" I squawked, surprised it was only caffeine he was offering. Jordan looked rueful. Jack's eyes were gone.

"I know. Stupid idea," he said, ducking his head.

"No, no!" I said, too loudly.

Jordan looked up, startled, and then gave me a grin, lopsided and impossibly sexy.

"Let's do it," I said. "Coffee, I mean." My naturally pink skin turned crimson.

Jordan grinned ear to ear at my embarrassment. "Follow me," he said, loping to his truck, his butt making an offer I couldn't refuse.

I ran behind it to my car, waited until the pickup pulled out, and then followed its tailgate to the exit. On the county road, Jordan turned toward Plenty. That gave me second thoughts, but I kept my speed steady at forty-five. When we pulled up in front of the Horn of Plenty Café, Jordan knocked on my window. His mouth formed my name with a question mark through the glass. I nodded, hoping my smile wasn't too uncertain, unbuckled my seatbelt, and opened the door.

"Do you know the Carlson family?" I asked as we climbed from the dirty street onto the equally dirty sidewalk.

Jordan stopped just short of the café door. "I do, Paul. It's a small town," he said apologetically as if he knew all about it, which probably he did. Then in a more adamant voice, he added, "Don't worry, buddy. I got your back." He ushered me into the café with his hand on it, like he meant me to take his words literally.

There weren't many people inside besides a middle-aged waitress at one of the tables and a Latino short-order cook I could see through the service counter. The waitress gave us a hearty wave and then went back to her conversation with one of the three or four older men, all dressed like cowboys, spread throughout the room. I didn't recognize anybody, thankfully, and Jordan didn't introduce me to any of them, just returning nods as we passed by. We settled into a booth in the back, far away from the plate-glass windows.

"Hi, Jordan," the waitress said, putting one hand on the booth partition behind him. She looked at me.

"Paul Dantly," I told her, jolting myself into motion.

"Dantly," she repeated, like she'd heard it before. Something clicked into place in her brain, and she smiled more broadly. "Well, welcome to Plenty, Mister Dantly," she said with a wink at Jordan. "Coffee?"

We both nodded.

"Menus?"

Jordan shook his head, and the waitress left.

"You hungry?" he asked belatedly.

"A little," I admitted.

"Damn, I shoulda let Nat bring 'em. Anyway, I got the list memorized." He began to recite, which made me laugh—which made him ham it up, inventing silly names for the fine food selections available. I was giggling uncontrollably—nerves, I suppose—when the waitress came back.

"What's so funny?" she said, setting two heavy coffee mugs down with a crash. "Black?" she asked, holding the glass coffee pot dangerously near my head. I waited for Jordan to answer. "Oh, I know how he wants his. How about you, honey? What do you like?" She looked at Jordan and then at me, trying not to smirk.

"I need room for cream," I said.

"I bet you do!" she said, pouring my coffee and slapping my back before she walked away, chuckling and looking over her shoulder at me.

Jordan dropped his smile when he saw my stricken face. "I'm sorry. Nat's my aunt. Well, she used to be," he said, looking confused. "Her and Uncle Lee got divorced. But she's still my aunt." He sounded defiant. "I don't think you should give up on people so easy."

I let the silence lie between us, thinking of Jack. Was I giving up on him too easily or too soon, exchanging Christmas presents with this kid from his hometown and playing kneesies under the table with him? *What in hell am I doing?*

"Everything okay?" Jordan asked.

I nodded dismissively.

He took a deep breath, like I'd knocked the wind out of him.

I tried to remember his recitation. "I guess I'll have biscuits and gravy," I said, as if he had asked what I wanted.

After I ate and we'd tussled for the bill, I returned my card to my wallet and began thinking it was time to drive back to Austin. "I'd better be going," I told him. "Thank you for everything." I started to get up. Jordan's words stopped me in midcrouch.

"Whach'all doin' tanaight?" he asked suddenly, blushing dark through his remaining summer tan. "I mean, it being Christmas Eve. You goin' anywhere? My sister's cooking us dinner, and I thought mebbe you'd like to come. I know it's last minute and all." He saw my hesitation and added, leaning forward, "I got my own place." He blushed. "Ah mean, if it gets too late..." He slumped in his seat, looking a little bewildered.

"I'm flattered," I answered, debating his offer. My folks weren't expecting me until tomorrow, but I didn't think I was up to meeting Jordan's family already—if ever.

What if they were another batch of Carlsons? On the other hand, my body was definitely signaling it was up for something. "Why don't we go to your place now?" I leaned in as close as Jordan had.

He shook his head. "Wouldn't seem right," he said, his mouth grim. "Your partner just passing and all." I was surprised—and embarrassed. I had totally misread him.

I thought about what he'd said on the lonely drive back to Austin. My mind agreed with him, although my body didn't. It would have been nice not to be alone that first Christmas Eve, especially in bed.

*

In January, I met Jordan at the café on a Saturday. He had arranged it online after tracking me down on Facebook and sending me a request. As we shook hands over the Formica table between the booth's faux-leather benches, I saw his aunt steaming toward us with a coffee pot and another mug. She had greeted me at the door as if I were one of her best customers.

"As I recall," she said, winking at me, "you like cream." She poured some into my mug before she added the coffee and did the same with Jordan's.

"I thought you drank yours black," I said, worried that I'd remembered wrong.

"Oh, he decided he likes cream too," Nat interjected. She cackled loudly enough for everyone else in the cafe to look, sure enough.

Embarrassment spread down Jordan's face and neck to the two open buttons of his red-plaid flannel shirt. I imagined my face looked much the same.

"Don't mind me," Nat said, laughing at both of us before she sauntered off.

"You been to the cemetery yet?" Jordan asked. Guilt hit me hard.

"Uh, I thought I'd go there after," I lied. "You know, on my way back to Austin."

He looked like he didn't buy that at all. "Here," he said, pushing a cheerful package across the table at me. "Happy birthday." My mouth fell open in protest.

"You shouldn't have! How did you know?"

"Facebook," he said. "I know I'm early but, well..." His voice trailed off and then came back strong. "Go ahead. Open it. Hope you like it." I loosened the ribbon and carefully removed the tape, like I planned on saving the paper, and maybe I did. It would be something of Jordan's back in Austin. I was getting tired of memories.

"Well, happy birthday!" Nat exclaimed. She was back without warning. Jordan and I looked up at her like deer in her high beams. "What are you—twenty-five, twenty-six?" she asked.

"Thirty-four," I said, itching to finish opening the package and see what Jordan had thought to give me.

"Well, honey, you don't look it. I thought you two was a lot closer in age than that." Her voice had a judgment in it, like *you're too old for my used-to-be nephew, mister*. I ignored it and pried the paper apart.

"Wow! Thank you!" I said, holding the red shirt up. It looked plenty big, even with the extra pounds I'd gained from all the wine and ice cream since Jack died.

"It's flannel," Jordan said hopefully. "I wanted you to have something warm to wear. For this time of year and all. I hope it fits. I kept the receipt," he added, looking so young. Maybe Aunt Nat was right.

"And it's just like yours, Jordie," she said in the midst of my doubts. Jordan gave her a dirty look. "Okay, I'm leaving. Are you hungry, Paul? It's on me." Maybe she didn't think I was a child molester after all.

They argued over whether the biscuits and gravy would be a gift from him or from her. The aunt won and went off to place the order and refill other customers' coffee mugs.

"Do you like it?" Jordan asked, sounding anxious.

"I do," I said. "Especially because it matches yours." He blushed again deeply.

"We'll go visit our loved ones after we eat," he said, trying to pretend nothing had happened. We were both relieved when our lunches arrived.

After thanking Nat for lunch, I followed him to the graveyard and eased my car next to his truck in the parking lot. "Did you remember the roses?" he asked, looking ominously at my empty hands. I nodded and ran to retrieve them from my car. I nearly fell on the ice and slush.

"I'll go visit Grandpa," he said, leaving me on my own.

I crunched carefully across dirty snow and cracking ice to the Carlson contingent. Jack's grave was as tidy as always, swept of snow and free of debris. I looked at the lines of other dead Carlsons. At the beginning, they bought land and then bought some more. They built up their herd, made money—lots of it—and now donated too many dollars to reactionary causes. I knelt on the wet earth and folded my hands in prayer without hesitation or a look around me. Jordan and I were alone in the cemetery, except for the wind.

"Dear God, thank you for Jack Carlson," I prayed. "Thank you that we met and loved. Bless his soul. I know he's in paradise with you now. Amen."

After I finished talking to God, Jack and I had the conversation I'd been dreading.

"I met someone," I said, looking over at Jordan, standing at the foot of his grandfather's grave, head bowed, still with the summer cowboy hat in his hands. He looked good in his heavy wool jacket cinched tight at the waist. "You probably know his family." I stopped talking, wondering if Jack had known Jordan in the biblical sense. For all his worry about me looking at other men, he was the one who fucked them. An open relationship, he called it. *Too open*, I thought, *but look at me now*. I wondered if he could.

"Did you know Jack Carlson?" I asked when Jordan joined me.

"I heard of him," he said. "I think my dad must have gone to school with him. Why?"

"Nothing," I said, trying to brush the wet off my knees and ignore the generation gap comment.

Jordan looked down. "Man, Paul! You 'bout ruined those slacks! Are they washable? I got a..." I kissed him to shut him up. He jumped away like I'd goosed him in the high school locker room. "Shit, man!" he muttered, looking around the empty cemetery. "I live here, dude. Besides, it ain't right." He nodded toward Jack's marker.

I folded my arms across my chest, frowning.

"Come on, Paul," he said peevishly. "This ain't Austin." That we could agree on.

"Maybe next time you should come there," I said, turning toward the parking lot. With a gulp of guilt, I turned back. "Goodbye," I told them both. Jordan put his hat back on, tight against the wind, and walked with me.

"Did you mean that?" he asked. "About Austin," he added, in case I'd already forgotten.

"Certainly...if you think that beat-up old pickup can make it that far."

He looked slightly outraged and then grinned and hit me with his hat. "Hey," he said in a voice the opposite of anger.

Back in Austin, I had second thoughts but decided to ignore them. Valentine's Day was coming up, and I didn't want to spend it alone. Besides, if I got Jordan out of Plenty, who knew what might happen? I sent him a message with a formal invitation.

If the weekend being Valentine's gave him pause, he didn't let on. *I'd love to* his answer read. I sent him my address and driving instructions.

*

On the day, I said, "You got here awfully fast!" when I heard Betty Anne's near-death rattle wheeze into my driveway, and I went out to meet him. He hopped out of the truck and reached behind the driver's seat, pulled out a black gym bag, and turned to me, smiling.

"Yep. Mighta got here even quicker if I hadn't followed your lefts and rights the last bit." I thought about my instructions. I guess it was a left at Hancock, not a right.

"Sorry about that," I said. "Come on in the house."

"Just a minute," he said and reached back in the truck. I picked up his bag and enjoyed the view.

When he pulled back out of the cab, he was wearing that same old hat. I gave him a kiss even though he looked nervous.

"This is Austin," I reminded him.

"I see," he said, setting his hat aright on his longish blond hair. "Well, we goin' in the house or not?"

I led the way up the sidewalk.

Jordan took his hat off when he stooped through the door. "Some place," he said, looking around the foyer. I set his bag down near the umbrella stand.

"Want a tour?" I asked.

"Later." He looked serious. "You been back to your partner's grave this month?" he asked, like he already knew the answer.

"No," I admitted, refusing to break eye contact with him. "Don't worry, I'll go." I headed into the parlor, and he followed. He looked around like he was in a museum.

"Mebbe this time you'll meet my folks," he said.

"Maybe," I said way too happily. I hung his jacket in the foyer closet next to our coats, Jack's and mine. I had been donating or throwing away some of Jack's things but hadn't reached the foyer yet. I put the straw cowboy hat on the shelf above them. "Let me show you the kitchen." Jordan held me back.

"Hold on there, cowboy," he said. "Here." He shoved a big red box in the shape of a heart at me.

I started sniffling.

"Whoa, buddy! I'm sorry. I didn't mean to..." He stopped in midsentence. He had no idea what he'd done. Jack had always given me a big red heart box full of chocolates too. Okay, his was Godiva, not Whitman's, but that didn't matter.

"I'm all right," I said. "I bought you something too," I said, wiping my eyes and handing him the beautifully wrapped package.

Jordan eyed it suspiciously. It was rather large.

"Looks like you spent way too much money."

"Sit down and open it," I told him.

He did as carefully and slowly as I had opened his present to me on my birthday.

"Oh, just rip it!" I told him, growing impatient.

"Nah," he said. "This paper's too pretty."

When he finally got through the wrapping and saw the manufacturer's box inside, he looked at me with mouth open and eyes wide. "You bought me a new hat!" he exclaimed. "Damn, Paul, it's a Stetson. Now, I know you spent too much."

"Open it," I repeated, starting to take the lid off myself.

"I will, I will," he said, slapping my hands away.

"Try it on," I told him. I had guessed at the size.

He stood in front of the mirror in the foyer. "Fits good," he decided, trying it at different angles. He looked at me in the mirror with it set back on his head, showing some blond hair, and winked. "Am I a bad guy?" he asked, looking mischievous and unbearably sexy.

I blinked and then realized he meant because the hat was black. "Definitely not," I answered, coming up behind him. He let me stay.

"I'm glad you're here," I said over his shoulder, hugging him tightly. "Happy Valentine's Day."

"Happy Valentine's Day," he said back at me, covering my hands with his. He looked pensive in the mirror. "You might not believe this, but I ain't had a valentine since fourth grade." While I considered whether I did believe that, he turned in my arms, crotch to crotch. "Now, how about that tour?" He held on to me.

"Sure," I said and tried to step away. He held me even harder.

"Let's us start with the bedroom," he said, letting me go and heading down the hall like somebody had told him where it was.

"All right," I called after him, jogging to catch up.

"That's it on the left," I said.

He peeked into the room. I stood behind him, letting him look. To me, with Jack's colognes, photos, and mementoes missing, it seemed too much like a motel room, but maybe, even with the absence of Jack's things, Jordan would still freak out. Maybe he'd think again it was too early for us. Maybe us was never going to happen. But, as my fears grew, Jordan looked around with Jack's eyes and a wide grin and asked, "Should I leave my hat on?"

March

One Plus One

My date stared longingly at a man across from us at Aslam's Rasol. *Who wouldn't*, I said to myself charitably. The man had those capturing eyes, the darkest dark, set wide apart in a strong, diamond-shaped face shaded a grayish brown. His hair sprang upward, obsidian black and gleaming, came close at the sides, and elongated down the jaws through deliberate stubble, ending in a Van Dyke beard precisely trimmed.

Because "Hank" gaped so openly, I debated whether to slap the maroon-colored menu down and declare our date officially over, but just then, our server Chanda came back with our drinks and her ready iPad.

"May I take your order now please?" she asked politely, her smile gracious in a pale North Indian face so unlike the handsome man across from us.

"I'll have the chicken tikka masala," I said without further thought or any reopening of the menu. The man with the capturing eyes glanced my way, lowered his head conspiratorially to his friends, and spoke inaudibly to them. His perfect lips moved silently, the upper formed of conjoined scrolls and the lower full and ready to be bitten. Now I was the one staring. Hank brought my attention back to himself by going through his resume. It would have been impressive—for a job interview.

Happily, our food arrived, which gave me something to do other than listening to my date's life achievements and impressive financial assets. I tried not to look at the nearby table. In any case, Hank continued looking often enough for both of us during his soliloquy. I was drinking the last of my second glass of wine when we heard the four men request their bill, pay, and rise. Hank stopped somewhere in a catalogue of his forties to stare hungrily after them as they left. I decided enough was too much and extracted sixty dollars from my wallet. I laid it next to Hank's pale-blue plate, wiped nearly clean with complimentary naan.

"What's this?" he asked, money apparently able to break his concentration.

"For my dinner. Thanks," I said perfunctorily, getting to my feet. The quartet of Indians was at the door, playing audience to our drama. Ignoring Hank's muttered curses, I followed them out of the door. They stopped on the Valencia Street sidewalk, speaking in some musical language. The handsome man shook his head at them and nodded at me. His friends all turned, expressed variations of "Ah!" and left us to it.

"Ganak," the man said in an unexpected baritone and extended his right hand.

"A.J.," I said, taking his hand.

He smiled more broadly. "We use that name, too, where I am from. In Malayalam, my language, it means invincible. Are you unconquerable, Ajay?" He flirted pleasantly. "It also means lovable," he added, not asking whether I was that as well.

Our handshake was interrupted by someone pushing through us. It was Hank exiting the restaurant. He scowled deeply at us both and stomped away south.

"Your friend does not look pleased," Ganak said with a suppressed smile.

"We aren't friends. We were on a Zoosk date," I said, wondering whether I should have. "No loss to me. It wasn't going anywhere."

"Yes," Ganak agreed, smiling sardonically. "He seemed to look more at our table than at you."

"You mean he looked at *you*," I corrected. Ganak blushed and dropped his head coyly.

"I did nothing to elicit it," he said in his clipped Indian-British voice.

"I know," I said, taking his hand back without thinking, but he let me keep it, and the next moment we were walking north along Valencia without a destination, chatting easily, our clasped hands sometimes swinging in delight.

I asked if he would like a drink somewhere.

"I don't drink alcohol," he answered, frowning with a sudden worry, but quickly added, "However, there is a place nearby which is sometimes fun. Do you know the Pi Bar?"

I shook my head.

His face brightened, and he tugged me further north.

Past Sixteenth Street, Ganak pointed with slender fingers to a Pi sign hanging above us. We dropped hands and walked inside single file. The feel of his skin lingered warm on mine.

There were more pi signs inside. Everywhere, in fact. On the walls, along the long mahogany bar. Ganak found us places at the far end of the bar on stools also shaped in the sign for pi. I appreciated the attention to detail.

"Why pi?" I asked after we had mounted our seats.

"They serve pizza," Ganak answered, stifling a laugh as the bartender approached.

"Would you like to see the menu?" he asked, leaning over the bar in a thickly muscled way.

"We are just having drinks," Ganak said, but the mustachioed man handed us a menu anyway.

"Our drinks list," he explained. Lots of beer, I could see. One caught my eye.

"I'll have a Blind Pig," I told him. Ganak's sharply arching eyebrows almost flew off his face. "It's from a microbrewery at the River," I said, wondering if he knew where I meant. "What will you have?"

"A lemonade, please," he told the bartender directly.

Ganak and I turned our stools to half-face each other, ready to exchange personal information. I told him I was from downstate Illinois and had rid myself of my southern accent at the Rhode Island School of Design, and after it, Harvard. I learned he had a Ph.D. from Cambridge and was from Kerala, an ocean state on the western coast of India.

"Like California," I prompted. He considered that for a moment and then shook his head.

"Not exactly," he replied. "Although both are beautiful." I loved listening to his choice of words and lilting speech pattern.

"What is it you do?" I asked.

"I teach maths at Stanford," he replied.

"No wonder you like this place."

"Oh, yes," he agreed, laughing gaily. "It is a mathematician's dream, a bar full of Pi. But you know maths as well," he said, his teeth flashing in a phosphorescent smile. "Being an architect." I had forgotten I had told him my profession.

"To math," I toasted.

"To maths," he agreed.

Our eyes locked over the respective rims of our drinks as we drank. Our legs were open to each other, crotches obvious beneath the fabric of our pants. Our conversation continued, but I'm not sure I could tell you what we said. I studied every detail of Ganak's body. When he excused himself to use the loo, as he of course called it, I took notes on the rotation of his ass in slacks otherwise loose through the leg, the gliding way he moved forward, the strict posture of his back and shoulders. *Like a dancer,* I thought, *a mathematical dancer.*

I was still thinking of Ganak's body when he returned. "Would you like to come home with me?" I asked abruptly as he sat down. "I live near the ocean, but I brought my car."

"I am afraid I cannot," he replied smoothly, although his face showed his surprise, and perhaps, regret. "I must rise early to catch the commuting bus. In any case, it would not be wise." He placed his hands on the bar, showing me his sinewy forearms. Sparse black hairs grew along their length. "Soon I am returning to India to become engaged." I am sure I looked surprised, if not shocked. "It is an arranged marriage." He sat taller, his voice rising too. "My parents are modern in many ways, but concerning marriage and grandchildren, they are still very traditional. Maneesha is my friend," he added before I could say anything stupid. "She is from a very good family. We will have children and make our parents happy."

Ganak's words sounded bitter to me, but perhaps that was the hope in me talking. I was one of the many who do not believe in love at first sight, but something about this man had me enthralled. I hurried to find something to say so he wouldn't leave. "When are you leaving?" I finally asked, settling for safe.

"April seventh, in time for Vishhukkani. I have purchased my ticket."

I didn't ask what Vishhukkani was. It didn't matter. What did was Ganak was leaving and would be unavailable when he returned. We had met and made a connection—or at least I had—and nothing would come of it. Unless…

"That's over a month," I said factually. "Can we have dinner tomorrow?" I knew I was being pushy, and I'd have to cancel my next mystery date, but that would be a relief. I was full up with too many sexless glasses of wine and ultimately empty cups of coffee.

Ganak frowned with disapproval but then sighed, agreed, and took my phone. His thumbs fluttered across the tiny keyboard. Ganak Varma and a 650-area code, the screen told me when he handed the phone back. "It saves time spelling," he explained.

"Don't you want my information?" I asked, as he rose.

"No," he replied, a little curtly. "I will leave it up to you to call or not. If you do, I will answer. Thank you though," he said with a kinder sound to his voice before declaring more resolutely, "it is time for me to go." I tried to stand but he placed a surprisingly definite hand firmly on my shoulder, keeping me down. *"Nale var."* He squeezed my shoulder gently and briefly, sending electric thrills down my body.

It would just be sex, I told myself.

The next morning, I called Ganak at eight. "Are you on the bus?" I asked.

"I am," he replied in a muted voice, like he was shielding the phone with his hand.

"Are we still on for dinner?"

He said we were, although I heard mixed feelings in the yes.

I suggested an Indian restaurant on Taraval, out my way.

"I fancy other cuisines besides my own," he answered sharply. "In any case, soon I will be eating too much of it."

My second suggestion was the Beach Chalet, near the ocean and even nearer to my house. "I'll pick you up," I offered.

"That won't be necessary, Ajay. I will drive. Is 7:00 p.m. possible?"

I agreed it was.

There was an awkward following pause on both ends of our connection. I imagined his fellow bus riders listening.

"Well, then. Goodbye for now," he said, clicking off.

I held my phone, looking at the eager screen fade to black. *It would just be sex*, I repeated.

I arrived too early. Ganak was neither downstairs in the exhibit area nor upstairs in the restaurant, so I returned to the portico, peering at every car entering the small parking lot. When a navy-blue Tesla Model S appeared, I trotted to it. The driver lowered his window and leaned his handsome head out. Ganak. My heart expanded in happiness, even if he looked distinctly peeved.

"There is nowhere to park," he complained.

"Try across the street," I suggested. "In the beach parking lot. I'll meet you there."

He nodded grimly and made his way across the Great Highway. By the time I had dodged bursts of traffic to join him, Ganak was out of his car and leaning against the crumbling seawall. "I never come here," he said, looking over his shoulder at the Pacific. "It is very beautiful."

"It is," I agreed and tried to take his hand, but he crossed his arms and turned to look west, groin against the seawall now. Somewhere west, thousands of miles away, was India. I wondered if his ocean looked like this one and if he were thinking of home.

"Will you come back?" I asked quietly.

He looked askance at me. "Of course. My work is here. Kerala either does not have enough jobs, or it has too many people. In either case, we leave. My brothers are in Saudi and Dubai."

"Are they married?"

He rolled his eyes. "Oh, yes—as is my sister—and they each have at least one child, but that is not enough. I must be married, too, and more grandchildren are required."

"Does your family know you're gay?" I asked tentatively.

"No," he answered glumly, looking west again.

"None of them?"

"None of them," Ganak repeated definitely.

"If you told them—"

"I cannot," he interrupted and turned, leaning on his side now to look at me. "You Americans think life is so simple. One plus one equals two. However, that is only true in a binary system. India is not binary," he concluded bitterly.

I told myself I should let him off the hook for tonight, think of some excuse he would too readily accept, but something in me wouldn't let me give up this chance, no matter Ganak's reluctance and good reasons. He would have to make his own choices. Ganak sighed as if he knew he was making the wrong one.

"Shall we go to the restaurant?" he asked.

I nodded, hands in my slacks.

He put his arm through mine, and my heart nearly burst with joy.

Upstairs at a window table, we watched the ocean and each other as we talked about our day, our work, the weather, the view—the simple end of day discussion I longed to have with someone, the same someone, every night. We ordered different appetizers and entrees and offered each other bites as if we were long familiar with the other's tastes. It was so easy and right—or so it seemed to me.

After our server and I exchanged the bill for a credit card, Ganak watched her walk away before he told me, "You have questions you are not asking, Ajay."

"No questions really," I said. "Just a wish."

He sighed deeply and played with his silverware, avoiding my hopeful face. Then, with a grimace, he tossed his napkin onto the table and screeched his chair back.

"All right," he said, seeming no happier with his second decision than with his first.

I gave him driving directions to my little aqua and lavender house. "Park in the driveway," I told him, repeating the street number.

We exited his car without words, the slamming of both doors cracking through the quiet weekday night. I waved at my next-door neighbors, returning from a walk. The Chins smiled, waved back, and tried not to be too curious about the stranger I was bringing home.

Upstairs in my bedroom, Ganak and I sat next to each other on the bed; I because I was ready, and he because there was nowhere else to sit. I unbuttoned his shimmering charcoal shirt and was surprised to see the sharply etched chest muscles below two prominent collarbones. Black hair outlined his chest, and small brown nipples dotted either side. I held him close, feeling his warmth through my shirt and into my hands. I kissed him slowly as if we had all the time in the world.

His resolve seemed to melt. "Let me see you," he whispered.

I energetically removed my shirt, pants, shoes, socks, and underwear. Ganak's eyes widened and his mouth gasped, for which I was grateful. I was more broadly built and more abundantly muscular than he. He put one hand over the center of my chest, and we both felt my rapid heartbeat.

I hurried him out of his clothing and arranged him on the bed. He looked up at me with half-lidded eyes and a mouth slightly open, hinting at teeth and tongue. I spread his dark legs and settled between them. We kissed for infinite delicious minutes.

"Go ahead, Ajay," he said, gasping as my kisses reached his chest.

I shouldn't have, I suppose, but the body has its own imperative, so I leaned over him to find a condom, put it on, and lubricate us both. When I entered him, his eyes widened and then he smiled, wrapped his arms around my back, and clamped his legs over my thighs. He moaned as I accelerated. I pushed into him, panting into his face, diving for kisses. His body moved with mine, crashing together and lurching apart over and over until we erupted simultaneously. I groaned an elongated ah. Ganak merely held on, catching his breath. I wanted to say it was my best sex ever but did not even though it was true.

Instead, I waited for Ganak to say something and he did. "I'm impressed," he said, and I believed him, but I didn't know what to say or how to say it in response, so I busied myself with cleaning us up. Then, when there was nothing left to do, I lay on my back and listened to my breathing, trying not to think or wish.

His fingers traced the outlines of my face.

"I wasn't sure you enjoyed it," I said before I could stop myself.

"It is so complicated, Ajay," he answered, removing his hand and looking west.

"I wish it weren't."

His eyes focused on me again. For several long moments we stared into each other, until I reached for another condom. There was so little time.

Ganak let me see him every night the following week. We met most of the seven at his place, a three-story Noe Valley renovated Victorian he shared with three friends, the same ones who had been with him on the day we met. Ganak lived on the ground floor, Padiril on the second, and Naveen and Vinay shared the top floor as a couple. There was a deck with doors from Ganak's bedroom and kitchen but shared by all. Steps led on either side to a small, sunny garden full of exotic-looking plants from northern India. Naveen was the gardener. "He is Uttarakhandi," Ganak said.

He had been teaching me Malayalam and bits of Hindi. "What does that mean?" I asked.

"It's a state," he answered. "Very beautiful."

So, thanks to Naveen, I awoke each morning I spent in Ganak's bed and arms to sweet, unfamiliar fragrances drifting over me through an open window. I tried not to think of marriages and return airplane tickets. Every day, I reminded myself instead, "We have this day," and was happy—or at least happy enough.

On our tenth morning, while we lolled on a Saturday bed, I asked, "Do you know what Tuesday is?" I could tell he didn't. "It is the mathematicians' holiday," I hinted.

"Pi Day?" he guessed, grinning widely.

I nodded, and he looked solemn.

"You know, Ajay," he said professorially. "What you say is only true in certain countries. Most cultures do not start with the month in dates."

"But we do here. Let's celebrate," I insisted.

"Oh, yes. We should," he agreed sarcastically. I smacked his firm butt, and he jumped out of bed.

"Did I hurt you?" I asked, my brow crinkling in concern.

"Not at all," he replied, sounding happy, not angry with me.

He slipped quickly into white baggy shorts and a pink sleeveless shirt. "Come!" he commanded, barely letting me pull on sweatpants before dragging me door to door in his building, knocking at his friends' flats, demanding entrance.

"We are celebrating Pi Day!" Ganak shouted at Padiril when he opened his door one floor up. He was wearing tiny, very tight red bikini briefs and nothing else, not even body hair. We unavoidably admired each other's chest.

"It is days away," Padiril said placidly in his accented tenor with a knowing smile at me. I felt our complicity, even if it was unwilling on my part.

"Come, come!" Ganak insisted, yanking his friend through his doorway into the hall. Padiril winked at me and let himself be led. All in a line, we thundered up the staircase to the lovers' apartment—Ganak leading, Padiril following, and me panting behind the impressive twin bulges of Padiril's bubble butt.

Naveen and Vinay answered Ganak's repetitive pounding clad in lungis, looking anxious and tousled, as if they had been interrupted during sex, but they good-naturedly followed us downstairs through Ganak's flat, with me last in line again and Padiril before me.

"You could at least provide us with tea," Padiril declared as he inserted his fine butt into one of the wicker chairs arranged neatly around the patio fire pit. Ganak obediently trotted toward the kitchen.

"I'll help you," I said, my voice rising in fear of being left too close to Padiril's impressive body.

"There is no need," Ganak said over his shoulder. He waved me down. "Sit, sit," he insisted.

After his friend's departure, Padiril spread his thickly muscled arms slowly and sinuously along the sides of his chair. When he opened wide his dark, nearly hairless thighs, I jumped up as if stung, knocking my plastic chair onto the wooden planks with a bang.

"I'll just help Ganak," I said, righting the chair and scurrying away. I heard laughter follow.

"I told you not to trouble yourself," Ganak said when I walked through the kitchen door, but he gave me a kiss, so I knew he was glad.

"I'll make the coffee," I replied, trying not to think of Padiril. "Does anyone drink it besides me?"

"Vinay," he answered as he poured steaming water over earth-colored tea leaves in a kitschy elephant teapot. The already familiar acrid smell snaked its way to me. Five minutes later, we joined his friends on the deck. Ganak carried the pots of tea and coffee, and I followed with a silver tray holding teacups, spoons, milk, and sugar. "Where is Padiril?" he demanded.

"Padu said his nipples were cold!" Vinay answered gaily. Naveen and Ganak joined him in laughing at their friend. I could only hope my face was not too obviously red.

"He is always mentioning his nipples," Ganak clucked in mock exasperation.

"If not his ass!" Vinay exclaimed.

"Oh that," Naveen said, waving away the image with one hand. "It is too big."

"Can an ass ever be too big?" Vinay asked, looking at Naveen's.

"Definitely," Naveen replied, sitting down.

Just then, Padiril returned in a short, dark-green terrycloth robe cinched tightly at the waist but open enough in the chest to show plenty of cleavage. He sat and spread his thighs again, displaying heavily muscled calves and salacious knees.

"And where are we to celebrate this Pi Day?" he asked, a jeer in his voice. Everyone looked at me. I dragged my attention from Padiril's legs too late.

"The Pi Bar, of course," Ganak responded quickly, looking with noncommittal eyes from me to his friend and back. His friends smiled at one another. They had heard the story of our first date, I was sure.

"And you are paying, Padu," Naveen said. "You should, you know. Are you not always telling us how much money you make at Apple?"

"More than you gross at that start-up, Navi," Padiril replied, grinning a broad, post-toothbrush smile.

"Don't pronounce his name that way," Vinay muttered. "It is a girl's name," he explained to me in an aside.

"Ah but after the IPO, I will be a millionaire!" Naveen shot back, without a flinch.

"Yes, then, I will gladly pay the bill, but where shall we be having dinner?" Padiril asked, looking at me as if he wished I were on the menu.

"Udupi Palace?" Vinay suggested.

"We always eat Indian," Ganak replied. His friends looked at me and stifled laughter.

"Ajay," Padiril began, straightening his face, "where would you like to eat?" I looked unavoidably at his crotch.

"The Pi Bar has food," I mumbled.

"Perhaps they are having a party," Vinay suggested, his face happy again at the thought.

Ganak did research on his phone and found they were. He insisted everyone take Tuesday afternoon off so we could be at the Pi Bar at 3:14 when it opened. "That is when the contests start," he said, as if that were a reason we could all give to our supervisors.

At three o'clock, there was already a queue waiting. "They don't take reservations!" Ganak shouted over his friends' complaints of incompetence. So, we waited. Ganak would not take my hand.

Once inside, we only ordered drinks. "It is too early to eat," Vinay insisted, looking at his partner.

"I had lunch," Naveen explained with a guilty duck of his head.

"You should not have eaten," Ganak admonished quietly.

"Yes," Padiril agreed—much less quietly. "You should most definitely eat less and exercise more."

Vinay frowned at Padiril and began a retort, which was interrupted by Naveen informing us, "They have a special. It is good until 6:28—$7.22 for a slice of pizza and a beer." Everyone laughed at the sequence of numbers, and there was no more talk of overeating or lack of gym time.

The Pi Day contests began at 7:22. Teams could only be comprised of four people so I remained at our table, admiring Ganak's excited face and trying to ignore Padiril's pumped-up body, which was all too obvious in his form-fitting white shirt and slacks.

After many mathematical questions, Ganak's team placed first and received a trophy of Atlas holding up the world. "It is Akapura," Vinay said in wonderment. His friends laughed.

"It is a man, not a turtle!" Naveen said, giving his lover a gentle bump with his shoulder.

"Here, you take it then," Vinay said, trying to hand him the award. Naveen backed away, waving his hands no and laughing.

"I will take it!" Padiril said. He grabbed the statue around the groin.

"No," Ganak decided, yanking it out of Padiril's hand. "It will go on the entrance table in the foyer." No one disputed this judgment, nor Vinay's declaration that it was time to go home. I joined them, of course.

When Ganak and I were naked and he was sprawled across the bed, I stood above him, snapping mental photographs for remembering. He had assured me over and over our relationship could continue after his marriage, but I always replied that wasn't the way I was built or raised. His eyes gazed languidly up at me, dark and dreamy, the most beautiful eyes I had ever seen, black diamonds in an ash-brown face.

I opened my mouth to say something we both might have regretted, but he reached up to me with open arms, and I settled instead for making love as well as memories.

We spent the rest of March together—nights in my bed or his, the two weekends away in Monterey and Napa. We continued to disagree on what we would be together—if anything—after his return in May with his Indian bride.

"It is just a marriage of convenience!" he yelled in an argument days before his leaving.

"But she will live here with you!" I reminded him, yelling back even though I worried our shouting would tear us apart before his departure did.

"Of course," he said, trying with great effort to regain his composure. "But Maneesha will have her own bedroom."

"And she will hear us fucking next door!"

"We can fuck at your house then! Is that all you are worried about?"

He knew it wasn't. But his solution was always the same compromise. I stopped telling him I couldn't live with it, and he finally stopped offering it.

We continued our truce for the remainder of his time as a single man and mine as his lover. Ganak began giving me peace offerings. The day before he was to leave, he surprised me with a plane ticket.

"What does this mean?" I asked.

"We are going to London," he announced.

"What about India?" My hopes rose that he had called the marriage off. Maybe London would be our honeymoon, not theirs.

He looked at me with his amazing eyes at full effect and replied, "I will go on to India, and you will return home."

I shook my head.

"Please, Ajay." His eyes pleaded too.

I shook my head more resolutely. "I would rather say goodbye to you here," I said, folding my arms across my chest.

Ganak stared at me for a long while, analyzing and reviewing, before he nodded and put away the tickets.

When the day came, he would not let me drive him to San Francisco International as we had agreed I would. "Padu will drive me," he said.

"Let me come with you at least."

"No," he replied firmly, his eyes insisting I not insist, so I finished my coffee, tried not to cry, and held Ganak for as long as he would let me before he closed the door on my back. I took the *J* train downtown and sat at my desk all morning doing nothing until my watch informed me Ganak's Air India flight had left. He hadn't texted or called. He said he wouldn't, but I had still hoped.

The morning after Ganak's departure, an almost familiar voice spoke when I answered my mobile. "Ajay, this is Padu. I am calling to tell you our friend Ganak has arrived safely in Kochi and is with his family." I thanked him for calling and was about to say goodbye when he continued. "Would you have dinner with us tonight, Ajay?" I missed Ganak so much. At least I could be with his friends.

We met at Holy Kitchen on Twenty-fourth Street in Noe Valley, not far from their house. The three of them were dressed in tech casual: Padiril in tight pale-blue jeans and a navy-blue-plaid shirt open three buttons at the neck and chest. His dark skin reminded me of Ganak's.

The four of us ate and drank and talked of our missing friend. The three of them joked about the impending advent of Maneesha in the communal home.

"You will not be parading around only in your underwear much longer, Padu," Vinay said mock seriously.

"Yes," Naveen agreed. "No cold nipples hereafter."

Padiril grinned a toothy smile and rubbed both nipples through his shirt. Vinay shot a quick look at me. I hoped my face did not disclose my thoughts.

As soon as was polite, I took money out of my wallet for my meal.

"You are going, Ajay?" Naveen asked, looking at me with surprise.

"Yes," I answered, avoiding their eyes—most of all Vinay's. "The ride is long, and I must make connections." I was beginning to phrase sentences like my Indian friends.

Padiril spoke up quickly, his voice almost purring. "There is no need to take public transportation, Ajay. I will drive you." He opened his wallet too.

I replied nervously that taking a bus and train was no bother.

"I insist, Ajay." He leaned over the table at me with his chest.

I accepted meekly, like a lamb being led to the slaughter.

The four of us walked to their house and Padiril's car. I said good night to Vinay and Naveen in the garage. Padiril clicked open a large, black Jaguar sedan, which, to my mind, didn't seem flashy enough for him. I eased into the comfortable passenger seat, we put on our seatbelts, and he backed out onto the street.

Padiril drove like he sat, with meaty legs open in invitation. I kept my hands nervously folded in my lap. We tried conversation, but it came only sporadically. The conversation between our eyes was more effectual.

Without asking me for directions, Padiril took Sloat Boulevard to Sunset Boulevard, turning south. "This is not the way," I said quickly, my voice breaking.

"There is such a lovely moon tonight, Ajay," Padiril said, continuing south. "Why don't we enjoy it a bit together?" He made a left turn at Lake Merced.

I looked out the windshield at a moon which was full and virgin white. I thought of it shining over Ganak a half day earlier and wondered whether he had watched it with Maneesha. Grief and loneliness welled up inside me, and just then Padiril chose to smile with all his teeth. *Why not?* an evil angel at my shoulder answered, although I had not asked. Padiril made a quick, right-angled turn onto a narrow, paved road leading to the lake. My body slammed against the car door, reminding me it was there and had its needs.

The car rolled to a quiet, braking stop, and without any further attempt to talk, Padiril leaned across the cup holders to kiss me, gently at first and then with much more force. His tongue was huge inside my mouth, battling mine and searching for my throat. I gasped for air and half-heartedly tried to break free of his hands at my back, keeping me in place. They clenched more tightly, and I gave in. He pulled away, looking at me with heavy-lidded eyes and a smile I had never trusted.

"There is more room in the backseat," he said seductively. Now I saw why Padiril owned a sedan.

"Please," I begged, sounding as virgin as the moon.

"You are so beautiful, Ajay. So blond," was his answer.

He began unbuttoning my shirt.

"No," I said, halting him with the flat of my hands against the mounds of his chest.

Padiril sat back in his seat, observing me coldly. "And why not?" he asked in a precise, very British-sounding voice. "I am not so worthy as our friend?" His mention of

Ganak sent arrows into my heart. Padiril saw this and pressed his advantage. "He is to be married, Ajay. Married," he repeated with greater emphasis. "I know you are attracted to me. You know I am attracted to you. Why should we not do this?"

I didn't need to ask what *this* would entail.

I thought a moment, scanning the moon for advice. *Why not?* the evil angel repeated.

"All right," I said and followed him into the back seat.

In no time, we were out of our shirts and our pants were down. Padiril was the aggressor. His hands and mouth and teeth were everywhere, rushing over my body, not giving me time to regret or remember.

"Yes, beautiful," he mumbled, quickly shedding the remainder of his clothes and mine. "So pale in the moonlight," he murmured as he lifted my legs over his shoulders and applied a condom.

I must admit Padiril was good at fucking. He took his time and let me take mine. Afterward, for long, quiet moments, he stayed on top of me. A dog barked somewhere far away. A plane roared high above us. I thought of Ganak and shifted my weight beneath Padiril. With a kiss, he withdrew and exited the car to dress. After a moment, so did I. Lights were on in nearby apartments. Could they see us? Did it matter? Padiril held me steady while I reinserted my legs into my pants.

We drove to my house, neither of us speaking except for the asking and receiving of directions. I left his car with only a whispered goodbye and walked, dazed, into my house, glad neither the Chins nor any of my other neighbors were out. Inside, I slumped into a chair and automatically checked my phone. There was one message.

I am coming home Wednesday.

My fingers hovered. *Is everything all right?* I finally typed.

Will explain when I see you. Can you pick me up at the airport?

Ganak gave me the flight number and arrival time.

I sent *yes* and started worrying. My next message was to Padiril.

We need to talk.

The next evening, he and I sat across from each other in an almost empty Pi Bar in the Mission. "Ganak is coming home," was how I began the conversation.

"Yes," Padiril said, looking unperturbed and unsurprised.

I started to say, "We have to..." but Padu held up his hand to stop me talking.

"We do not *have* to, Ajay. Ganak is my friend. He was getting married, and I thought there would be no harm but now..."

"Wait," I said. "But now what?"

He looked at me intently and then leaned closer, smiling again. "You do not know."

"Know what?"

"Ganak is not married. He is not going to be married. At least," he added, with an odd smile, "not to a woman."

"Why?"

Padiril stared as if he couldn't believe my stupidity. "Because of you, Ajay! Because of you," he said more quietly, looking around the nearly empty room. "He told his parents about you and him." He shifted excitedly in his seat at each word. "Oh, the uproar! I can imagine if I told such a thing to my family!"

"He told you this?" I asked, angry Ganak had not told me.

"No," Padiril answered. "He told Naveen, and Naveen told Vinay, and Vinay told me. We were not supposed to tell you but now…" He didn't finish that sentence. Instead, he sat forward, clasped his hands, and began another one. "Ajay, you cannot tell Ganak about you and me. There was only that one time anyway. I had hoped you would like me, but… In any case, we don't want to hurt our friend," he concluded, back on the firm ground of logic.

"I can't lie to him."

"I am not talking about lying, Ajay," Padiril said firmly. "He will not ask. He does not know."

"But we do."

Padiril leaned back again and sardonically appraised me. "You Americans can be so naïve. He does not know. He will not ask," he said again, with greater emphasis.

"I don't know if I can live with it," I replied.

"Oh, stop thinking only of yourself, Ajay. Think of Ganak. His family talks of disowning him. He has shamed them in front of their friends and Maneesha's family. They are all conservative people." His eyes showed disgust. "India is not San Francisco, Ajay. Ganak has been very brave. Do not let him have been brave for nothing." He stabbed his finger at himself and at me. "You and I will forget last night happened. What was it anyway? Nothing," he answered, waving away the word. "We will not speak of it again, not to Ganak, not to ourselves, and not to others. Have you told anyone?" He looked apprehensive.

I shook my head.

"Very good. Neither have I. So, we agree?"

I didn't know if I could do what Padiril advised, but I accepted his offered hand. He held on tightly. "You are promising to me and to Ganak, Ajay. Do not fail us. Or yourself," he said.

"I won't," I told him, trying to believe what I said. He let my hand go and signaled for the check.

On Wednesday, I waited outside customs for Ganak's handsome face and slender body to appear. When it did, my heart jumped, and my face almost split in two from smiling. He waved, smiling just as broadly, and once through the gate, dropped his bag and held me so suddenly and so closely, I could barely catch my breath. I kept his head against my heart, and when he looked up, I kissed him. People in saris and western business clothes stared. I didn't care. I kissed him again and again.

"You have missed me a bit, I think," he said, looking mischievous. I picked up his bag.

"Is this all your luggage?"

"Yes," he said, looking suddenly serious. "Everything else I could leave in India."

We walked toward my car, hand in hand. "I have something to tell you," he said before we had gone very far.

"I know," I said.

He looked perturbed. "I told Naveen not to tell you."

"He didn't."

"Who did then?"

"Padiril," I said, hoping I was not turning red.

"Padiril?" he asked in a wondering voice. Then, the lightbulb lit. "I cannot say anything to any one of them. Oh, well." He smiled up at me. "Are you happy?"

"Yes," I said, squeezing his hand. "But it has caused you so much trouble. I'm not happy about that."

Ganak dismissed the trouble with his free hand, making me flinch. It was the same gesture Padiril had made about our secret. "Maneesha is the only one I am worried about, but she insists she is fine," he said. "She prefers to marry for love as well." His face tightened and relaxed in an array of emotions.

"But your parents? Their friends?"

He kissed me. "They will either get over it or they won't. Now, where shall we eat?"

I let him discard the topic and took a deep breath. "I have something to tell you too." Ganak gave me a quick look. I had to tell him. I took another deep breath. He waited. Ganak began to look afraid. "I missed you," I said, exhaling.

He smiled wickedly at me. "You will buy me dinner first?" he inquired.

"I will buy you a ring," I blurted. His eyes danced, and his smile broadened, but he did not stop our walking toward the car.

"I will have to buy new clothes then," he said. "I left my wedding kirta in India."

"We can go shopping together," I said.

"We can do many things together," Ganak agreed, smiling lasciviously.

We were at the elevators. I punched the up button. Once the doors closed, we kissed until level five. The doors opened on the surprised eyes and open mouths of a young Indian couple with two small children. Ganak spoke to them in Hindi and they smiled, making room for us to leave. "*Badhaee!*" the woman called after us.

"What does that mean?" I asked.

"Congratulations," Ganak replied happily.

I turned to thank her, but the doors had closed.

As we drove north on 101, I asked Ganak to choose the restaurant.

"I am thinking pizza. Let us go to the Pi Bar after," he said, before turning to me with a sly smile. "Sex always leaves me so very hungry."

"You have changed your mind then?"

"Yes, Ajay," Ganak sounded serious. "I have changed my mind, but I'm glad you didn't," he whispered, taking my hand and looking ahead out of the windshield.

I had to tell him.

"Ganak—"

"Yes?"

I heard Padiril's words in my head. *You are promising to me and to Ganak, Ajay. Do not fail us.*

"I love you."

"I love you too!"

I drove on.

April

Ripe Fruit

"Can I help you?" a male voice asked.

I turned, ready with my list of questions. A young Chicano was standing behind me, the fabric of his forest-green polo shirt stretched almost to bursting across his chest.

"Sir, can I help you?" his voice repeated. His eyes were laughing at mine, like they'd seen this all many times before.

"Uh, yes," I stuttered. "Uh, I'd like to buy some trees."

My eyes shifted rapidly to the brightly colored photos of ripe fruit on tags hanging from a row of trees. Juicy Gravenstein apples. Dangling Anjou pears. Darkest red Bing cherries. Fecund Honey Babe peaches. I felt so embarrassed.

"You are looking for fruit trees?" the young man asked, following my stare.

I nodded yes guiltily.

"What kind of fruit?" he prompted, taking a fatal step next to me. I willed my hands to remain at my sides.

"What do you suggest?" I asked, blushing as red as a Washington Delicious.

"You like Fuji apples?" He moved down the row. My eyes followed his rotating walk, his khakis riding low on his hips, his green shirt tucked haphazardly into his pants. "Produces good if you have a lot of sun," he informed me.

"I have lots of sun," I confirmed enthusiastically.

He nodded and bent over, exposing brown skin and a glimmer of red underwear.

I wiped sweat off my forehead.

"Here are a couple good ones," the young man said, straightening up. He held two young trees like dumbbells. My eyes grazed from tree to tree across his chest. His nametag read Alejandro.

"Which one do you like? A thicker trunk is better," he prompted. Alejandro had a thick trunk and a Mayan face. I thought of museum statues of squat, muscular men, stolen from Mayan architecture. Alejandro would look like that—if he were naked. A film rolled in my mind.

He shook the trees at me to bring my attention back to commerce.

"That one," I said, indicating his right arm. Alejandro pointed it at me. I accepted the tree. It was heavier than it looked.

"Anything else?" he asked. "Pears maybe. A ripe pear is really tasty."

I nodded vigorously in agreement.

"Here's a bosc. It keeps better. Or maybe you'd rather have a Bartlett?" He bent over again, checking tags.

"Bosc," I managed to squeak out.

"It's a little more money." He turned around to look at me. His eyes widened. "*Tan grande*," he whispered.

I said I'd take the pear tree, too, without asking how much money *tan grande* was.

"How about a cherry and a citrus?" he asked, his eyes still focused on my crotch. "Then you will have ripe fruit all year."

"I'd like ripe fruit all year," I said in a stronger voice. The longer he leaned over, the more definite I felt about it. Maybe I should... I squashed my maybe like a bug. He was way too young.

"Why don't I get a cart?" the kid said decisively and moved off toward the main building, his ass swinging rhythmically from side to side.

My brain intervened during his absence. How much was this costing me? I totaled the price tags. Over two hundred dollars before tax! Did I even have space in my new backyard for four trees? How big would they get? What would my neighbors think? Maybe I should put one back—but which one? I really did want ripe fruit all year— firm, fresh, nubile. Squeaking wheels made me jump. Alejandro was pushing a trolley straight at me. He stopped just before he hit the apple tree, which he took from me and placed on the trolley, followed by the pear.

He chose a cherry and an orange with a raised eyebrow in my direction. *Young, too young,* I chanted under my breath as my arm reached out to accept his selections. My fingertips grazed a knuckle, totally accidentally.

Alejandro jammed his hands into his pockets, which made him look even younger. "You need any soil amendments?" he asked, rocking back and forth on his feet.

I said yes without really understanding the question and stumbled after him as he steered the cart toward stacks of plastic bags. I trailed behind, imagining another film starring just the two of us. We were naked on the stacks after hours on a warm summer night, like this one promised to be. I...

"How many you want?" he asked, leaning against the trolley. I blinked several times. It was strange to see him back in clothes so suddenly.

"Two," I said assertively. "Two big ones."

He hoisted the bulky bags like they were Kleenex boxes and plopped them onto the trolley with a double thud, dusting imaginary dirt off his clothes afterward, carefully and repeatedly. I envied his fingers as they worked industriously across his chest and crotch.

"You know," he said in a seductive sales voice. "We deliver free on an order this big. We also have a planting service. Twenty-five dollars an hour. I'd be the one doing the planting. Three hours. Minimum," he concluded in a more businesslike voice. I wasn't sure what he was selling, but seventy-five dollars seemed like quite a bargain.

"Sign me up," I responded quickly, like it was a time-limited offer.

Alejandro accompanied me to the cashier and told the woman in Spanish what to charge. He gave me a 10 percent discount, she said to me in English; I hoped that meant he liked me. When we left the counter for my car, my heart was beating almost as loudly as the squeaking trolley wheels.

"Nice ride," he said as he opened the tailgate of my Jeep Grand Cherokee. "I like red too." I reminisced about his underwear while he went on with his story. "I drive a red pickup," he informed me. "Dodge Ram." The word *ram* made my erection thump inside my pants, like a dog wagging its tail. "*Chulo papi*." A hint of tongue appeared between the boy's Bing cherry lips as he whispered, but his eyes darted toward the garden center main building, and he hurriedly started loading trees and bags into the car. I didn't see anything when I looked.

"So, when should I come?" he asked when he was finished, looking again at the building and relaxing.

I mused over his word choice but roused myself in time to say, "Whenever you're available."

He thought a moment.

"Tomorrow is Arbor Day, you know," he announced decisively. "Good day for planting trees. Usually, Saturday is extra but for you, *papi...*" He gave me a wink and a leer. I nearly dragged him into the nearby thicket of pink and red oleanders. Instead, we agreed on 10:00 a.m. and he shut my rear door.

"So," he said, settling against the back of my Jeep, the business part of our conversation over. "I haven't seen you here before." He folded his arms across his chest, which created even more cleavage, and spread his legs. My left brain explained I'd just moved into the area while my right brain enjoyed another fantasy starring the young man in front of me. He said he went to school; I hoped he meant college.

He suggested I call him Alejo. I told him my name was Doug. We talked about him working for his father, who owned the Sunshine Garden Center, and what I did in tech. He was twenty, which was a relief. I didn't tell him I was thirty-two. I moved closer to him, hoping to make fantasy reality—at least a small part of it, but something behind me caught his attention and he stood up abruptly, almost at attention. I looked over my shoulder. An older man stood outside the garden center building, arms folded across his own ample chest, staring at us. He looked a lot like Alejo.

"My dad," he muttered. "I better get back to work. See you tomorrow morning, Doug." He used my name for the first time, which sent a thrill up my spine. I watched him run across the parking lot, leaning into the cart. His father spoke to him harshly in Spanish and looked at me in anger. I decided it would be best to drive away.

Saturday dawned bright and sunny. The forecast said ninety-five with a late afternoon breeze. I shaved and showered carefully, dressed in clean work clothes, and looked at myself in the mirror. "What's up with you?" I asked my image. "You're not usually interested in men this young." Just then the doorbell rang. My image shrugged.

"Happy Arbor Day, Doug!" Alejo said when I opened the door. I could look right over his head at the huge red pickup parked in my driveway. I hadn't realized how short he was. For the first time in my life, I was glad I was only five foot ten.

"Happy Arbor Day, Alejo," I replied, trying to match his level of *bonhomie*. "Would you like some coffee?"

As he followed me to the kitchen, I heard him mumble, "Nice *nalgas*."

"What does that mean?"

"Nice house," he lied.

Mugs in hand, we left the kitchen for the patio and each took an Adirondack chair, drinking strong, black coffee and talking as if we had all morning, which we did since I was paying for it. Anyway, if Alejo and I worked together and worked hard, it wouldn't take us three hours. Plenty of time for other activities. A new film started airing.

"Isn't it cool?" he asked enthusiastically, interrupting my screening. "It's Arbor Day and we're planting trees! My dad and I plant trees in city parks every year. We put in ten trees already this morning." He puffed out his chest proudly.

"You must have gotten up really early," I said, picturing him in bed, the sheet thrown artfully across his groin, big chest exposed, one hefty leg showing...

"Doug! Doug?" I heard him saying.

"Oh! Excuse me," I said, seeing his coffee cup was empty. "Let me get you a refill."

"That isn't what I was asking." He looked at me curiously. "But, okay!" he finished brightly.

We talked over the second cup of coffee, too, but about us, not Arbor Day. Alejo was studying to be an accountant. "I'm really good at figures," he boasted. I said I bet he was, and he giggled. He thought it was cool I was a CPA.

"We're both into money," he said. That made me take several silent sips of coffee. He looked at his watch and chugged the rest of his.

"You want to get started, Doug?" he asked, standing up, fantasy crotch suddenly within real groping distance. "Where do you want the trees to go?" Temporarily wordless, I pointed toward a weedy section along the back fence.

Alejo headed for the side gate in strides long for his height. I hurried to catch up. He extracted the apple and the citrus from the bed of his truck, and I reached for the pear and the cherry. "We gonna do this together, Doug?" he asked me, wiggling his eyebrows at me.

"You bet we are," I answered, wiggling mine back. He giggled again, which was becoming disconcerting. He was young for twenty, museum-quality body notwithstanding.

We returned for the soil amendments. There were four bags, not two. Alejo giggled again. "No extra charge," he said reassuringly and hoisted a bag over each shoulder. "I estimated we'd need more."

I staggered after him with the third and fourth bags wrapped insecurely in my arms.

"*Eres fuerte*," he said, looking back. I hoped that meant something good. "You work out?" He grinned.

I nodded as butchly as I could before one bag slid out of my grasp and dropped to the ground.

"That's okay, Dougito," he said without looking back or stopping. "I'll come back for it."

Dougito, I mused to myself. *Little Doug? Dougie!* I liked it.

Alejo and Dougie worked side by side, clearing weeds, spading the ground, and mixing in bags of compost. Four turned out to be just right. By the time the plot was ready, we were both soaked in sweat. Alejo looked like he'd been in a wet T-shirt contest—and had won.

"Let's take a break," I said. "I'll get us a beer."

I nearly dropped both Dos Equis when I returned to the patio. Alejo had his shirt off and was using it to wipe sweat off his nearly hairless body. His chest was as massive as promised and hung high and wide, nubile and inviting. The nipples were small, maroon, and tight. My fingers twitched.

"That for me?" He pried a beer out of one of my hands. He clinked the neck of his bottle against mine and said, "*Salud*."

"*Salud*," I repeated. He took a lengthy pull from the beer, his Adam's apple gulping down several swallows, his lips wrapped tightly around the head of the bottle. I fanned myself and mentioned how hot it was getting.

"Why don't you take your shirt off too, Dougito? You'll be cooler," Alejo suggested, staring fixedly at my chest. Hadn't I heard those words in a movie?

I slowly complied, wondering if I were too pale. My chest certainly wasn't as impressive as his. *Oh, well,* I thought. *Here goes.*

Alejo gave me a thumbs-up and we drank our beers, eyes on each's other mammary glands. After he tipped the bottle back, draining every drop, I asked if he wanted another.

"Maybe later, *Papi*," he said. "We're making real good time. Probably finish early. You got anything else for me to do, boss?" He gave me a saucy look.

"Oh, we'll think of something," I answered as nonchalantly as possible, watching him rotate his assets on the way back to work. He began digging a hole, foot on the shovel, pushing it in, lifting the spadeful with straining arms, stretching his body as he deposited the amended earth beside him. "Ripe fruit, ripe fruit," I kept muttering as I went to help him.

Alejo positioned the apple tree inside it and asked me to hold it straight while he filled the hole twice from the hose. After the water soaked in, he knelt at my feet to push soil around the roots and pack it solid. I couldn't resist tousling his hair with my dirty glove.

"Oh, I'm sorry!" I said, snatching back my hand.

"No problem, Dougito," he said, grinning up at me from the doggy position. "Let's do the pear tree." He crawled to the next hole, his jeans barely hanging onto his ass.

"Ripe fruit," I said to myself, grabbing the pear tree.

"What did you say, Doug?" he asked.

"Nothing," I said. I wasn't as good at lying as Alejo was.

He waited a moment, the cat watching the mouse, before shrugging his shoulders. "No problem. What you want next—the orange or the cherry?"

"The orange," I said, barely stifling the urge to say what I truly wanted.

"Oh," he said, smirking up at me. "You saving the cherry for last?"

I started digging the last hole as quickly as I could.

After we had popped the cherry into the ground, we removed our gloves and stood, admiring our work. As natural as anything, Alejo put his hand around my waist and I not nearly as naturally extended my arm around his shoulders. His skin was smooth and warm. I pulled him against my hip, and he turned into my arms. Enough was enough. So what if he was young? So what if he giggled a lot? I squeezed the broad, thick muscles of his back and kissed his soft, thick lips. I looked at my watch. We still had thirty minutes.

We used several of them kissing and exploring each other's bodies with curious fingers but when my neighbor fired up his mower and I suggested we go inside, Alejo looked at his phone.

"I probably better go," he said, looking alarmed.

I offered my shower, but he shook his head and pulled his green shirt over his head rapidly. "No worries, Dougito," he said, his voice muffled inside the shirt. "They expect me to be dirty. I have clean clothes at work."

"Any plans for tonight?" I asked, biting my lip too late.

"Maybe," he answered, his head on view again. "*Quizás, quizás, quizás,*" he sang. "You know that song?"

"No," I said, fanning myself. "But are you sure you don't want to shower?"

He shook his head no, gave me a quick kiss, and ran out of the side gate. I stood there, watching the gigantic red truck speed off toward the east. Somewhere that direction was Indiana. *Well, Doug, you're not in Indiana anymore.*

I retired to the privacy of my upstairs bedroom and closed the blinds. In my mind, Alejo hadn't left. He and I were still in the back yard, still kissing and exploring. I took my jeans and Jockeys off.

"*Ay, papi,*" he said, a little breathless.

I removed his pants and underwear, which of course were red. He got down in the doggy position without being prompted. He was ripe all right. I pulled the condom out of my pocket, glad I'd planned ahead...

And then the phone rang. It was my mother. "How hot is it out there?" she asked.

"Pretty hot, Mom," I replied. I got up to put a robe on, opened the blinds, and walked to the kitchen for another beer, all the while saying, "Uh huh" and "Really?" to my mother's monologue.

Later that afternoon, I received another phone call. I hoped it was Alejo saying he was available that evening so we could make fantasy interruptus reality, but instead of his tenor, an unfamiliar baritone asked, "Mister Webster?"

I answered yes, wondering who it was.

"My name is Garcia," the accented voice announced. "Alejandro's father. From the Sunshine Garden Center?" he added in case I still didn't get it. I got it all right.

Mr. Garcia came to the point quickly. "Tell me, *señor,* how old are you?"

"Thirty-two," I answered, gulping hard.

"Mister Webster, forgive me. I do not judge. People are what they are. But, please, find a man who is your own age. Alejandro is just a boy."

"He told me he was twenty!" I blurted out.

"He is seventeen," Mr. Garcia said sonorously, like the sentence of doom.

Fuck! I thought. What was the age of consent in California? Oh, my God! Maybe his father was going to have me arrested!

"I swear he told me he was twenty!" I said, feeling sweat flow inside my shirt for the second time that day.

"Do not worry, *señor*. My son told me this too. All I am asking is that you have..." He hesitated. "No more relations with Alejandro."

"But I haven't had any!" I yelped. "Relations, I mean."

Mr. Garcia's breathing sounded skeptical. "Please, *señor*," he said.

"Okay," I said. After all, I had had carnal knowledge of his son—in my mind.

"And I still welcome you as a customer. We understand each other, yes?" he asked, striving for good customer relations.

I nodded at the phone and then squeaked out, "*Sí*."

Mr. Garcia sighed and disconnected.

*

I did not return to the Sunshine Garden Center and Alejandro Garcia and his father. I found another nursery to buy supplies from and other men to have sex with—and I made sure they were all in my age category. Mr. Garcia had given me good advice as well as saving my ass from a lawsuit. Still, images of Alejo's body came frequently to mind in the weeks that followed with the original mental film replaying itself frequently. Sometimes, even at work, I had to take an extended bathroom break.

"Douglas Webster," I said crisply into my office phone one day. It had been a busy morning in the CPA biz.

"*Señor* Webster?" a deep, slightly familiar voice asked in a Spanish accent.

I almost said "*sí*" but caught myself and merely answered, "Yes, this is Douglas Webster."

"Alfredo Garcia," the deep voice intoned.

"Yes, Mister Garcia," I said pretty calmly, I thought. "How can I help you?" Maybe he needed a CPA. He ran a business after all. I could only hope.

"My son," he began, and my heart sank.

"I haven't been anywhere near him!" I croaked defensively.

"I know, *señor*. I know." He took a deep breath. I imagined the father's impressive chest expanding inside a forest-green shirt. "My son is unhappy, *señor*," Garcia said, bringing me back to the phone conversation. "And I thought..." He hesitated. "Perhaps you would like to come to dinner," he finished rapidly as if he had to hurry the sentence out or he wouldn't say it at all.

"Excuse me?" I asked, sure I'd misunderstood or that it had just been more film dialogue in my head.

There was silence on the other end of our conversation. "Mister Webster," the voice finally said. "Maybe we should talk."

By the time I hung up, I had a coffee date with Alfredo Garcia. Under different circumstances and with a different sexual orientation on his part, that might have been a good thing.

The Starbucks in Lafayette was crowded, but I found Mr. Garcia when he stood up and waved. He looked great in his work uniform—tanned, mustachioed, and almost as muscular as his son. We shook hands and sat across from each other. I pretended not to ogle his chest, and he pretended not to notice.

He offered to buy me a coffee. I accepted a latte.

He walked to the counter, his body moving sensuously inside his clothes, the son matured by twenty additional years of living and definitely in my age category. I sighed in spite of myself. *If only,* I thought, reviewing film of an older Alejo and myself living happily ever after. I was jolted back to reality by Mr. Garcia handing me a hot cup of coffee without a sleeve.

"My son is unhappy," Mr. Garcia repeated after I had thanked him. "He says I am not a good father." My urge was to pat his solid-looking shoulder and reassure him, but I restrained myself. "He says he likes you," Mr. Garcia continued. "He says you are a good man. He says I am a homophobe." That word did not seem to roll trippingly off his tongue. "Mister Webster..."

"Doug," I said, thinking we'd had enough of mister and señor.

"Alfredo," he replied, trying to smile. He looked so much like his son when he smiled. I took several nervous gulps of foamy latte. "I knew what Alejo was before he told me. It was not easy, but I accepted it. Marta, my wife, and I had many conversations." He sighed. "It was easier for her. But, Alejo is my firstborn. You understand," he said confidentially as if I did.

"It's never easy for parents," I said, thinking of my own father's threats to disown me, which he had yet to carry out, and the uneasiness between us to this day.

Alfredo gave a sad nod of his head.

"You were just protecting him, like a parent should," I said, now thinking of my mother who always left the room when my father and I argued. "He's young. You didn't know what was happening. I could have been...

"But you are not." Alfredo Garcia smiled more easily now. "I see that now. And truly," he said, sounding proud, "my son doesn't need to be protected. He is a man."

"Not if he's seventeen," I reminded him.

Alfredo gave me a rueful smile. "Being a man is not always a matter of age, Mister Doug," he told me. "And besides, my son is no longer seventeen." My expression must have changed. Or maybe it was my mouth dropping open to my chest. Mr. Garcia chuckled and put a hand on my shoulder, its grip strong but gentle. "He goes to college soon. Locally," he added.

I liked the feel of Alfredo Garcia's hand on my shoulder, but I shook that thought off. I must have also shaken my shoulder because Mr. Garcia removed his hand quickly as if stung. I wanted to tell him I didn't mean to brush him away, to explain, but decided things—and hands—were better left where they lay.

"So, Mister Doug, you will come to dinner? My wife is a very good cook. *Muy buena comida*," he added. I wondered if that was her specialty dish. I really should take Spanish lessons now that I lived in California.

"Just Doug, please," I answered.

"Doug." Alfredo's smile spread his black mustache wide above his slightly chapped lips. Images of me kissing those lips came to mind. "You will come to dinner?" he asked. The streaming of kisses ended abruptly.

My eyes roamed from his expectant face to the bags of coffee on the shelves near us, the highly polished tile floor beneath our feet, and the black-and-white photographs of nineteenth century Latinos arranged periodically along the store's walls. Garcia senior was fortyish and unavailable. I hadn't seen Alejo in months.

"I think maybe not," I said sadly. "Your son is so much younger than I am. Maybe it's best if we leave things as they are."

Alfredo Garcia looked both disappointed and relieved. We talked a few minutes more while I finished my coffee, about my fruit trees mainly, although the movie starring him and me resumed in my head. Mr. Garcia assured me I would have ripe fruit all year.

"It may take a couple of years. You should give them time to mature."

Good advice all around, I told myself as we shook hands.

That evening, urgent knocking made me rush to my door. Maybe one of my neighbors needed help. However, it was not the Wongs, the Chaneys nor the Petersons. It was Alejo Garcia, wearing a white T-shirt and dark-blue jeans, both more than amply and attractively filled.

"You shouldn't be here," I said, barring the way. I felt noble and self-sacrificing in the face of all that male pulchritude.

"My father said he spoke to you," he said, looking angry and furiously sexy. It may have been my imagination, but he looked a little older too.

"You told me you were twenty," I said, trying to sound stern.

"I'm sorry, Dougito," Alejo said, his anger dissipating. "I shouldn't have lied."

"No, you shouldn't have," I agreed, dropping my arm from the door jamb. "Your father could have had me arrested."

"He is not like that," Alejo said, looking up at me through his father's heavy eyebrows. My heart lurched, but I remained externally adamant. "Why won't you come to dinner?" he asked peevishly, reminding me he was eighteen, not forty-two. "My mother wants to meet you." If I had hoped to escape explanation, I had been wrong.

"Didn't your father tell you?"

"What?" he said, defiant again. "That I am too young? There is not that much difference."

"Fourteen years," I subtracted for him.

"We are both men." He folded his thick arms across his thicker chest and held his handsome head high. *That chest,* I thought. *Those eyes.* He was growing a mustache, like his father. I couldn't take it.

"Come in," I said, standing aside.

We sat at either end of the couch.

"We need to talk," I began.

He nodded, scooting closer.

"I'm nearly twice your age," I said, as he butt-hopped the rest of the way. "I..."

He put a hand on my thigh.

"You..."

And then we were kissing and pawing each other as if the director had said *action*. I watched him remove my clothes and his as if this were another fantasy. My brain advised critically it was not, and I should get off the couch immediately, but the rest of me ignored its advice. When we were done, he asked me how the trees were doing.

I replied, "Fine. Now, let's talk. You..."

"Show me," he said, rising and putting his briefs back on. He led me into the backyard, only one of us in our underwear. We stood side by side, arm in arm, appraising my mini-orchard.

"Looks good," Alejo said, his happy eyes taking in the present. My eyes, however, saw the future. In twenty years, he would look like his father. Okay, that was not a discouragement. In twenty years, he would be older than I was then, and thirty-eight is very different from eighteen, I reasoned sagely. *In twenty years, you will be in your fifties*. That final point won the argument.

"I'm too old for you," I said to his happy smile, which was replaced quickly by a frown.

"You are not," he argued. "You were like a bull in there." He nodded toward the house.

"You need to know other men," I said gamely.

He shook his head.

"You're going to college. You'll meet—" I started to say nice boys your age but chose my words more carefully. "—men your own age."

Alejo grinned at me. "Give up, Dougito. I have made my choice."

He wrapped his arms around me and stood up on tiptoe for a kiss. Somewhere, I heard a director yell *cut*.

May

Someone I Didn't Know

I decided not to go home for Mother's Day even though my sister invited me out to Douglaston. I opted instead to spend the day in the Metropolitan Museum but avoided madonnas, pietás, and all mother and child scenes painted down the centuries.

As I gazed at the muscles of a marble Heracles, a vaguely familiar voice behind me said, "Hello, Dave." I turned, smile on automatic, and saw someone I didn't know. Whoever he was, though, he was good looking in a deliberately rough trade kind of way, with the *de rigueur* two day's growth of beard covering strong jaws and a jutting chin. Full red lips pouted provocatively at me. Sunglasses hid his eyes. *Really*? But what I saw below the chin made me forgive and forget. A tight yellow dress shirt open several buttons down the chest displayed a deep tan and deeper cleavage. Jeans formfitting in the crotch and thighs covered and accented the stranger's own heavy musculature. Heracles had a rival.

"It's Bruce," the stranger said, removing the shades. "Bruce Sonnenschein. From high school?" The name evoked memories, which the man in front of me did not. I repeated the name uncertainly and hurt appeared in the dark-blue eyes. I recognized him now.

"Bruce Sonnenschein," I repeated a second time, still trying to reconcile the present person with the past. The fey voice was gone. So were the fluttering hands and the overly coy pursing of lips. This Bruce Sonnenschein was butch to the nth degree.

The man in front of me put his hand on my shoulder in a consoling way. He said, "I'm sorry your mother's dead," and I frowned. If I lived another hundred years, I never wanted to hear that sentence again, but I liked his hand on my shoulder. It did feel consoling.

"Thank you," I managed to say. "How did you know?"

He dropped his hand and shrugged. "My mom still keeps in touch with some people in Farmingdale. Would you like a coffee? Or brunch?" The segue was abrupt but his tone and look said he was confident I'd say yes. "There's a cafeteria downstairs."

"No," I answered curtly, coming back to myself. I didn't need that depressing place with its manufactured light and sickly color—especially that day—and anyway, I wasn't sure I wanted to be with Bruce Sonnenschein. Seeing him again made all the guilt rise up in me, but something else had risen as well, so I agreed.

"Okay but not there," I said more politely.

"Where?" he asked. "On Madison maybe? Do you still have your sticker? In case you want to come back?"

He smirked, clearly messaging his total disbelief anyone would leave him for a museum. He touched the proof of payment situated on the center of my chest, which activated my fourth chakra. I visually located his, strategically placed just above his right nipple, erect and obvious through his shirt, which activated chakra number two.

"Wherever you want," he said in a slightly pleading voice.

"I know a place on Madison," I said in a rush.

That made him smile, which made me glad. Now, at least, I had done something that made him happy.

He pivoted and walked toward the exit in long, manful strides. My eyes followed him before my legs did. I remembered walking behind him down high school hallways, thinking the same lustful thoughts I was thinking now. At the exit to the gallery he looked back, smirked again as if he had read my thoughts, and waited while I caught up.

We walked side by side to the main entrance, down the steps, and across Fifth toward Madison. The hostess at the café smiled appreciatively at Bruce and led us to a window table. When we were seated and our drinks had been ordered from a waiter who couldn't take his eyes off Bruce, I enthusiastically stated the obvious. "You look terrific!"

"You do too," he replied. "But then, you always were so handsome." His voice sounded wistful and his eyes had a yearning in them I couldn't look at. I remembered that yearning. I had looked away back then too.

"Have you been home lately?" I asked, feeling my cowardice, past and present.

"You mean Farmingdale?" he sneered. He draped one arm over the back of his chair. "I don't think of that place as home. I only lived there our senior year. When I went to college, I got an apartment in Manhattan. My folks moved to Rochester a couple years later. They're in Paris now." He thought a moment. "Yeah, Paris. Rome is in three weeks."

It surprised me to hear Bruce had gone to college. I don't know why. I couldn't remember if he had been a good, bad, or indifferent student. We only had one class together, and that was PE. He definitely wasn't any good there. It was where the teasing began: jokes about his voice and mannerisms, questions about his sexuality, intimated violence. Never anything actually physical but still, relentless. I had watched it all, heard it all, and done nothing. I could have, I told myself, then and now, but I was in the closet and afraid of the door being opened. My reputation, after all. I was football and basketball captain, student body president: a high school bigshot—for what that's worth now, ten years later, which isn't much.

I realized Bruce had stopped speaking. "Lucky them," I said quickly.

"Mother's Day gift," Bruce explained concisely as the waiter returned with our drinks. Bruce had ordered a Bloody Mary. It came with the longest, thickest stalk of celery I'd ever seen stuck in a glass. I was confronted by my white pomegranate Cosmobellini with its teeny tiny sprig of basil. Mirror, mirror on the wall, now who is the butchest one of all?

I thought of all the Mother's Day gifts I'd handed over to my mom, from the kindergarten drawings to perfumes best called "exotic" to, more recently, cards containing fifty-dollar gift certificates. *I should really call my dad*, I thought. *I really should have gone to Sharon's for Mother's Day. I really...*

My father's face merged into Bruce's. He was waiting again.

"Excuse me," I said, with a start. "What did you say?"

"Not me," he said. "Him."

I looked up into the smirking face of the actor/singer/model waiter and ordered a cheese-and-herb-soufflé omelet with sausages. Big ones. The waiter's smirk widened.

Bruce said, "Thank you," with the barest of phony smiles, and the waiter's face fell. He left, his disappointment preceding him.

"I went to Hunter," he enunciated precisely as if I were hard of hearing or new to English. "What about you?" He sucked more Mary up his straw while I answered.

"Harvard for undergraduate."

"And Yale for law school," he said, an eyebrow raised.

"Good guess," I responded, wondering what the eyebrow meant.

"Where else?" he said with a sting. Then he frowned. "You're an attorney."

"Huddleston, Hembry, Albright, and Webb," I recited. His face returned to neutral, making no further judgment on my chosen profession.

"What about you?" I asked.

He waved away the question with the celery stalk from his drink. "I'm a clerk. I do a little modeling too," he continued, showing me his profile, whether intentionally or not, I couldn't tell. "And some porno," he added, leaning forward and letting me look further down the several open buttons of his shirt. I nearly dropped my drink. "You ever see any of my videos?" he asked as our orders arrived. The server snorted, like he certainly had.

"Anything else I can do for you?" he asked Bruce, with an emphasis on the personal pronoun.

"No, thanks," Bruce answered, watching my face.

The waiter flounced away, terribly offended. Well, points to him for persevering.

Thinking about it, I did remember one video. At the time, a man in the cast *had* reminded me of Bruce. There was a pickup with the driver's door open. The man who sort of looked like Bruce was sitting facing out, his pants and underwear down to his ankles. Another man was giving him a blow job. My face reddened, and Bruce chuckled. As quickly as I could, I took up my knife and fork and assiduously divided the sausages on my plate into three equal sections each and crisscrossed the omelet into bite-sized portions.

"Have you seen anyone else from high school?" I asked, trying to say something, anything. I popped the first sausage third into my mouth.

"I hated high school," Bruce said fiercely.

I chewed quickly and swallowed hard. "I know," I said. "I'm sorry." *Keep going*.

But Bruce spoke before I could. He looked resigned and then angry.

"I didn't blame you. Anyway, you tried. You were the only one who did—including all those sorry-ass teachers!"

"I didn't try very hard," I said, quickly gulping at my drink for additional courage. "Look, I want to apologize for not trying, for not intervening, for not—"

Bruce put up his hand, palm facing me, the lines making me try to tell his fortune.

"If you had, they probably would have turned on you too. Assholes," he muttered. His look softened. "I've thought a lot about you."

"Really?" I yelped, like a happy puppy.

Bruce nodded grimly. "Yes. I'd be thinking how shitty that year was, and then I'd remember you and feel better."

How unbelievably sweet that sounded. My emotions leaned in Bruce's direction as well as my body.

"I've thought of you too," I said. "So many times. I wish—"

Bruce reached across the table, breaking my train of thought. Our hands met. Our fingers intertwined.

"I wish we'd done this in high school," I finished, letting the feeling of him soak into me.

"Me too," he whispered, rubbing my thumb with his. Back and forth, back and forth…

"How is everything?" the waiter's voice asked archly.

"Wonderful," Bruce said to me, his face young and happy.

"Let me know if there's anything else you need," the waiter told us. He handed me the bill on a black plastic tray. Bruce snatched it out of my hand.

"I invited you," he said.

He placed the tray to one side and started eating again, giving me another chance to look for vestiges of the boy from senior year. Then, he wore glasses that did nothing for his face. When he took them off in gym class, he was so shockingly good looking I had to suffocate a gasp. His eyes recognized my reaction, though, and his face beamed with hope. I remember turning away quickly. When I looked back, the hope was gone.

I also remember trying not to watch while he got into or out of his gym clothes. His body was another surprise, naturally muscular: chest defined, arms reasonably thick, and very good legs. The first time we changed near each other, my mouth fell open so fast I was sure everyone had seen, but apparently no one had. No one turned on me, called me fruit or fag, or gave me the limp wrist like they did with Bruce. I told myself to be more careful. And I was.

I moved to a different row of lockers, but Bruce did too. I tried to avoid showering with him but there'd he be, next to me. When I was ready to leave for lunch, he followed me out of the door. I never invited him to join me at the jocks' table.

I did, however, when no one else was around, talk to him, and I guess that crumb was enough to make him forget everything else I didn't do.

"I had such a crush on you."

Bruce was speaking but it could have been my own thoughts. Yes, I had a crush on him. Wouldn't my high school friends be amazed to hear that? Dave Hoffman had a crush on Bruce Sonnenschein.

"What?" I asked, although I'd heard him fine.

"I had a crush on you," he repeated more loudly. Couples around us looked, first at him and then at me and then back at Bruce. "Why wouldn't I? You were—are—so handsome. And you were so nice to me."

I didn't know how to respond. Guilt and desire were still battling it out inside me.

"Would you like to go out sometime?" I heard him ask in a more business-like tone.

I almost sprayed the sip of Cosmobellini I'd just taken.

"Sure," I answered, putting my glass down with a shaky hand. Desire had defeated guilt, at least for the moment.

"Great!" Bruce said and segued into, "How about dinner?"

"Tonight?" I asked. I pictured how we might spend the intervening afternoon.

He smiled indulgently. "I have an appointment. What does your week look like?" We checked our schedules. The best Bruce could do was Thursday, and even then, he said he'd have to move things around.

"Don't do that for me!" I told him.

"Why not?" he asked with his sexy stranger's smile.

We got down to logistics. Both of us lived in Brooklyn, me in Park Slope and him in Red Hook. He said he could come to me, so I booked a table at Jardiniere on Fourth Avenue, a bistro run by friends of mine.

When Bruce showed up in a light-yellow sports coat, white V-neck T-shirt, tan slacks, and camel-colored shoes, heads snapped as he sauntered through the restaurant to me. With his tan, yellow was definitely his color. I felt dowdy in my red khakis and blue cotton blazer, but he complimented me as he leaned in for a quick kiss on the lips.

Even though it was the briefest of kisses, I was Sleeping Beauty awakened by the handsome prince—only in my scenario SB was a nymphomaniac. After our lips grazed one another, I could have knocked flowers, napkins, silverware, and glasses onto the floor and fucked Bruce on the table in full view of our fellow diners, but luckily, another waiter appeared, requesting our drink orders, and I had time to reconsider. I gave the man his instructions *en français.*

"How'd you get so good at French?" Bruce asked after the waiter left. He didn't remember I'd taken French four years in high school, but why would he?

"French minor in college, a year abroad," I answered. "I lived near Paris."

"I love Paris." He gazed dreamy-eyed into the distance before abruptly staring at me intensely. I wasn't able to break the hold of his stare, as I had so easily in high school. "We should go," he said, sounding like the period was on the sentence.

"Paris?" I asked stupidly. He gave me a look that would make men strip naked immediately.

"Why not? My folks are there." His fist banged the table, rattling our silverware and making me jump. "Wouldn't that surprise them," he said, like he'd just planned a major counteroffensive in a long-running battle.

The waiter arrived with our wine, and I accepted mine gratefully. Bruce and I clinked glasses. "Santé," he said.

I tried speaking with him in French, but he answered in English, so I didn't try that again.

We both ordered the hanger steaks—mine well-done, his medium-rare. He shared my pommes frites and made me eat some of his escargots. We drank several more glasses of wine.

"Next time," I said, hoping I wasn't slurring my words, "we'll have to order a bottle."

"Or two," he said, laughing. He shifted in his seat, his chest following, taking my eyes along with it. The alcohol didn't seem to affect him, except perhaps to make him happier. He pushed back from the table. "Y'know. We really should go to Paris."

Just then, my friend Gilles arrived at our table, wearing his chef's uniform minus the health code headgear.

"Ah, *mon ami*. Good to see you," he said to me, kissing one cheek and then the other. He snatched a chair from another table and sat between Bruce and me. "Benoit will be so disappointed," he continued in French. He looked at Bruce, who didn't seem to register what Gilles was saying. "He's in Paris. Researching suppliers." He rolled his eyes. Gilles scanned Bruce's body. "This one is very hot, *n'est-ce pas*? I hope he fucks as good as he looks, my dear. Let me know. *D'accord*?"

He switched to English. "How was your meal?" he asked us.

I gave an enthusiastic review, and Bruce nodded once in agreement.

Gilles took another long look at him and wiggled his eyebrows at me. "Dessert is on me." He waved for a server. "But," he added, switching back to French, "maybe what you want for dessert is not on our menu, *mon ami*."

"I don't really eat sweet things," Bruce said.

Gilles winked elaborately at me. "Very tragic," he said. "Our friend David is very sweet, don't you think?"

Neither Bruce nor I replied.

"*Eh, bien.*" Gilles slapped his thighs and got up. "I will comp the wine."

I started to protest, but he shushed me.

"It is decided," he said mock sternly and then relaxed into a smile. "When Benoit returns, the four of us will have a party, *d'accord*?"

I looked at Bruce, whose face was noncommittal. Gilles excused himself and returned to the kitchen.

"That was nice of him," I said.

Bruce took a sip of the free wine without responding. Maybe he didn't like the party comment.

"He was just kidding about the foursome," I explained.

Still nothing.

We drank our wine and looked around the room.

"Well?" he asked after our long silence.

"Well?" I answered, staring back, pissed in more than one way.

"Do you want to go to my place?" he asked.

I debated my answer. A hint of concern appeared in Bruce's eyes. *Good,* I thought. I let him wait a little while longer.

"Mine is closer," I said and signaled for the waiter. Bruce paid again, despite all my protests.

Outside, I told him, "It's only a few blocks" and began walking toward Eleventh Street, but he stopped me in midstride, grabbing my hand with his, the strength of all those muscles not at all a surprise.

"I drove," he said, keeping my hand and leading me around the corner to a deep-blue Mercedes convertible, the same blue as his eyes.

"Wow," I said when he released the door locks. "This smells new."

"It is," Bruce confirmed as he opened my door and closed it behind me.

Where does *his money come from?* I asked myself for the fortieth time as I gave him directions. He pushed a button and the top went down for the short ride to my flat. People stared as if we were in a parade. I gave them the queen's wave.

"You're drunk," Bruce said, laughing.

"Not too drunk," I told him, wiggling my eyebrows like Gilles. Bruce laughed again and took my hand across the steering column. I edged closer for easier access. He moved his hand to my thigh and inched it upward.

Miraculously, he found a parking space on my block. Otherwise, I think we might have had to head for some bushes in Prospect Park. He put the top back up, opened my door for me, and actually gave me his hand to help me out of the car. Was this a signal he wanted the top bunk? I began to worry.

Bruce stayed close behind me on the stairs to my flat, timing his steps to mine, which made his crotch bump frequently against my ass. I began to worry some more.

As I inserted my key into my door, Bruce put his arms around me and pressed close. He was erect and eager.

"Maybe we should talk," I said.

"Talk?" he asked as I closed the door behind us.

"I'm a top."

Bruce laughed loudly.

"You really haven't seen any of my videos, have you?" he said, unzipping my pants deftly with one hand while unbuckling my belt with the other.

"No," I replied as he knelt in front of me.

*

"I can't believe it!" Bruce said after we had moved to the bedroom, removed the rest of our clothes, settled onto the bed, and made love. It felt like making love with him, not just having sex. Was he this good in the videos? Maybe I *would* have to check them out.

"What can't you believe?" I asked, kissing the top of his head. He was lying on his back against me, my arms wrapped around his chest, my legs cradling his.

"Dave Hoffman fucked me! My mother would be so amazed."

"I'm sure she would be," I replied, trying not to imagine his mother observing what we'd been up to five minutes before.

"We should really go to Paris." He twisted onto his front. He was as eager as a kid asking to go to Disney World. "I'll get us tickets," he continued as if the decision had been made. "Don't worry," he added, mistaking my look. "They're free."

I considered how a clerk could fly often enough to get that many miles or points or whatever it was. For that matter, how could a clerk afford a Mercedes convertible? Porno must pay really well.

Bruce looked perturbed. My thoughts must be showing again.

"Look," he said. "Would you let me worry about this? You just decide whether you want to go." He looked tough again for a moment and then high school Bruce returned. "My mom would be so happy."

"Your mom?"

"Yeah, she always thought you were the king or something."

I had been king, actually, at Junior Prom and Senior Ball.

"She never even met me," I said. Or had she? I couldn't remember but it was pretty unlikely, given how much I tried to keep away from her son.

"Oh, I told her all about you," Bruce said, leaning on his side, his chest shifting left while his abs and stomach stayed tight. "She always said you sounded like a wonderful young man." He looked embarrassed. "Like I said, I had a crush on you."

"I wish I'd known you better then."

"I wasn't me yet," he said, sitting up and pulling his legs under him.

I couldn't argue with that. The man sitting next to me in bed didn't look much like the boy I didn't really know in high school.

"We could make it just be for the weekend, Thursday through Sunday," Bruce offered, going back to the topic of Paris. I must have still looked doubtful. "Okay, Friday through Sunday. Do you mind a redeye?"

I didn't say yes, but I didn't say no.

While I was thinking about it, Bruce took me to a play he had comps for and then back to Brooklyn to my place for the night, followed two days later by dinner at Le

Grenoble in Manhattan. I couldn't imagine how he got us a reservation on such short notice.

And he insisted on paying the check.

"How can you afford this?" I asked, still holding out my gold card.

"I can," he said, looking impatient. "Stop worrying." The server took his platinum.

"You aren't just a clerk," I said like the brilliant trial attorney I was working extra hours to become.

"You're right," he agreed, holding my gaze. "But I don't want to talk about it here." He signed the receipt and stood up. "Actually, I don't want to talk about it at all. Shall we go?"

I stayed seated, with my arms crossed. "Why not talk about it? What exactly *do* you do?" I imagine mobsters and drive-by shootings.

He pried my arms apart and pulled me up like a weightlifter performing a clean and jerk. "Come on," he said, and half dragged me out of the door. I felt frightened of him.

Between my fear and Bruce's anger, we were wordless while we waited for the valet to retrieve the Mercedes. Bruce held onto my hand like I might run away.

"Will you still go to Paris with me?" he asked.

I tried to pull out of his grasp. "Still? I haven't said I would yet."

He dropped my hand and stuffed both of his into the pockets of his cream-colored slacks. "My parents are leaving Paris next week," he said. "I have the tickets in my jacket. We could go tonight."

"I can't go tonight," I responded automatically. "I've got clients tomorrow, cases to prepare for—"

"Fine," he said, taking the keys from the valet, who flashed a clear I'm-available smile at him and looked at me like I was out of Bruce's league and he wasn't.

"All right," I said, staring down the valet. "I'll go."

Bruce handed the keys back to the abashed young man and took both my shoulders, his face glowing with happy light. "Oh, Dave, really?" he said before he gave me the most tender, most romantic kiss I'd ever had. I felt as if we were in a movie, and it was anything but porno.

The valet cleared his throat.

"Yes," I said, deciding to keep it simple for all our sakes. I retrieved the keys from the now very disgruntled valet and handed them to Bruce. Before I knew it, we were on the FDR.

"We'll go to my place first. Then yours," he outlined cheerfully. "Get our passports and maybe a change of underwear." He gave a happy laugh and several delighted glances at me while he drove, and I ran through a string of second and third thoughts.

Part of me insisted I *could* make calls in the morning; I *could* rearrange my life for a couple of days. *Why not?* And, although I had a half dozen very sensible whys ready, none kept me from mentally packing. Bruce wanted me to go, and there was something about him that made me want to go. There had been that something in high school, too, and I had ignored it. *Not this time,* I told myself.

I lifted his right hand off the steering wheel and held on, feeling the warmth of his palm and the little hairs on the tops of his thick fingers. He placed our coupled hands on his wide, steely thigh and smiled beatifically. Was I as happy as he looked? I checked the sideview mirror.

"Don't look back," he joked.

We held hands across the Atlantic and summarized two lifetimes in six hours. The feeling of wanting to protect the man in the first-class seat next to me returned, although, to look at him, no one would think he needed it.

It was afternoon in Paris when we arrived at Charles de Gaulle, early morning in New York. I sent texts, and Bruce called his parents from the first-class lounge. By the time we were outside the terminal, we had a double date for dinner, and my clients would see me Monday.

Bruce gave the taxi driver an address in the Marais.

"You do speak French," I said, wondering if he'd understood my friend at Jardiniere after all.

"Enough to get by," he replied, taking my hand again.

The cab stopped outside an elegant Haussmann-style building in perfect condition on a wide street lined with old trees. "Home, sweet home," he said, handing euros to the driver and sliding out of the door. An ironwork elevator pulled us slowly to the top floor. He opened the heavy oak door and ushered me into a period flat.

"Is this your parents'?" I asked, ogling the opulence.

Bruce chuckled and tossed the apartment keys onto a small gilded table under an elaborately framed mirror. I looked at my reflection, swamped by all the second thoughts I'd tried to leave behind in New York. Bruce's brow wrinkled behind me in concern.

"What?" he asked.

I waved my arms helplessly. "All this. The flight. You. It's... It's..."

"You're just tired," he said. "Let's get some sleep."

"Look," I said, holding him back. "I'm here. Tell me. What do you do?"

"What difference does it make?"

"I want to be sure before..."

"Before what?" he asked, homing in on my confusion.

I straightened my shoulders, raised my head, and forced all the emotion out of my face. "Just tell me."

Bruce trudged into a parlor and slumped on an uncomfortable looking settee, his cream slacks badly wilted from the flight. He inhaled deeply, exhaled, and said, "I'm a whore. All this..." He waved one hand at the room. "I pay for with sex. Everything I own, everything I wear, everything I do, I pay for with sex. Now you." He yanked me down onto the settee with him.

"I told you what I do," I said, trying to get up. His hand was clamped like a vise around my arm.

"Why are you here?"

I didn't reply. All I could think of was how much he was hurting my arm.

"Let me guess," he said, eyes narrowed, mouth curled in a snarl. "You liked the fantasy. Muscle man porno star. Well, you wouldn't be the first. It's how I make my money." He dropped his hand and folded his arms across his chest, on guard.

I considered what he'd said. An attorney has to deal with testimony.

"No," I concluded. "You wanted me to come, and I didn't want to disappoint you...again. And, anyway—"

He kissed me quickly but followed up on the *and*.

"You know," I said.

"Guilt," he muttered glumly.

"Not anymore," I answered but thinking maybe it still was, at least in part. "I'm attracted to you. I always was." *Good*, my better angel whispered encouragingly.

Bruce hugged me violently and covered my face in kisses. I tried to make some breathing space between us. "But..." I began.

His face fell, and the kissing stopped.

"Sometimes I see you, and sometimes I don't."

"What do you see?" he asked, choosing the positive. An incipient smile tried to grow at the corners of his mouth.

I thought a moment, examining his face and then his chest, groin, and legs. "I see Bruce Sonnenschein's eyes and a stranger's body."

He held me close again, his face video seductive. "You'll get used to the body. It has its advantages." He nuzzled my neck, knowing how I like that. I pried him off me. There was more to say.

"But you're fantasizing, too, aren't you? Fucked by David Hoffman, high school hero? High school was ten years ago. You're star fucking, and I'm not even a star." He started to protest, but I shushed him with my hand on his lips. "Not anymore. I'm just a junior associate in a second-tier law firm." I walked to the window, remembering we were in Paris and wasting it. What a shame. Why didn't we say all this in New York? *But then, I thought, we might not be in Paris now.* It was so beautiful outside. "We hardly know who each other is," I said, still looking out of the window.

Bruce came up behind me. "What better place to become acquainted?" he said, putting his arms around me and nuzzling my neck again. He unbuttoned my shirt and unbuckled my belt, one hand going to my chest and the other to my cock. "You didn't say anything about my confession," he whispered into my ear just before he licked it.

"Plenty of people would say my job is worse," I answered, turning in his arms to hold him off half-heartedly—but that didn't last long.

Several hours later, I looked over his bare shoulder at the clock beside the bed. We had fallen asleep postcoital. Bruce's back was against my front in spooning position. His head turned, and his eyes opened. "What?" his groggy voice asked.

"What time are we meeting your parents?"

"*Vingt heures*," he answered.

I tried to get up. "We better start getting ready." Bruce pulled me back down and wrapped his beefy arms and legs around me.

"There's still plenty of time," he said, grinding against me.

Thirty minutes later, I looked at the clock again. "Shit!" I said and jumped out of bed.

We spent ten minutes bumping into each other in the bathroom, dressed in five, and ran to the restaurant, which was only two blocks away, arriving somewhat disheveled and definitely sweaty. Bruce looked good a little messed up.

He straightened his light-blue summer suit and retucked his white dress shirt. I buttoned my jacket. We went in the door, holding hands.

Bruce explained us in English to the tuxedo-clad, hatchet-nosed man at the podium, who led us to a table in a window corner. An older man seated there stood as we approached. I didn't remember him, or the woman seated beside him.

"David Hoffman!" the woman exclaimed. "You haven't changed a bit!"

I shook the man's hand, and Bruce kissed his mother's cheek. "Oh, he has, Mom. Believe me," he said, giving me a wink. "Happy Mother's Day," he added, giving her a second kiss on the other cheek. His mother looked at me more carefully.

"You're right, dear," she agreed. "I think he's taller."

During dinner, I often found her glancing from me to Bruce and smiling while Mr. Sonnenschein talked about all the things they'd done and seen. At one point, he asked what I did.

"I'm an attorney," I told him and mentioned the firm.

"Then, we have something else in common," he said, winking at his son. A family of winkers. The name of his firm was much more impressive than mine. "How long are you two in Paris?" he asked.

"Just the weekend," Bruce answered for us. "David has to work." I loved that he called me David.

"Come see me when we're back in New York," Mr. Sonnenschein said to me and gave me his card.

"No business," his mother commanded, frowning at her husband, and then smiling at Bruce and me. "It's too bad you don't have more time. I wish you could join us next week in Rome."

"I have work, too, Mom," Bruce said, shoulders tensing. His parents looked at each other, both seeming to bite their tongues. I wondered whether I'd be biting my tongue as well in future. Was it too soon to ask that question? I decided not to worry about it.

On the way back to the flat, Bruce and I walked hand in hand. "Mom likes you," he said.

"Didn't she always?"

He grinned. "Well, yeah. But now she knows you. Dad likes you too."

"I know," I said, laughing in turn. "He asked me in for an interview."

Bruce maintained a silence about things legal, while swinging our hands back and forth as we walked. I saw the horse chestnut trees lining the sidewalk. I hadn't known what they were when I'd first come to Paris, but they were everywhere so we had become well acquainted. Whenever I came across a chestnut vendor in New York, memories of Paris came drifting back like leaves in fall.

Behind us, I heard unfriendly voices. Gradually, the French they were speaking broke through my happiness. "Look at the homos. Dude, that's disgusting. Fags! Let's get them!"

Bruce and I turned at the same time as if we'd coordinated our reaction. There were four of them. We met their intended blows with restraining hands and punches to midsections and knees to groins. The fight was over in seconds. Seeing the four of them writhing on the sidewalk and hearing them complain made my heart feel good.

"I wish I'd punched a few stomachs and kneed a few groins in high school," I said.

"Me too," Bruce agreed, looking rumpled and sexy again. "We make a good team," he said and retrieved my hand.

I thought about that. Yes, we were a good team in the fight though perhaps an odd one in life. A lawyer and a prostitute. Oh, well. Maybe Bruce could talk me into making a career change.

We turned to go, leaving our attackers moaning and groaning and bravely yelling French epithets at our backs. Bruce looked over his shoulder and so did I. The boys had managed to get to their feet and were running or hobbling away.

Bruce yelled after them, "*Vous ferais mieux de courir, enfoires!*"

"So, you do know French," I said, slightly amazed at his use of slang.

"*Bien sur, monsieur,*" he responded.

We walked another block, Bruce's hand warm and strong in mine. "What do you want to do tomorrow?" he asked.

"Besides fuck?"

He winked. "Well, there is that, although I was thinking of a museum."

"No museums," I insisted. "Only on Mother's Day."

"Is that our anniversary?"

Why not, a voice asked me. "Maybe," I said out loud. "In the meantime...I'll race you to your apartment!"

I took off running, and Bruce ran after me. I hadn't run the four forty in years, but training will out. Besides, it was only a half block. I beat him to his door by a couple of steps. At the threshold, he grabbed me and hugged me tight. "Open the door," I told him, between catching my breath.

"*A ton service, mon amour,*" he said, winking at me.

I was beginning to appreciate the winking. And the French. There were things left to consider—but not today. I followed Bruce inside and shut the door behind us. Life and the Louvre could wait.

June

The Man in the Photo

"Welcome to the unit," my new commanding officer said. He stood to return my salute before shaking my hand. I couldn't believe how much he looked like the man in the photo—or at least like him if he'd lived.

"Take a chair, son. Tell me about yourself," Colonel Markham said, giving my hand a friendly final squeeze before sitting back behind his desk.

The word *son* echoed loudly in my ears.

"You graduated from West Point like me, I hear," he prompted when I didn't immediately respond.

My brain snapped back to reality. Best to stay in the present tense. "Yes, sir. Nineteen ninety-four," I said. I was at Fort Riley, Kansas, again. Just another duty rotation: stationed overseas two years, Fort Riley for one or two. The life of a career infantry soldier.

The colonel smiled, just a whisper of one, like the man in the photo. "Nineteen seventy-eight for me. Just missed Vietnam." He looked regretful. I'd had two wars so far, Afghanistan and now Iraq. I'd give him one of them— gladly.

While I recited my resume, I subtracted 1978 from 2004 and added twenty-two to calculate the colonel's age. He looked good for forty-eight, very good. His chest swelled nicely inside his khaki shirt. Short sleeves showed off muscular biceps and dark hairs down sinewy forearms. When he stood, I could see he hadn't developed a gut sitting behind a desk.

For thirty minutes we talked about where we'd served in the army—including how many times we'd been at Fort Riley, what we'd done, and whom we both knew—until a knock on the open door made me jump as if we'd been up to something.

The colonel barked, "Come in!" and I looked around, locking eyes with another captain. I recognized that look.

"Excuse me, sir," the young officer said, crossing the threshold. He was blond, blue-eyed, and very well-built. "General Cameron is on the phone, sir. I didn't want to interrupt but—"

"Of course, Captain." Colonel Markham cut his junior officer off briskly. "The CO," he said to me in confiding tones, one hand on the receiver and another poised above the extension button. "See you tonight," he added before taking the call. I saluted although the colonel was already speaking. He returned my salute automatically.

"We're all looking forward to your welcome party," the blond captain whispered as he ushered me out of the door, hand firmly on my back. A little too firmly, but I understood where he was coming from. I'd been there.

Outside the colonel's office, he introduced himself as Captain Jensen even though the insignia on his starched collar and name tag on his ample chest had already told me as much. "Kevin," he added, waiting.

"Jamie," I said after a moment's hesitation. We both carried the same rank, but that wouldn't be for long. I had passed my board and was finally on the list for major although I'd done my best to avoid it. My buddy Pete said

I didn't want to make rank because my father, James Sr., had died a captain. I told him he had taken too many college psychology courses. Being promoted meant assignment to a staff position. I wanted to be fighting, not sending men to fight for me.

CPT Jensen cleared his throat. "Why don't I show you around?" he suggested seductively. Hadn't he heard about Don't Ask, Don't Tell?

We started the tour with my own small office next to the colonel's, my prison cell for the next two years. I looked around without looking. Jensen was chatty in a flirty kind of way some men have—even straight men—and would have taken a seat if I hadn't asked him about directions to the party.

"I'll give you a map," he said and left my office.

I didn't think that was necessary since I knew the layout of Fort Riley really well, but I followed his butt, which was as ample as his chest, into the main office. We stopped at his desk where he handed me a map of the post and the town around it. A line was drawn from the Bachelor Officer Quarters to an address in Junction City.

"Colonel Markham doesn't live on post?" I asked, surprised my official welcome wouldn't be within walking distance.

"No..." the captain answered, like he could say more but was trying not to. I analyzed his face while he debated. His lynx-blue eyes were small and too close together, and his lips were thin and tight. I liked his chin, though, how it jutted down and out. Very butch.

He noticed me staring. "Can I help you with anything else, Captain?" he asked, stifling a smirk and squaring his shoulders, which thrust his big chest out at me even more. I gave it a good look before I answered.

"Thanks, Captain. There is something. Would you please introduce me to the staff?"

He looked annoyed. Poor kid, he wasn't used to men rejecting his assets, but this was work and work was the army. I, for one, wasn't bucking for a dishonorable.

We started with the lieutenants and progressed to the sergeant major. Jensen would have left it at that, but I continued to the rest of the enlisted staff. The hunky captain followed me closely desk to desk, too closely. A dozen pair of eyes were following us. I was sure they had Jensen's number; I didn't want them to learn mine too.

When I'd made the rounds, Jensen walked me outside. I didn't start my new job officially until the next day. "I could give you a lift tonight," he offered. "I live in the BOQ too. Second floor." I was surprised he didn't add his room number.

"Not necessary, Captain, but thanks," I replied. "I picked up my car on leave."

"Call me Kevin," he reminded me. "What do you drive?" He grinned with huge wolfish teeth.

"Thunderbird," I answered, leaning out of biting range.

He took a half step closer. "I've got a Dodge Ram 1500 quad cab. Never know when you might need a back seat," he said and gave me a wink. I wondered if the noncoms passing by noticed it. "Maybe we can try it out sometime." He smirked. "The T-bird, I mean," he amended and, with another smirk, took the other half step, bringing us almost belly to belly, near enough for me to feel his body heat and smell the strong man scent of him. It was a good smell, but I had sucked enough cock to know what I wanted, and it wasn't Kevin Jensen, so I said goodbye without a smile and didn't look back.

At the BOQ, I took the stairs two at a time to the third floor—they had already put me up with the majors—found my apartment, locked the door, and turned my Nokia off. I had the TV and video player to myself.

I had watched the video a thousand times. My father, Captain James Clayton, Sr., on R and R in Hawaii with my mother—so beautiful—my sister Emily, who was three, and me, two months old. Dad, dark-haired and torso tanned, splashing through the surf on his own, dancing with Emily on the toes of his long white feet or cuddling me in his sinewy brown arms against his hairy chest.

When the video finished, I took the photo out of my wallet. It was Dad in fatigues, leading a company of infantrymen through a rice paddy in Vietnam, an army publicity shot taken just before he died. I was right. The man in the photo and the one in the video looked a lot like my new colonel must have when he was younger.

I had lunch in the officers' mess, wrote a letter to my folks, and sent some emails before I dressed for an early dinner in the Officers' Club and drinks with friends— other captains and majors I'd been with at West Point, Fort Riley, or overseas, including Pete—Major Peter Williams III—also West Point '94, my best friend and periodic fuck buddy.

When I told my friends I had to leave after only one drink, everyone complained long and loudly except Pete. He just smiled and said he'd see me later. We always gave each other quite a welcome back. After the one scotch, I waved off their hoots and hollers and headed out.

The colonel's house was in a subdivision on the far side of Junction City. It didn't look much different from its neighbors. They were all shades of tan like a formation of soldiers in their summer uniform. All of them had a regulation two-car garage and a lawn badly in need of water. I parked the T-bird and walked to number 718, sweating in the July heat and humidity, even after dark. The air smelled like corn, wheat, and freshly plowed earth. *Yes, Dorothy,* I told myself, *you are definitely back in Kansas.*

Colonel Markham opened the door with a smile and another strong handshake. He led me inside, saying words I didn't quite hear. My mind was on the rough feel of his hand and the black-and-white chest hairs I'd seen above the open collar of his baby-blue dress shirt.

"Any trouble finding me, Jamie?" he asked. My name on his lips sounded like a bugle call.

"No, sir."

"Kevin's map worked then?"

I agreed it had.

While we spoke these innocuous words, my eyes were on my colonel's face and body. It might have been my imagination, but his seemed to be on mine too.

We were interrupted by a loud, "Jamie!" Hot and hunky Kevin was framed decorously in the archway to the living room. He was wearing loose shorts that showed off his muscular legs and a tight, white polo shirt that outlined everything else. "What are you drinking?" he asked.

"Scotch on the rocks, Kevin," I answered, trying not to stare at his crotch.

"A scotch man, too, huh?" Colonel Markham said heartily, his hand squeezing my shoulder, sending shivers down my body. "Captain, pour this man some Glenlivet!"

"Yes, sir!" Jensen shouted. I could see how he was around the colonel. I wouldn't have been surprised if he had clicked his heels. He double-timed into the living room ahead of us, grabbed a glass smartly, inserted two cubes of ice, and poured precisely two fingers of liquid. If we had been strangers in a bar, I'd have given him a good tip—and maybe my number. He handed me my two fingers worth, letting his digits linger on mine while I took the glass. If he weren't so obvious...

I looked around the room. There were three choices—Jensen and the single officers, the single enlisted men, and several couples seated on chairs and leather couches across the room. I decided to check in with the officers and then introduce myself to the wives. They always had good information about any new posting.

I talked sports with the first group and my marital status with the second. Once the women ascertained I was single, they began making plans, as military wives always do. I knew there were plenty of single Kansas girls working on or near the post.

I asked about Mrs. Markham, assuming the colonel had a lady. I assumed incorrectly, however, one of the wives informed me. Everyone else carefully said nothing, paying attention to their hands or to their drinks.

"They're divorced," Mrs. Billikens told me, her drawl identifying southern origins. "Oh, it was years ago. Wasn't it when you were still a staff sergeant, Jack?" she asked her husband, the sergeant major.

"Oh, not that long ago," he answered, giving her the shut-up-now look.

"Do they have any children?" I asked. If they had a son, he'd probably be about my age, maybe a little younger. Everyone gave me a funny look.

"No," Mrs. Sergeant Major said like it was an opening statement and then clammed up. Her husband was now giving her the look that made brave enlisted men tremble.

I smiled at everyone and went back to the other single officers.

The party progressed well enough with good music, loud conversation, and plenty to drink. I kept thinking about the man in my wallet and the man in front of me while keeping up my end of several conversations. Jensen tried chasing me around the room a few times, but I knew how to handle that. When the sergeant major and his wife made their move to leave, the room began to empty. Soon everyone but Jensen and I had followed them out the door.

"Thank you, sir, for the welcome party," I said to the colonel, preparing to go.

"You're welcome, Jamie," he said jovially. "We try to make our young officers feel at home." I saw Jensen smirk. It was not a good look for him.

"Guess I'll be going, too, sir," he said, casually stretching his arms and body for full effect.

Colonel Markham gave the two of us a strange smile.

Jensen and I walked out of the door in single file, him giving me precedence, but he moved next to me on the walkway to the street, leaning in, brushing against me, speaking in low, almost cooing tones. He stopped at a big black truck parked just past the colonel's driveway.

"Feel like a nightcap?" he asked, a hand in each back pocket, thrusting his pretty chest and full crotch at me. My body said yes, but I overruled it. Pete would be waiting.

"No, thanks," I answered, trying not to look lower than his chin.

"Another time?" he asked, moving closer, restless hands now out of his pants.

"Maybe," I said, my resolve beginning to melt as something else solidified. His lips moved in for the kill. I did an abrupt about-face and jogged to my car.

I called Pete's number, horny as hell. He gave me directions to his off-post apartment, and I shifted the Thunderbird into first. On the way, I unavoidably fantasized about Colonel Markham and the voluptuous Kevin Jensen, but at Pete's apartment, the handsome (and equally horny) major made me forget all about them.

Peter Bartley Williams III had been the closest match to the man in the photo before Colonel Markham, but he had always been too young to be Dad. I have to say, though, he always made me forget about my father when we got together. He had an easy smile, intelligent mind, and ready body. He made me laugh. We had great political discussions and outstanding sex.

We had fooled around carefully at West Point and then slightly less carefully overseas and in between assignments. Now, we were both at Fort Riley again, and Pete's apartment had a king-size bed. As the weeks went by, I spent almost as much time in it as I spent in my own.

I didn't always say yes, though, no matter how good Pete looked. One Friday after dinner at the O Club, when I wouldn't go home with him, he followed me out of the door and, at my car, asked, "Is there somebody else, Jamie?" like we were a couple or something.

"Come on, Pete. Somebody else? You know—"

"I know more than you think, Jamie," he said, his full mouth grim and his dark eyes glowering. He was still in his fatigues, sleeves rolled up exactly as they should be, tufts of dark chest hair showing above his undershirt. He was beginning to gray at the temples. I resisted the urge to pull out the photo and compare.

"Okay," I said, staring at the man he wasn't.

"Okay what?" he asked belligerently, arms across his chest, legs spread, crotch full and beckoning.

"Okay, I'll go," I told him. "But you have to keep the fatigues on—at least at the beginning."

He broke into a toothy laugh, like my dad does in the video when the waves hit him unexpectedly. "No worries," he said, taking long, loping strides toward his more sedate Chevy sedan.

We were barely inside his apartment door before he unzipped his fatigue pants and pushed me to my knees. "Do your duty, Captain," he said. His voice was stern, but he caressed my head gently while I did it.

Saturday morning, gulping coffee in his tiny kitchen, another set of crisp fatigues covering his body, Pete suggested I stay. "You can hang out all day since you're just a staffer" is how he put it. I said okay and snapped the dishtowel at his olive drab ass as he trotted out the door. He was in a line unit and had weekend duty with the recruits. Part of me envied him. It wasn't war, but at least Pete still had time in the field even if it was only a former Kansas wheat field.

The apartment was quiet now, absent Pete's laughter and our conversation—and the noise we made in sex. I could have climbed back into my civvies, grabbed my wallet, sunglasses, and car keys, and locked the door behind me with the key Pete had given me the night before, but I had said okay, and it was something to look forward to Pete coming in the door after work. He'd be all sweaty and rumpled like the man in the photo. We could take another shower together. I had no other plans anyway.

Pete's refrigerator and cabinets were well stocked and admirably organized, so I put on a pair of his shorts and one of his T-shirts, made myself some breakfast, and drank more coffee on his patio, enjoying the view of a busy

Saturday morning golf course. Pretty nice, except for the errant golf balls. Pete played and kept threatening he'd make me learn but shied off when I said he'd have to take up tennis in return.

I took my empty coffee mug back inside, rinsed it, and wandered around the apartment, reminding myself who Major Peter Bartley Williams III, US Army, was. His place was like him: all comfortable furniture, colorful paintings, and hardcover books. He always stored everything when he rotated overseas. I only kept the T-bird and some clothes at my parents' house in New Jersey.

I read the new Carl Hiaason novel a while, lying on the sofa in Pete's clothes until I started feeling like lazy scum and got myself up to dust and vacuum. As a reward, I changed from his shorts into a pair of his swim trunks and did laps in the communal pool. At five fifteen, I ran from the pool, stripped off the trunks, and greeted him at the door naked. That led to another great roll in the sheets, dinner out, and a second consecutive night in his bed.

Monday at work, I daydreamed about playing house all weekend with Pete until Colonel Markham buzzed me on the intercom. He said to shut the door behind me, and we went over his week's appointments and events with just the desk between us. I could smell his aftershave and see the flesh starting to sag along his jawline. His warm brown eyes and easy smile held my attention until he said we were done.

Back in my little office, I mulled over my life, staring at the map of Fort Riley behind me like it would tell me which direction to take. I took my wallet out to look at the man in the photo. He looked more like Pete than the colonel.

"Who's that?" Jensen's voice asked over my shoulder. When had he come into my office, and why hadn't he knocked?

"My father," I told him, putting the photo back in my wallet and the wallet back in my khakis.

"Looks familiar," he said with his trademark smirk. He flopped into my one guest chair and spread his legs, giving me a good look at his always bulging crotch. I wanted to tell him I'd seen better last night *and* this morning but just asked, "What do you need, Captain?"

He stood up, smirk gone. "Nothing. I was just passing by on my way to the colonel." He did an about-face and strode oh-so-manfully out of the room, butt cheeks popping up and down like pistons. I heard him knock next door and went back to work. Pete Williams, Jensen, the colonel. It didn't matter. I was still a soldier, and I wanted to keep it that way.

My life at a desk went on. After three months, I finally got my unwelcome golden oak leaf. I stood at attention in the autumn chill listening to my promotion orders being read, looking out at the sea of men just back from war or waiting to return to it, and asked myself what the hell I was doing at headquarters, lusting after my commanding officer, pushing papers, and wasting the government's money. To hell with that, I said to myself while the battalion paraded in front of me. I was a soldier, not a bureaucrat. It was time to go to war again. The next morning, I asked Colonel Markham if I could speak with him in private.

"Sounds serious, son. Something personal?" he asked just as someone knocked on the closed door behind us. His kind eyes waited for me to answer. Louder knocks banged the door in case we hadn't heard.

"At ease!" the colonel said, raising his voice. He lowered it speaking to me. "Why don't we have a drink in the O Club? Early. Say, five thirty? Plainly, we can't talk here." He inclined his head toward the door.

He didn't wait for an answer. "Come in!" he barked to the person outside it. I rose as Lieutenant Evans entered, looking contrite.

A drink with the colonel! I walked in a daze the whole ten feet to my office. Ranks aren't supposed to fraternize, but I could say this was work related—in case anybody questioned it, which Pete did when he called and asked me to meet him after work.

"You're having drinks with your colonel?" he said/asked, like I was cheating on him.

"I want to talk about reassignment."

Surprisingly, he didn't pursue that topic. Instead, he asked in an acidic tone, "I suppose you've noticed how much he looks like your father?"

"No," I lied. He waited. "Okay, but so what?" He waited some more. "It's work," I whined lamely.

"Sure," he said and hung up.

That put a big-time damper on my afternoon, but when the colonel appeared in my open doorway and asked, "Ready, Major Clayton?" I jumped up with renewed enthusiasm although it was still weird to hear my new title. Captain Clayton sounded so much better.

"Yes, sir," I answered, following him out of the building. We were in our dress greens, about the same height and body type but otherwise, opposites. I am sandy-haired like my mom, with a tendency to freckle. My eyes are blue—azure, Pete calls them. I thought about Pete as the colonel and I walked. He was jealous. *Well*, I thought, looking at the fit older man beside me, *maybe he has reason to be.*

Colonel Markham and I walked in step, being saluted and saluting along the way. Inside, he steered us to a quiet corner, ordered us scotch on the rocks from the eager server, leaned back in the faux-leather chair, and asked, "So, Major, what's on your mind?"

I tried to ignore the familiarity of his smile and said, "I'd like to request reassignment, sir."

Colonel Markham put down his drink and shifted his chair closer. "What's wrong, son?" he asked in a more intimate voice.

"Nothing, sir," I said. "I just think it's time to do my bit again."

"You need to do your bit here, too, Jamie," he said, moving a knee close enough to come to rest against one of mine under the table. He smiled beneficently while pressing against me. "I know you'd rather be in the field, but you've only been with us—with me—a few months. You haven't given it a fair shake yet. We need you here, Jamie. The army needs you. I need you," he finished softly.

I gulped nervously.

Thankfully, he removed his knee, and we went on to other topics, mainly about the office, the wars, the civilians running the army. Nothing personal and not a word more about my request. We drank two additional drinks.

Suddenly, in the middle of one of my sentences, Colonel Markham asked, "I'm feeling a little woozy, son. Think you could run me home?"

The colonel didn't look woozy. He looked like a man who could hold his liquor under all circumstances. But I agreed and we walked to his Buick. I could always call Pete for a lift or a place to stay overnight.

When we arrived at the colonel's house, he asked me in. He removed his jacket and tie and insisted he take mine.

"Relax, son," he said.

I said no to another drink but accepted his invitation to sit next to him on the sofa.

"There's something else bothering you, isn't there, son?" he said. "I'm probably the same age as your dad, aren't I? Pretend you're telling your father if that helps."

I looked into his face, my father's face. And then it happened. Colonel Markham abruptly pulled me to him, placed his lips on mine, and kissed hard. I tried to pull away, but he held on tight, his mouth moving vigorously against the outside of mine, and his tongue probing my dental work. His hands found the buttons of my uniform shirt and the hem of my undershirt, and in no time, I was half naked, and his lips and tongue were on my chest.

He whispered, "Relax," and I did, wondering if this was how my father's lips and tongue felt. My father's eyes stared back at me as I considered this. His fingers manipulated me right and left.

After a few minutes of foreplay, the colonel stood up and took his own shirts off. His torso was lean, well-muscled, and hairy—the body of a man who took care of himself but who also was not a kid anymore. I had found the man in the photo, twenty years on. He put his hands on his hips and nodded down at his crotch. I knelt and undid the button of his slacks, slid the zipper down, and took him into my mouth.

"Damn, son!" he hissed. He started pounding my face right away.

After he'd finished, I waited for him to say the magic words no man had ever told me. Instead, he zipped up and said, "That was mighty fine work, son. Mighty fine," like it was my annual evaluation. We stared at each other across the decades.

"Well, Major, I'll see you in the a.m.," Colonel Markham announced jovially. "Better get your clothes on. And tie your tie. Don't want to make the neighbors talk. Here's the number for a taxi." He gave me a business card, looked at his watch, and didn't say another word.

When I was dressed and the taxi had arrived, he escorted me to the door. There was no goodbye kiss, handshake, or even a salute.

"Where to?" the driver asked.

I told him how to get to Pete's place.

The porch light wasn't on, but I knocked anyway. I heard heavy footsteps thud through the apartment and the peephole click open.

His deep voice yelled "Just a sec!" through the door as his fingers undid the locks. He was in his go-to-bed boxers and nothing else. He looked so good. He looked familiar.

"Come in," he said and walked me to the sofa, his arm around my shoulder. "What's up?" he asked.

"I had sex with someone else," I said, putting it on the table. Pete flinched and removed his hand from my thigh. "I'm sorry," I told him. He ignored my apology.

"Colonel Markham," he said flatly.

"He looks so much like my dad," I said.

To his credit, Pete did not point out how sick that sounded. He just stared at me, eyes hard and face in neutral.

"Maybe—twenty years later. But he isn't the man in the photo, Jamie. I am. Or, hadn't you noticed?" He snaked one long, summer-tanned arm along the sofa back behind me.

"I've noticed," I mumbled. I couldn't look up; I knew what I'd see.

"Show me the photo," he commanded, and like the good soldier I am, I lifted my wallet out of my back-left pocket and extracted it. Pete took it out of my hands and held it next to his face. "If you want Daddy, here he is." His words sounded like a final offer.

My mind started whirling. What the hell was I doing? It was late. I had to get out of there. I stood. "I have to go."

Pete yanked me down again and, with two long arms, surrounded me with warmth and history. He gave me kiss after kiss: on the mouth, on my face, on my neck, and back to my mouth. They were more in a long series of kisses we'd shared—at West Point, Fort Riley, saying hello, saying goodbye, ignoring both in his bed or wherever we could find. I felt familiar hands.

When Pete finally let me go, I said, "Hold the photo up again." *Yes*, I thought. "Yes," I said.

"Finally," Pete said, pulling me against him for more kisses.

We took the familiar path to his bedroom. I shed my clothes while he lay on the bed and watched, head propped up by one arm, the other stretching along the curve of his body. When I was ready, he made room for me and I settled beside him. I could feel his heartbeat. I felt safe. Did he feel safe too?

"You can call me Dad if you want," he said, completely seriously.

"I'll think about it."

"I love you, Jamie."

"I love you too," I answered. Pete stared at me with my father's face. His face. Their face.

"What's my name?" he asked.

I waited, debating my answer, and he rolled on top of me. "Son," he said, and we began.

July

That July I Learned to Surf

"Hey brah, you okay?" the stranger asked, a concerned frown temporarily wrinkling his otherwise flawless face. One second, I had been thinking about lunch, and the next, I was looking up into sky-blue eyes and a tan chest abundantly covered with dark-blond hair. I managed to nod yes, and he helped me to my feet. "Jonas," he said, giving me the waggling thumb and pinkie surfers use.

"Jared," I responded without the salute, trying to ignore the fact we both were naked and my elbow and ass hurt. A lot.

"Cool! The two J's!" he said. His voice seemed to blare in the long open space, but no one seemed to be paying any attention to us but us. Jonas high-fived me and went back to showering, chattering away like we were old friends. I tried to listen and not ogle. He said he had just moved to San Ramon. I promised to introduce him to my friends.

However, Jonas Michaels didn't need social assistance from me and my middling popularity. All he had to do was walk down the halls at Cal High, grin, and say, "Hey brah!" and people fell in love with him. I don't know where he got the "Hey brah" from, but if you heard it, you knew who was coming and you prepared to be happy.

It didn't hurt that Jonas had money although money is in very good supply in San Ramon. He had his own car—a BMW z4 hardtop convertible—one key indicator of family wealth. A second was his home. The first time I saw Jonas's house in the new Bella Vista section of town, I knew the Michaels family had means way beyond their end. It was an Italian villa-style mansion built on three levels against a hillside with terracotta tiled roofs, various balconies, and a bell tower with a significant telescope but no bell. On our arrival, one of three garage doors opened, and Jonas eased the BMW inside. The other two stalls were empty.

The invitation to his house had mentioned a pool. We changed in Jonas's bedroom, which was as big as my parents'. I turned my back on his shedding of clothing and stepped into navy-plaid swim trunks. When I dared look again, my eyes followed the treasure trail down his abdomen and belly into minimal turquoise-colored cloth and the conspicuous bulge inside it. Jonas laughed at my open-mouthed stare and took off running. I ran after him through the house and into the pool. He parted the water with a competitive dive, and I followed with mine a second or two later.

"You've got a good stroke, J," I heard him say after I came up for air at the end of a lap. "Ever surf?"

"No," I admitted. "I was on the swim team though," I offered as an alternate credential.

"Oh, man, it's so sick. I could teach you," he responded, brushing aside my varsity swimming experience.

"Maybe," I said, trying to sound interested before I pushed off for another lap. I was afraid my other interest was showing through my shorts.

After our swim and one of his dad's beers, we sunned ourselves until Jonas decided it was time to go to the mall.

"That's okay," I said. "I better go home."

"Nope," he said. "You need to update your wardrobe." Jonas snapped the elastic waistband of my baggies, sending sexual reverberations up my torso.

"I thought surfers wore board shorts," I said as I pretended to readjust my attire. I was saving for a car and wary of spending money on anything else.

"On a *board*," he emphasized. "But around the pool you need to get a tan."

At Stoneridge Mall, we walked right past the Mainland Surf and Skate Shop.

"Hey," I said. "It's back there."

Jonas looked over his shoulder. "Not there, brah. Macy's is having a sale."

A well-groomed, citrus-scented salesman followed us into the post-summer swimsuit clearance section. I admired the sale prices until I noticed the clerk hovering near Jonas, but Jonas ignored him and burrowed hurriedly through the piles under the Speedos sign.

"What's your size?" he asked.

I started to say I had several Speedos from being on the swim team but just answered, "Thirty."

He looked up with that happy, lopsided grin of his. "Hey, same as me. Here," he announced, back to business, handing me a swimsuit with barely enough fabric to qualify as a garment. "You like red, right?"

I did from then on.

The handsome salesman turned snooty when he turned to me. "You'll have to try it on over your underwear," he pronounced crisply like I was the deformed twin in the movie *Basket Case*.

Jonas frowned deeply and jabbed the clerk once in the name tag with a long index finger. "Look, *Seth*," he said. "If it fits, I'll buy it. If it doesn't, I'll still buy it."

Seth lost the attitude immediately. "Okay, okay," he said, hands up, backing off. He was just another twentysomething poser after all.

On the way to the changing room, Jonas kept muttering "underwear" and "cocksucker" under his breath, looking back at Seth. He only stopped when we were in the changing room. As far as I could tell, we were the only ones there.

I chose a cubicle, stripped fast, and slid the Speedo up my legs equally quickly, worrying about inopportune erections. When I exited the cubicle, Jonas whistled, which made me blush and worry even more.

"Hey, studmeister!" he exclaimed and then turned me around, holding onto my shoulders while he looked. He stopped me facing the mirror. "Hawt, brah. You like?"

"Yes, but—"

"But what?"

"Nothing," I said, silenced by the strength of his hands and the growing excitement inside my Speedo.

He gave me a playful shove. "Hey, I'm gonna get one too. Here, let me try yours on." He yanked the Speedo down my legs before I knew what was happening. Jonas grinned. "Uh oh, somebody's feeling sexy. Step out of this thang and get some clothes on. Seth might not be able to control himself." He started discarding his clothing while I got into mine.

After I pulled my shirt over my head, I saw him modeling in the three-way mirror. All three ways looked mighty good to me.

"I guess it would be too matchy-matchy if I got a red one too," he said, not really asking. "But I've already got blue and yellow. Hell!" he answered himself, stripping the tiny swimsuit off his perfectly tanned thighs and exposing the perfectly pale skin inside his tan lines. "Who cares?"

He tossed the suit to me. I decided then and there I'd never wash it.

Seth was standing guard outside the changing room. "How did it fit, sir?" he asked me, all politeness now. Maybe he'd heard Jonas whistle.

"Great," Jonas said. "Really hot," he added, giving Seth a nudge and a wink. "We'll take two, Seth. This thirty and another thirty. Both red."

"Two?" Seth asked like he didn't understand.

"One for me," Jonas explained. "And," he said, putting his arm around my shoulders, "one for my buddy here."

Seth looked at me like I was the luckiest boy in the whole wide world.

Outside Macy's, Jonas laughed and asked, "Did you see his eyes bug? Oh, man, hilarious!"

"Hilarious," I echoed, remembering other things I had seen.

Jonas looked at the time on his phone. "Hey, let's hit it. I'll drop you off at your place."

I gave directions to my less-Italian, less-affluent neighborhood in San Ramon. Our house was a perfectly nice four-bedroom ranch on a pretty street lined with full-growth trees, but it was no villa, and there wasn't much of a view unless our neighbor's massive purple bougainvillea across the street qualified.

"Hey," Jonas said as he pulled the Beemer into our driveway. "Why don't you catch a ride with me to school?

We could hang out every day at my place and get some use out of these things." He reached into the backseat, grabbed the Macy's bag, extracted his half of the purchase, and handed the bag to me.

"Okay," I agreed, my voice muffled by the weight of all the possibilities hanging out almost naked with Jonas might bring.

He made good on his offer the rest of the week—him honking every morning and me sprinting outside to get him to stop—followed by a swim after school and us sunning side by side in our red Speedos and deepening tans on multicolored tiles around the aqua-bottom pool. Heaven. By the following Friday, however, there was trouble in paradise. Jonas had a girlfriend, and I assumed my Beemer rides were over.

"Nah, Cecil's got her own car. We meet up at school," he said when I asked if I should plan on taking Mom's Van Service again. "You're stuck with me, brah." He flashed the impressive results of many dental dollars spent.

I did earn the rides though. Jonas talked, I listened, and the subject was always Cecily. I should have told him they weren't right for each other. She was a senior, head cheerleader, and ex-girlfriend of about every good-looking guy in school since the eighth grade.

It all came down at Christmas. The day after Cecily opened her plentiful presents, she broke another date with Jonas, and he sent me a text.

She bailed on me again. Want to take a ride?

That meant Jonas driving the Beemer out into the country, parking in a turnout with a view of the Tri-Valley area, lighting up a joint, and him talking for an hour or two. Jonas put the top down even though it was cold. We reclined our seats in unison and looked up at a trillion stars.

He started with "Man, fuck that chick!" and handed me the doobie. "I'm sick of her. Do you think I should break up with her?" He usually answered his own questions, so I didn't respond for a few seconds while I held the smoke in, but when I realized he was waiting, I exhaled quickly.

"I don't know, Jonas. What do you think?" I asked like my mom did when I brought up life-changing questions.

"I fuckin' think I should. Shit, there are plenty of hawt girls at our school." Even though that was true, I was about to say something about "hawt" maybe not being the most important quality in a girlfriend when Jonas interrupted me. "That settles it. I'm telling her tomorrow. Fuck it! Bet she'll be surprised. Thanks, dude."

I had heard this before. The surprise would be if they actually broke up.

He looked at the sky. "Man, I wish we could go surfing."

I chuckled, and he glared at me. "I mean, it's pretty cold," I explained.

"Yeah, the current's cold up here," he said, misunderstanding me. He folded his arms across his puffer jacket. "Have to use a steamer even in the summertime, I bet." He looked at me, frowning. "You should really learn to surf, brah."

I had heard that before too. Maybe he needed a surprise himself. "Okay," I said, looking sideways at him.

"Really, dude?" he yelped, looking like he might kiss me. He leaned in my direction, and I closed my eyelids, but nothing happened, of course. When I opened my eyes,

Jonas had settled back into his seat. "Next summer then. We can take a road trip up north somewhere. My mom keeps talking about some place called Mendocino."

I was going to ask why not a day trip to Santa Cruz but bit my tongue. There was no way I would give up a chance to be alone with Jonas off on our own for several days. I daydreamed scenarios. Jonas leaned into my line of vision for a response.

"Sounds good," I said, nodding belatedly.

He nodded back.

"You can borrow my steamer; I should get a new one anyway. You need your own board though," he said sternly.

I folded my arms and looked away. A room and food, yes, but a board sounded like an optional expense to me. I had been saving for a car for years, and I was so close. No optional expenses allowed.

"I'm saving for a car," I reminded him.

Jonas grumped, "Okay, we can take turns with mine."

While we waited through the winter to surf, we swam on the same relay foursome, took longer drives in the country, smoked more pot, and discussed Jonas's second, third, and fourth girlfriends—all with male nicknames. We doubled at the junior prom, Jonas with Girlfriend Number Four, and me with Emily Sciavone, who was probably a lesbian.

And then, it was June, and we were seniors with the summer off. Usually, I worked—the revenue augmenting my car fund—but Jonas talked so much about all the things we could do together before school started again I decided his company was more important than money and my future car at least for a couple of months. There was only one obstacle to our togetherness: the annual Stromson family vacation.

"So, you're really leaving Sunday?" he asked the last day of school like he didn't believe my family was going to someplace called Minnesota. We were lounging in the bell-less bell tower.

"Yew betcha," I told him in a bad Minnesota accent. "Got ta visit Gramma, doncha know?"

Jonas ignored, or didn't hear, me and continued to look through the telescope toward the ocean. Then, he made a slow turn with wide blue eyes that made my heart leap. "We're still gonna go surfing, right? When you get back?"

Like I hadn't promised him a thousand times already.

"Fer sure," I told him, giving him the surfer salute.

Minnesota was hot, humid, and lonely. Even though I loved my grandparents and my cousins were cool—for Minnesota—I missed Jonas. Although we talked every day on Skype and sent a thousand texts and tweets, it was never enough—for either of us. It made my heart flutter and my cock rise to hear him say he missed me. He was staying busy, though, driving to Santa Cruz frequently to surf. I wondered if he'd meet a new best friend, somebody else to take drives with, some guy who already knew how to surf. Maybe I should have bought that surfboard after all. More than anything now, I wanted to go surfing. I could not get home soon enough.

"Hey brah! You're back! Your dad made great time," he yelled into the phone after we pulled into our driveway, back from San Jose International. I hadn't even said hello. Thank you, caller ID. "I'll be over in five." He hung up.

"I thought you'd be in Santa Cruz," I told him when he arrived.

"No, dude, I..." he started to say but then his frown turned into a grin and his fists pretend-pummeled my shoulders. I loved every blow. "Very funny. Hey, you still up for our trip?" he asked.

I nodded enthusiastically.

"Good! I made the campground reservation, and I got a new steamer."

I remembered trying on his old wetsuit one rainy winter afternoon in his room. I felt naked even though I was covered in neoprene from neck to ankles. I felt sexy, too, which was new for me. It didn't hurt that Jonas was running his hands all over the wetsuit, which meant all over me.

"Looks like it fits you, brah. Oh, man! I can't wait!"

Me either, I thought to myself.

After Minnesota, Jonas and I hung out every day at his place. We swam laps, baked side by side in the sun, and planned our trip. Well, I listened, and Jonas planned. My mind wandered in and out while he talked, until he brought up some girl he'd met in Santa Cruz.

"When did you start dating her?" I asked, trying to sound nonchalant.

He looked at me just as casually across one brown shoulder. "I'm not dating her, brah. I just met her. She's hawt though."

"They always are," I muttered to myself.

"What did you say?" he asked, looking suspicious and a little scary.

"Nothing," I answered meekly. "Do you have a photo?" He happily brought up selfies of the two of them in bathing suits on the Santa Cruz beach, boardwalk, restaurants, and parking lots. She was beautiful and well-endowed, like all of Jonas's girlfriends.

"Her name is Dawn. Hawt, right?"

"Definitely," I said, although I was referring to him, not to her.

The night before we left for Van Damme State Park, I stayed at Jonas's, which wasn't new, and we had dinner with his folks, which was. I watched Mr. Michaels barbeque by the pool while Jonas was off somewhere in the house, and Mrs. Michaels was making a salad in their state-of-the-culinary-art kitchen.

Mr. Michaels was like Jonas with darker hair—and older, of course. He looked almost as good as his son, though, in his fitted khakis and light-blue oxford shirt open two buttons at the neck. I wondered if it were like father, like son in other departments. I laughed at myself and thought, *You must be really horny, Jared!*

I was.

Mr. Michaels smiled back at me while he flipped our steaks. "Where are you boys going?" he asked, making conversation.

"Van Damme State Park. We're camping out. Jonas is going to teach me how to surf," I answered in a hurry, trying to give him a summary.

Mr. Michaels's face was blank as if none of that was important to him. "You'll have your mobiles?" I felt my pocket automatically and nodded. "I hope they have cell service at this park," he said. "Where is it?"

"Near Mendocino," I answered like I knew all about the place.

"Eleanor would like to go there someday." He gazed down at the browning meat as if it would tell him whether they ever would. "Of course," he added meditatively, "not much time for that right now." He lifted his eyes from the meat to me. They were Jonas blue. "Jonas says you're an excellent student." He stared at me with his son's face, and horniness reared its ugly head again. "Have you thought about going into law?"

I gulped at what I was really thinking and replied demurely, "No, sir, I plan to study art and animation." I wondered if my erection were showing through my cargo shorts. Mr. Michaels was looking at my crotch like Jonas did sometimes. A strange smile crept across his face.

"Eleanor was an art major for a couple of years before I met her," he told me through the smoke. "At SC, the University of Southern California?" he asked to confirm I knew what the initials meant.

I nodded.

"Of course, she eventually changed her major to something more practical." The burning meat drew his attention for a few moments before he spoke again. "I know people at SC, if you need my help."

I'd been thinking of Stanford or Cal but politely said, "Thank you, sir," and returned his stare.

Mr. Michaels was looking at me or through me, I couldn't tell. I was relieved for several reasons when Jonas came bounding out of the house, wearing only his red Speedo and two darker red, patterned towels slung over his shoulders. I wondered if Mr. Michaels's body had ever looked like this. I wondered if it still did.

"You ready?" Jonas asked, eyes eager and his facial expression so much like a dog anticipating a walk I almost laughed.

"Jonas, we're eating in fifteen minutes," his father warned, watching me peel the camos off my ass and the orange shirt off my back. Did he notice our swimsuits were both minute and red?

"Just a couple of laps, Dad," Jonas assured him, jogging toward the pool. I felt Mr. Michaels's eyes on me while I shed my low-cuts and ran after Jonas as quickly as I could. I needed to hit the water fast.

"One, two, three!" Jonas yelled, and we dove into the pool in a racing start. My outstretched arms pierced the water, cool extending along the length of my body. I forgot the father, swimming alongside the son.

We did four laps, the regulation relay legs: breaststroke, backstroke, butterfly, and freestyle. Jonas pulled slightly ahead of me in the breast, but I caught up with him in the butterfly and beat him in the free. I was wiping water from my eyes when he touched the wall.

"Radical, brah!" he said, slapping me a high five. "Next year, Cal High is going to swim the shit out of everybody!" he predicted. Water streamed down his head and body. My eyes followed it down his chest and abs into the pool.

"Boys!" Mrs. Michaels called. "Time for dinner!" She was holding a salad bowl full of greens, sprinkled with red, orange, and yellow bits of other vegetables. It reminded me of a pointillist painting.

Jonas and I dried off quickly while his parents waited—not very patiently. I reached for my shorts, but Jonas shook his head, so we sat side by side at the clear glass table in our soggy red swim togs. In other words, basically naked.

Mr. Michaels spoke serially to my face, my chest, and—through the glass—my groin while he dished food onto his plate and handed the platters around. "You swim really well, Jared," he said, passing me the A.1., which I didn't use. "SC has a really good swim team, by the way. Think about what I said. You could probably get a scholarship. Athletic, I mean."

Jonas laughed. "Is my dad trying to recruit you for the alma mater, J?" He elbowed me in the side, almost making me stab myself with the steak knife. "Anyway, don't worry, Pop. Jared will get a scholarship for sure. Academic," he emphasized. "Straight As, extra points," he said in between chews. "He wants to study art though so don't get any ideas about the law school," he warned, smiling to make it digestible.

"Really?" his mother asked, showing interest in me for the first time since Jonas had introduced us months ago.

"Yep!" her son replied, spearing a potato chunk viciously.

"Jonas is going to SC," Mr. Michaels said, looking from me to his son and back. I wondered what he saw.

"Yeah, we could pledge the same frat, brah," Jonas said. "Lambda Chi Alpha! Huh!" he shouted and grunted in *basso profundo*, looking at his father, who kept his eyes on me, ignoring his son.

"Think about it, Jared," Mr. Michaels said. "You and Jonas could room together." I nearly choked. Mrs. Michaels turned the conversation to art, for which I was grateful, and the rest of the meal went down more easily. After dinner, Jonas and I played Resident Evil in his room until ten when he announced we were going to bed.

"Got to get an early start, brah," he explained, shedding the Speedo he still wore and turning the television off. I took my swimsuit off more slowly, wondering what was next, fantasizing possibilities. We hadn't slept naked together before, even in my dreams. I followed him under the bedding but avoided touching Jonas with any body part, especially my erection. He would have to make the first move. I thought he might because he was so chatty. Usually, he fell asleep almost immediately.

"You ever wish you had a brother?" he asked. "I have. Y'know, you're kinda like my brother."

I made myself breathe again and say, "I feel the same way, Jonas."

"Thanks," he said and then was quiet like he was falling asleep. I rolled over on my side. Behind my back, his voice said, "It would be cool if we both went to the same college and shared the same room. Y'know? Like brothers do."

I rolled back to face him, and his eyes sent messages I couldn't read. Then, he clicked the bed lamp off, said good night, and turned away from me, exposing the unblemished, well-tanned expanse of his back. *Touch it!* half of my brain yelled. *But what if he jerked away?* reasoned the other half. What if he called me a faggot? I couldn't imagine losing him, so I just waited and hoped until I heard his breathing slow. I sighed and closed my eyes.

The next morning Jonas was snuggled up against me, one of his arms splayed across my chest. When my eyes opened, his were staring back at me. "Sorry, brah." He rolled away from me and sat up. "Morning wood," he said casually in warning. I watched him head for the bathroom, a bobbing erection leading the way. After he closed the door and turned the fan on, I wondered what he was doing in there and whether he was thinking of me.

Mrs. Michaels coerced us into having breakfast before we loaded our luggage and attached Jonas's surfboard to the carrier on the roof of the z4. I chatted with her about Chagall and Diebenkorn over bacon and eggs while Jonas smiled proudly at both of us.

"I'm sorry I talked so much," I said as Jonas pulled out of the circular driveway onto the empty street.

"No worries, brah," he said happily. "I like hearing you talk, and it's cool you and Mom get along so well." If we'd been a couple, I would have taken his hand and given it a squeeze, but we weren't, so I didn't.

The drive north sped by. Jonas and I talked so much I hardly noticed the world-famous scenery outside the car, not that it mattered. I had seen it all plenty of times with my family, and anyway, Jonas's eyes were a more beautiful blue than any ocean.

In the middle of our continuous conversation, a sign suddenly announced we had arrived at Van Damme State Park. Jonas took the left toward beach parking, rather than the right toward the ranger station. We came to a stop in a space with an ocean view. I hadn't noticed before that the beach was so small or the waves were barely worthy of the name. I hoped Jonas wasn't disappointed.

His enthusiasm didn't seem to diminish, however. "Come on, brah! Let's go surfing!" he yelled, tumbling out of the car and snatching bungee cords off the surfboard. "Get out of those clothes, buddy!" he commanded, words I so wanted to hear but in a different context.

I removed my clothing deliberately, folding as I went and worrying about unwanted erections.

"Come on, J," Jonas said impatiently, already entering his wetsuit.

I tossed my shorts haphazardly onto my otherwise tidy pile and tried to insert a leg into his hand-me-down.

"Here," he said impatiently. "Lean on me," and so I did, feeling again the proximity and hope I had felt all those miles together from his house to here. "Hurry, brah!" he urged, his lips so close they grazed my ear. "I'll zip you up." As his hand carefully pulled the zipper up my back from butt to neck, I wished he were pulling it down.

"Now me," he demanded.

I watched the muscles of his back disappear underneath my fingers.

"Ready to surf, brah?" he asked rhetorically before he scooped up the surfboard and ran with it toward the water. My eyes followed his neoprene-encased body over the rocky sand, and I belatedly ran after he yelled over his shoulder at me. Halfway to the water, Jonas dropped the board onto the sand, the fins lodging it in place. "Practice first, J," he admonished sternly. *Yes,* I thought, *more like the father than the mother.*

We thoroughly reviewed the instructions I had followed in his bedroom. Once he approved of my stance and balance, he took up the board and sprinted for the water again.

"Cowabunga!" he shouted at me over his shoulder, laughing joyously. He was so handsome and, in memory, so young. "Watch me!" he instructed as he hit the water. There was nothing in the world I wanted to do more, so I waited in knee-deep cold water as he launched body and board, paddled with strong strokes through the miniature surf to where the waves were bigger and, in one fluid move, came to his feet, arms out for balance, legs set like an Egyptian statue, body turned toward the beach. The board moved, propelled by the wave, picking up speed. Jonas aimed it right at me. I let it come.

At the last minute, he hopped off into the water, an arm halting the board. "Let's do it, brah!" he screamed into my face, eyes wide, face contorted with happiness. I knew then I'd do anything for that face. Anything.

We swam together out to the easy breakers—ankle biters, Jonas called them—me on the surfboard, my arms acting like oars now, and Jonas swimming easily beside me.

"Up!" he commanded. I got to my knees and then struggled to my feet, but there was no forward motion.

I looked down, confused. Jonas was holding onto the board. "Balance, J," he cautioned and made it wobble.

I used my legs and arms in time and didn't fall.

"Cool," he said, climbing on behind me. His crotch landed next to my ass. "We're doing it tandem, baby!" he yelled up my back.

The board started moving and I nearly fell off, but Jonas's hands grabbed my waist. He leaned over me and said, "I got ya, brah," softly into my ear. I could feel his leg between mine, his crotch on my ass. The board moved faster under us, riding the wave.

"Jared!" he yelled, pressing his crotch more snugly against my ass and hugging me around the stomach. "You're surfing, brah!" I looked over my shoulder at his excited eyes and parted lips. I wasn't sure what was more amazing, our very sexual position or that Jonas had called me by my actual name.

By the end of the day, he was talking about Santa Cruz and debating which surfboard I should buy. We hadn't ridden another wave together. Jonas bodysurfed while I used the board. "You need the practice, brah," he explained.

It was nearly five when we eventually checked in at the drive-through ranger office. We were still in our wetsuits. The twentysomething ranger on duty was stern at first. "You just made it," he said. Then, he looked into the car and smiled appreciatively. "Not much surf today," he said, clearly to Jonas and not to me. Jonas agreed and the two of them chatted at some length.

"I'm hungry," I said, interrupting. The two of them bumped knuckles and said "see ya later" simultaneously before Jonas drove into the campground. I glanced into the rearview mirror. Ranger Boy was still looking and still smiling. Jonas seemed deliberately not to be checking any of his three available mirrors.

Our tent site was across the Little River, which deserved its name, in a cul-de-sac by itself. We changed into shorts, erected the tent, and prepared to shower.

"Here, dude!" Jonas said, handing me four quarters. "You'll need these for the showers."

After we were clean and fully dressed, we drove the few miles into Mendocino for a way-too-expensive dinner of free-range, locally sourced food, which Jonas insisted on paying for. It was dark when we got back to Van Damme. Jonas was uncharacteristically quiet on the return drive. I wondered whether he wanted to talk about some girl, probably Dawn. I waited but he was silent all the way back to our tent.

He flicked on the solar lantern, and we stumbled and crawled out of our go-to-dinner clothes. Jonas didn't add any clothes to his underwear so neither did I. I settled back to read while he rummaged in one of his bags. With a flourish, he produced a bottle of bourbon nearly two-thirds full.

"Where did that come from?" I asked in a squeaky voice.

Jonas snickered. "The Michaels family liquor supply," he answered, twisted off the cap, and took a long swig. "Here." He handed the bottle to me.

We took turns drinking and talking about everything but where we were headed until the bourbon was gone. Jonas tossed the bottle aside and lay back, hands behind his head. His erection loomed up and out impressively under the thin cloth of his Calvin Kleins. I stared unashamedly in adoration.

He grinned at me and scooted out of the briefs. "Suck it for me, brah," he said in a throaty stranger's voice, and I did—gladly, until Jonas pushed me away. We stared at each other across his body.

"You saw *Brokeback Mountain*, right?'" he asked.

"Yes," I answered nervously.

He got to his knees and turned me away from him. I heard him spit, lubricate himself, and then spit again. His fingers moistened me, one entering, then two.

"It's gonna hurt, J," he whispered, clamping a hand firmly over my mouth. "But it'll feel real good real soon. I promise," he said, easing himself in. He was correct on both counts.

When he finished, we remained on all fours, locked together, Jonas dead weight on my back. By then, I hadn't wanted it to end. Jonas slid off me and flopped onto his back. "Man, I'm bushed," he said, yawning demonstratively. "You wore me out, dude." He turned on his side and went to sleep. After a few moments of remembering so did I.

The next morning, I woke up alone, momentarily displaced. I rubbed the sleep from my face, remembering where I was and what had happened. I scanned the interior of the tent, wondering whether Jonas had left. Buyer's remorse maybe. I panicked. How would I get home?

The sounds and smells of food cooking entered the open flap. "You ready for breakfast?" Jonas asked when I poked my head out. I nodded, smiling in relief and instantaneous happiness. "Good," he said. "I made coffee. Man, I needed it this morning." He gave me a lecherous grin.

I got into shorts and drank a steaming cup, surprised at the absence of a hangover. I watched him prepare our bacon and eggs. He was fully dressed in shirt, shorts, and flip-flops.

"You up for more surfing, brah?" Jonas asked, plating our food. "I think you earned your own board last night," he said *sotto voce* and winking.

"Jonas, I don't..."

"Eat," he commanded.

I ate and then, almost before I knew it, we were in the car and in the surfing store. Jonas picked out a board—consulting me only aesthetically—and handed the clerk his credit card.

"I'll rent it," I said, reaching for my wallet.

"Don't stress, J," Jonas said, pushing my card away. "You earned it," he repeated, close to my ear. The clerk looked at us like he'd seen it all before.

Outside, I told Jonas I'd pay him back. "It's a gift, baby," he said, looping bungee cords around the carrier built for two. "I know you're saving for some wheels, brah."

"Let me pay for it, Jonas," I insisted.

"Get in the car, J," he said just as firmly, clicking the doors open.

"Jonas..."

"In the car." He sounded exactly like his father.

I got in the car. I'm sure Eleanor would have too.

At the beach, our disagreement forgotten or at least sidelined, we paddled out past the ankle-biters to the real waves and made several runs. Jonas was always touching me, giving me a high five, pounding my back, slapping my ass. Once he even grabbed a handful underwater, sticking out his tongue and rolling his eyes comically. When we finally left the ocean to other swimmers and surfers, after all the bumps and clutches, I was looking forward to being back inside the tent alone with Jonas and naked.

On the way to his car, two guys a little older than us passed us, carrying surfboards, heading for the waves. "Fags," I heard one guy say to his friend. They both laughed. Jonas whirled around.

"What did you say?" he asked, dropping his board and striding over to them.

"Nothing, man," the guy said, hands up, trying to stifle a laugh.

"Take it back," Jonas said, pushing hard against the laughing man's chest with both hands.

"Okay! Okay! It was a joke."

"Some joke," Jonas muttered. The two strangers walked leisurely away from us toward Japan. The one who said fags leaned close to his friend and said something else. They both laughed.

"Shit," Jonas muttered and started after them again. I grabbed his arm.

"Let's go."

He let me pull him to the car, but he still glowered over his shoulder.

After lunch in what passed for the town of Little River, we spent the afternoon hiking along trails away from the beach. Jonas found frequent opportunities to drag me behind trees and into thickets for languid kisses and full body groping. There were several near misses at being discovered, but Jonas laughed them all off.

That evening, we had dinner again at another elegant Mendocino restaurant. Jonas ignored my insistence we at least split the bill. He even ordered champagne, and the gay wine steward didn't refuse. Our gay server smiled at us benevolently and supplied us with a complimentary slice of cheesecake, two forks, and a knowing smile. On the way out of the restaurant, Jonas took my hand in the dark. He was gentle and considerate during sex that night. If this was how he treated girlfriends, I was surprised they ever broke up with him.

As we packed up, I wondered more and more. Why did they break up? What didn't I know about him? I decided to find out on the drive home.

"Why do you break up with your girlfriends?" I asked before we'd gone around the first curve. Jonas leaned away me with one eyebrow arched and both hands clenching the steering wheel.

"You know why, brah," he said, still inspecting me. "So, what's the real question?" I looked away. "You afraid I'll break up with you?" He gave me an exasperated look. "For a very smart guy, there's a lot you don't know. I like you, Jared. A lot. You like me, too, right?"

I wanted to say I loved him, but I didn't dare.

Jonas pulled over abruptly, slamming me against my side of the car. We were too close to the edge of a very sheer cliff. I could see whitecaps straight down below.

"What do you want, Jared?" he asked, looking so much older than I felt. "Jesus!" he exclaimed without waiting for an answer. "It's all the same. I thought you were different. I thought it would be different with a guy— with you." He punctuated his sentence with an enraged sounding, "Shit."

My chance was slipping away. "I love you," I said, quietly but urgently.

"What?" he asked, as if he hadn't heard, and then lunged at me across the gearstick. "Oh, man! I love you too," he mumbled in between kisses and an active hand inside my shirt. "I never felt this way before with anybody, Jared. Really."

I thought he'd start the car then, but he just held my hand, staring at it like he'd never seen one before. "So," he asked. "Are we rooming together at SC?"

After our declarations of mutual love, what choice did I have? I nodded yes. Jonas turned the ignition but, before he put the car in gear, said cheerfully, "My dad is going to be so happy—especially if you go into law." He gave me a wink, the storm vanished from his face.

I sat back and let him drive, wondering if this was how it had happened for Eleanor too.

August

Kachina Dancer

My hands fumbled across the bed for Joao's back. There was nothing but air and rumpled sheets. Had he left already? I opened my eyes. No, he was sitting on the edge of the bed, pulling up his socks. They were always white unless he went out. We had stayed in last night.

I pushed up, twisted onto my back, and sat up against the beige wall of our Best Western Window Rock king-size, feeling sadness creep up on me again.

"Leaving?" I asked, trying not to sound too pitiful.

"Got to, Davi. You know," Joao said in his soft Brazilian accent. When he stood and stepped into his jeans, I lunged across the bed and tried to pull him back down. "Let go, *irmão*. I gotta get ready," he said, laughing and pushing me away but only getting the tight jeans halfway up his thighs. I buried my face in his white underwear. He turned around. "You want some more, baby?" he asked, small dark eyes dancing.

"Yeah," I said.

He pulled his briefs down and pushed in between my lips and teeth, muttering, "*Tão loiro tão bonito*" over and over as he moved in and out of my mouth. I knew what that meant because he said it a lot. "So blond, so pretty," he told me when I asked, looking at me, well, looking at me like he meant it, I guess.

"Ooh, Davi. You got the sweetest mouth," he said in a voice I could barely hear. One arm stretched down my back until fingers found the elastic of my underwear and slid inside. His breaths grew louder and heavier, and he started muttering in Portuguese. *"Chupa me, baby. Chupa me,"* he whispered. *"Boa,"* he said, over and over.

I brought him close before his fingers along my jawline signaled me to stop. His eyes were half hidden by their pale-purple lids. "You got any condoms left, baby?" he purred. I started to pull away to get him one. *"Ainda."* He kept my head in place with one calloused hand while the other groped for an unopened package on the nightstand. "Get on the floor, Davi," he said, as he slipped the rubber on. "I gonna ride you like a brahma bull. Gonna fuck you good so you don't forget me before Albuquerque."

I got on the floor and into position. Joao knelt behind me and began riding me hard. In just a couple minutes, he went wild, fucking me like I guess the bulls fucked the cows in his father's fields back home, banging away and bellowing. I loved hearing him.

"Sorry it was so quick, Davi," he said. "But you know I gotta go. You gotta go too." Joao was right—another day, another rodeo—so we cleaned up and dressed, grabbed our bags, and went outside to our trucks, my beat-up old Ford next to his brand-new Dodge like before and after.

"So, you going to Zuni next, right?" he asked. I nodded yes, knowing he wasn't. Too small time for him now. He entered only major rodeos in huge arenas while I was still pissing around in small towns.

"I'll see you in Albuquerque," he promised. I nodded again but that was two weeks away and a lot could happen. It probably would. I had heard the rumors. But, fuck, I didn't have a ring on my finger and neither did he. I did stuff too—for money mostly, sure as hell not for love or whatever it was Joao and I had. I wondered how much longer whatever it was would last. I saw men stare at Joao's big chest inside his tight cowboy shirts—and at his crotch.

"I'll book us a room," he said, with a silly grin and goofy eyes. I wanted to say I'd split it with him, but I hadn't made any money in Window Rock, and my wallet was pretty thin.

"You're in Payson next," I said, to say something. I hated silences. They meant we didn't have anything left to say to each other. I also hated goodbyes. In my experience, you couldn't tell when they meant forever.

I must have looked worried because Joao winked at me and gave my shoulder a playful shove. "See you in Albuquerque, Davi," he said. "Don't be late. I gonna buy us plenty a condoms," he promised, giving me another wink and another shove that almost became a caress. I watched as he walked the few steps to his truck. It was like a gift was being taken away from me.

He waved from behind the wheel and then looked over his shoulder and in his rearview and sideview before backing up. He was a careful man. I liked that. Nobody else in my life had ever been careful.

He leaned forward so I could see him, waved, and then only a dust cloud was left to remember him by.

I glared at my pickup, kicked at an imaginary rock, and cursed. I leaned against the hood for a while, thinking, before I got in the crappy old Ford, slammed the rusty door, and headed for Zuni, blasting gravel of my own out of the Best Western parking lot.

I'd been rodeoing for three years without much to show for it but Joao. When I turned sixteen, I left school—and West Texas. This had been my life since—cheap motels and third-rate rodeos. At least now I had a boyfriend.

Joao was twenty-three. He had been a real cowboy in Brazil, rodeoing on weekends before he and a buddy decided to fly north and try for big money like so many other Brazilian cowhands before them. We had met over a year ago. Back then, we were both on the same circuit. I'm not that great at rodeoing, but I can make a living if I stick to smaller shows like Zuni, enough for burgers at Mickey D's and a room at Motel 6. That's a hell of a lot better than hanging around my dad's ranch and hearing him bitch or living with my mom in Lubbock and watching her drink.

Zuni wasn't far. It was a Native American town, one of those pueblos you hear about in New Mexico. Its rodeo was pretty small, but that meant I might have a chance to make the money I needed for Albuquerque. Even if Joao paid for the room, I wanted to buy my own meals and liquor.

I made good time on Highway 53. I arrived early. The little town looked busy like they were having a fiesta along with the rodeo. I found a motel to stash my bag and drove over to the fairgrounds, ready to ride. At the end of the day, I did pretty good. Placed second on the broncs, third on the bulls, and shit out of luck in everything else. If I did as well the second day, the prize money would pay my bills and get me to Gallup. Maybe I'd do okay there and make my Albuquerque money, or maybe I could pick up some odd jobs in between. Or, more likely some old guy would need a blow job bad enough to pay for it.

After my last event, I drove my saddle and gear back to the motel and took a long, hot bath and dried myself with two thin towels, put on fresh jeans and a crisp white shirt—thanks to the Best Western laundry and Joao's credit card in Window Rock—and stopped by the office to ask what nightlife Zuni had to offer. The clerk had a Native American face and a big belly.

"You're in luck, cowboy," he said with a nasty smile. "There's a dance on tonight."

"Dance?" I said. That sounded promising. Straight guys get horny around pretty women.

"Yeah. The kachinas are dancing," the clerk said, staring at me like he knew I didn't know what the fuck a kachina was, which I didn't. I stared back so he'd also understand I didn't give a shit. "They're Zuni gods," he said, his eyes stuck on me like I was flypaper. "Men dress up like the gods and dance through the main part of town. The costumes are real pretty," he said, with a kind of sneer. "You Native?" he asked me.

I shook my head no. *I'm five foot ten and blond. You figure it out, buddy.*

He looked me up and down. "We sure do need the rain," he said like it had something to do with our conversation.

"What does that mean?" I asked him.

"Maybe you'll find out," he said, laughing real creepy-like. I felt like punching him in the face or maybe his fat gut, but I needed a room to sleep in, so I didn't.

"When's this dancing start?" I asked.

"About dark. Head over to Pincion Street. You'll see 'em," he said, sticking his tongue out a little.

I kept my fists down and walked out. After I located the McDonald's and ate my fill of Big Macs and fries, I wandered into a bar and had a few with some of the locals and a couple other boys from the rodeo. I convinced them to wander over to Pincion Street with me after the third beer.

There was a pretty good crowd for a small town, mainly Native American but not everybody. I recognized more riders and ropers from the fairgrounds. We hooked up with them and talked shit while waiting for something to happen. I asked them if they ever heard of these kachinas. The Arizona and New Mexico boys started telling me *all* about them. Luckily, the music started, and they shut up. It was mainly flutes and like nothing I ever heard before, spooky, like someone was going to die. The crowd had quieted down, so you could hear every note float away like smoke into the sky.

The flute players were mainly old guys in headbands and blue shirts. They came down the street first, followed by the kachinas. At least, I figured that's what they were because they were dancing and wearing costumes in all kinds of crazy designs and colors.

My eyes went to one of them right away. It, he, whatever, was the tallest one and bare from the waist up except for the mask. His chest was really muscular and so were his abs. This kachina worked out. He was wearing a kind of skirt, white, with a fancy belt that hung partway down his right leg. He had leather armbands on his upper arms—which were pretty big guns—and beaded gloves on his hands, blue and yellow leggings on his thick calves, and high-top moccasins. When he danced, the skirt flew up a little, showing how beefy his thighs were.

He moved really well, rolling his abs and lifting his chest and shaking it. He had plenty to shake. The muscles in his legs worked as he danced, tensing and relaxing. It was real hot watching him so long as I didn't look at his mask. It was white like his skirt and way bigger than a human head with fancy designs for hair and ears and a mouth. The eyes were wide black holes. You knew there was a man inside, but you couldn't see his eyes. Gave me the creeps.

"Which one is that?" I asked.

Gonzalez tried to see where I was pointing. "You mean the antelope kachina?"

I guessed that was right because the mask had horns. "Yeah. What's he do?"

Gonzalez yelled in my ear, so I'd hear over the flutes. "His name is Chop. He brings the rain." Didn't make much sense to me, an antelope bringing the rain, but, hey, it was their story, not mine. The Native Americans around us looked pissed like we weren't supposed to talk, so Gonzalez and I shut up and watched the show.

Chop was coming closer. Every once in a while, he bent over and touched the ground with the two poles he was carrying, making like he had four feet, I guess. He was an antelope after all. His skin was tanned reddish-brown. It was smooth and shining with sweat. Drops fell from him onto the ground when he bent over. It was like he was raining.

The kachinas were alongside us now, and Chop was on our side of the street. He danced toward us, step-stepping and bending over with those poles, making me hornier than I already was. I still couldn't see the human eyes inside the mask, just those big black holes, but it was like Chop was looking right at me. I looked away, but Alvarez nudged me.

"He likes you, Davey."

I looked back at the street. Antelope Man had stopped in front of me. He was bent over with his poles and pushed his antlers at me. When he stood up again, I could finally see his eyes. They were the darkest brown I had ever seen, darker even than Joao's, and just staring. I stared back. Then, I don't know what came over me. Probably the beer. Anyway, Chop started dancing again—still right in front of me—and I did, too, imitating his steps. I could hear the rodeo rats laughing at me. I knew I was making a fool of myself, but I couldn't stop. It was like the damn kachina's eyes were hypnotizing me.

I was close enough I could hear his raspy breathing. He shook his shoulders at me and thrust out his groin, grinding it while he danced. I felt like I could do something crazy if Chop asked me to. If he'd wanted to fuck me in the street, in front of the whole crowd, I would have done it, I guess.

And then the music stopped, and Chop and I stopped dancing. He took one of the pole things he was carrying and poked my chest with it, easing it inside my shirt and holding it against my skin like it was a branding iron. He said something in Navajo, which I didn't understand of course, and then, when the music started again, danced away down the street, real slowly. I stared after him, watching his ass move in his skirt. It looked mighty good, powerful. Something you could hold on to. He turned around once and gave me that look again.

"Man, that was weird," Jenkins said, snapping me out of it.

"Yeah," I agreed, scared at how hard I was breathing. "Let's get out of here and find some more beer."

A couple hours later, drunk and alone, I staggered down empty streets back toward the motel. I could hear drums and singing coming from the pueblo. I thought about joining them. Maybe the guy playing Chop would be there. But I had to get up early again and try to make some more money, so I kept walking. Hadn't been any takers on a blow job, even a free one.

The motel wasn't far when I heard a flute behind me. I tried to ignore it even though it seemed closer than the drums. I thought I heard footsteps, too, like deer hooves on hard stone. When I whirled around, there weren't any deer, of course, nor a man either.

"Aw shit, Davey," I said out loud. "You're drunk."

I started walking again but kept listening, just in case. A drunk cowboy on a lonesome street is an easy target, not that they'd get much off a me. Then, sure as hell, I heard little clickety-clickety footsteps behind me and the flute again. The hair rose on my neck and arms. I hated to look back. but I did, really slowly. The antelope kachina was behind me all right, maybe twenty feet, dancing in slow steps like before, pointing one of the poles at me. I tried to run, but my boots had melted into the pavement. It was Chop's eyes, the black holes. I couldn't get away from them.

I wanted to yell, but I couldn't do that either. I couldn't move, couldn't speak, almost couldn't blink. All I *could* do was wait for Chop and watch while he caught up with me, taking his time like he knew I wouldn't run.

When he was within reach, he poked me with one of the poles, tapping my shoulder, nudging me around, and then poked my backside to get me moving like a damn sow in the show ring. He kept tapping me right and left, herding me forward, until we were past the motel, past all the houses, out in the desert, surrounded by dark shapes I hoped were rocks. Finally, I was able to say something, stupid as it was.

"What do you want?" I asked him over my shoulder, my voice cracking.

He poked my ass with one of the poles and said something in Zuni or whatever.

"No way!" I yelled and finally found legs to run. I didn't let anybody up my ass but Joao. Sure, I sucked a guy off now and then, but let him fuck me? No way and sure as hell no way if the dude was wearing an antelope suit.

I ran farther into the desert since Chop was between me and town, my legs pumping as hard as my high school four forty experience could make them. Running was about the only thing I did right in school.

I didn't hear Chop following me—or the flute—so I stopped to catch my breath and figure out where I was and how to get back to town and into my motel room. But, when I looked back to see how far away I was, there was Antelope Man, dancing toward me, step by step like he still heard the music. And then, I did too. Flutes were playing all around me. The sounds were soft and pretty, not scary at all. I relaxed and let the music enter me. My feet shuffled like I was dancing again. I told myself to stop, but I didn't listen. I closed my eyes and lifted my arms, turning this way and that, keeping time with my feet. There was magic all around me—and inside me too. Everything was magic. I wasn't me anymore. I was everything.

I forgot all about the kachina until the music stopped and I heard his breathing. When I opened my eyes, he was right next to me, but I wasn't scared of him either, not anymore.

He said something in Navajo, and this time I understood him. "Follow," he told me and danced farther off into the dark. I looked back toward town; I could still see some lights. This was my chance. Chop wasn't even checking on me. But, as soon as I decided to make a run for it, I heard another flute, just one, coming from the direction Chop was going. It was beautiful. He was beautiful. I danced after him like he told me to.

We came to an outcropping of rocks like you see in the desert. Chop turned, danced in place, waiting for me. When I was about five feet away, he stopped dancing, held up a pole to stop me, and slowly, as slowly as he danced, took off his clothes. First, the yellow and blue belt and then the skirt, moccasins, and leggings. His body was perfect, big and thick everywhere.

I shucked my clothes as fast as I could while Chop step-stepped over to me with everything jangling around. He stopped an inch away. Strong hands pushed me onto my knees. I took the head of his dick. I didn't think I could manage more than that. At first, like usual, I thought of Joao. But, every time I looked up, I saw Chop's mask and his eyes, his chest and his arms, and pretty soon I wasn't picturing Joao anymore. The mask leaned back, and I saw more of Chop's size eighteen neck. The small brown nipples on his chest were like magnets, and I yanked them hard. That's when Chop grabbed my hair, held on, and rammed all the way in. I didn't even choke.

He pushed in and out, in and out like a slow piston. I didn't have to do a thing. Then, just like that, he stopped. "Stand," he said in this deep, scary voice.

I stood up right next to him. I could see the man's eyes inside the mask. He wasn't no god, and there wasn't no magic. I should have left when I had the chance. But, before I could try, Chop had me lean against one of the boulders, arms out, legs wide, ass up.

When he had me set up the way he wanted, he worked himself inside me, inch by inch. It hurt like hell and felt really good at the same time. When he was flat against me, the slow piston started up again. Whoever this guy was, he knew how to fuck. I didn't even try to think about Joao.

The dude grunted, and I moaned like a damn cow. The noise we made bounced off the rocks as much as we did, and dogs barked, way off, like they could hear us. I didn't care. Once, I tried to look over my shoulder, but Chop clamped a big hand around my dick and started jerking. Pretty soon, I exploded, yelling and cursing like I never had before.

The kachina started bellowing and going crazy in my ass. I felt the scratch of hair against my back, the flash of hooves on my shoulders, and antlers holding my head in place. I thought he'd never stop. I didn't want him to. And then it began to rain, rushing down our bodies, in between us and all around, a downpour. Chop had finished and was squashed against me, breathing hard.

"*Lidokkya,*" I heard myself say into his ear. Rain. I let it cleanse me. And then Chop began again, in and out, in and out, slowly, so slowly. The rain was warm and flowed strong down our bodies and around the connection between us. The more Chop fucked me, the more it rained, harder and harder throughout the night. He didn't stop, and the rain didn't neither.

The next thing I remember was waking up in the motel bed. My clothes were on the floor where I must have dropped them. My ass didn't ache at all. It would have hurt like the dickens if anything had really happened. It hadn't. I had been drunk. There had been no antelope god trailing me, no stumble into the desert, no all-night fuck against the rocks. Just a crazy dream. I got up and took a shower, warm and strong, like in my dream. In the middle of it, I heard my phone ring.

"I got us a room in Albuquerque, a suite," Joao's voice said when I answered, still wet. I wanted to tell him he was spending too much money on me; I wasn't worth it, but I just said thanks. "I got something else to say, *meu amigo*," he said, his voice catching.

"So, say it," I told him after only hearing him breathe for a couple of minutes.

"No, *pirado*! In Albuquerque. You gotta ride today. Me, too, *meu amado*." And then he hung up, leaving me wondering what the hell he wanted to say and why he couldn't say it over the phone.

I thought about this as I tossed my saddle and bag into the cab of the pickup and walked to the motel office for some free coffee and to settle my bill. The guy on duty wasn't the same one from yesterday. He was Native American all right but tall and well built—really well built. He looked up from his computer.

"Thanks for the rain," he said, his dark eyes not smiling at me. I knew him then. When the flute started playing, I wasn't surprised. "Sure you can't stay another night?" he asked when he saw my wallet. "We need more rain real bad.'

"I can't," I told him, hearing the flute playing louder and louder. "I got a rodeo to ride in Gallup."

"You sure?" he said, smirking and coming around from behind the counter. My vision blurred, and for a minute I thought I saw Chop wearing his mask and kachina outfit, his chest bare and brown, his legs strong and dancing.

"Please," I whispered. Chop snorted inside the mask. My vision cleared. The clerk was leering at me.

"Tonight. On the street outside the motel. Midnight," he said in Chop's deep voice. I nodded my head and took the room key back from him.

With the door shut and locked, I flopped onto the unmade bed. What was I going to do? I thought of the night I'd had with Chop and unzipped my jeans but stopped, disgusted with myself. I had to ride today, and I had to go to Gallup. I had to make some money. I had to see Joao in Albuquerque. Wanted to see him. *Call Joao,* my brain told me.

"Davi!" he said when he answered. "*Que saudade.* You okay?"

"Yeah," I lied, my voice shaking. "What is it you want to say to me?" I asked him. Maybe it would make a difference.

"Can it not wait until Albuquerque, *meu xodó*?"

I thought of Chop's eyes. "I don't think so," I said. "What is it?"

Joao chuckled. "I miss you, too, baby. Well, okay. We been going out nearly a year now, and I want you to know...um...how much I like you." It had been over a year, and I already knew he liked me—or at least my ass. I started to say something smart-alecky but Joao interrupted. "Just listen, *moço*. Okay?"

I shut up, trying not to think of Chop's chest.

"You know I don't wanna stay here in the States a long time," Joao said. "I'm saving for my own ranch in Mato Grosso, and the way I'm making money, I figure it's only gonna take me another year, maybe less."

So, he was telling me we had a time limit? I knew that already too. I let myself visualize Chop in his mask but out of his clothes, naked and ready for me.

"I want you to go with me," Joao said loudly like I hadn't been listening the first time he said it. The vision of Chop disappeared.

"To Brazil?" I asked.

"*Sim*," he said, waiting to hear if I would agree.

I listened to him breathing. I thought of him there in Payson, his handsome face, of how well our bodies fit together and how loving he was, of how much I missed him. While I was thinking, the flute began to wind its way through my mind.

"Did you hear that?" I asked.

"What?" Joao asked back.

"That music."

"Must be coming from next door or outside maybe. So, you gonna come with me, Davi?"

I didn't need to think any more. "Yes," I said, taking forty-five bucks out of my wallet and tossing it and the room key onto the bed. "I'll see you in a couple hours in Payson," I told him.

"I thought you was supposed to go to Gallup," he said, sounding confused and maybe a little happy.

"Not anymore," I told him. "I'll see you in Payson."

"Okay, baby!" he said, definitely happy now. "You want me to enter you in the broncs? I pay the fee for you. No worries, Davi."

"Okay," I told him as I opened the motel room door. "I'll see you at the arena."

"*Beijos*," he said.

"*Milhões de beijos*," I said. Joao laughed at my Portuguese and hung up.

I ran for the truck, ignoring the flutes trying to hem me in, opened the door, jumped inside, and locked both doors after me. I turned the ignition on, put the Ford in reverse, and then in first. I hit the gas, burning rubber. The clerk ran out of the office with two poles. I put my blinker on and accelerated out of the parking lot, heading north. I didn't check my mirrors. There wasn't anything behind me I needed to see.

September

Garden Party

"Henry, what you doin' for Labor Day?" my friend Bill Barnes drawled at me after plopping his long, lean body onto one of the green fabric chairs facing my desk.

"Nuthin," I drawled back. Which wasn't precisely true. I had an invitation to drive home to Nashville for a family picnic, but that could wait if Bill Barnes had a better idea. I loved my family, but I'd been after my colleague for years.

"Good," he said, slapping his well-tailored thighs and standing up. "You're coming home with me then. We can leave work early on Friday. Old Man Lafferty's bound to announce an early closing. Bring a suit or two."

"Wait! Where are we going?" I asked before his bodacious ass could sashay out of my door.

"The Delta, Henry. We still on for lunch?"

I nodded, sitting back in my chair. The Delta with Bill Barnes, his home territory. Well, I swan—as my granny used to say. The possibilities made it difficult for me to concentrate on the Smallsby case. I had heard about his family's house, with its fluted columns and full-frontal verandah, often enough to wonder whether it truly existed. People do make up stories about plantations and civil war family valor. Wanting Bill Barnes and wondering about the house had come together in my mind, all part of my family's upward social trajectory.

On the day, bags in hand, we ambled through heat and humidity toward the parking garage, Bill Barnes talking all the way. Mr. Lafferty, our managing attorney, had indeed let the staff leave early and given us attorneys the option. Normally, I might not have taken it, but I would follow Bill Barnes's smile anywhere, anytime.

I gave God a little thank-you Bill had a convertible. The weather was so hot and heavy I had sweat through my dress shirt already. We headed south on US 61—the Blues Highway, Bill called it—through fields of farmers' market gardens. I'd been to some on weekends.

"Do you like the blues?" I asked him.

"Not really. How about you?"

"Not really," I repeated, staring at the mound of his left pectoral exposed by the wind sluicing through the car, made possible by Bill undoing at least three buttons after he removed his tie. "I'm looking forward to meeting your family," I said, trying to take my mind off his chest.

He gave me a funny look, but it vanished, and he slapped my thigh. "Hope you like crowds!" he exclaimed.

Just north of Clarksdale, a town I'd only seen on a map, we did a jog west and then south again on a narrow state highway, flanked by telephone poles along one side and a line of cottonwoods on the other. We drove fast through one disintegrating little southern town after another until Bill announced, "Here we are! Rosedale, Mississippi, my hometown." I had imagined rows of elegant mansions and manicured lawns, given Bill's often recited family history, so Rosedale with its rundown, ruined, and empty storefronts was quite disappointing. I wasn't sorry when Bill didn't stop.

On the other side of town, we passed through a brief forest of sweet gums and more cottonwoods into a wide field of low green plants.

"What's that?" I asked, nodding right.

"Our soybeans," Bill answered. "We're close to Beaulieu now."

He eased his Audi A5 around a curve, and the air grew heavier still. I could see the Mississippi on our left through groves of cypress trees. At a promising drive, we turned right, passing under monstrous oaks hung with Spanish moss into a clearing with a grand two-story white mansion at its center. Beaulieu did not disappoint me. It had the requisite four central pillars and second-story verandah. Two wide wings flanked the center, like bodyguards.

"Is this Beaulieu?" I asked, just to make sure.

"Nah, son, we're just stopping to ask directions." Bill deadpanned before he whacked my shoulder and grinned at me. He eased the Audi into a parking space between a Lexus and a Buick and honked three times. People ran from the house, yard, and who knows where to greet us, all talking at once.

"Billy! You're late!" yelled a young woman who could have been his twin, all sunny-blonde wavy hair and golden skin. I made a note of her nickname for Bill Barnes; I might be able to use it someday. Others shouted similar greetings except one young man with a deeply tanned olive complexion and curly black hair. He hung back as if he were shy or not really part of the group.

"Everybody, this is my friend, Henry Williams from Nashville," Bill said to the assembled dozen or more.

They all yelled "Hello!" or "Welcome!"—even the retiring young man. I saw his lips move, and pretty lips they were.

"Henry, let me introduce you to my cousin Jamie," Bill Barnes said, wading through the crowd toward the solitary figure. "Jamie Battle," he said, "this is Henry Williams. You'll like him." The two of us shook hands, both wondering, I suppose, what that meant. But then I was swept away to meet more cousins, two sisters, a brother-in-law, Bill's mother and father, and an uncle and aunt. No one else looked like Jamie Battle, even the brother-in-law. Maybe he was adopted.

We flowed up the broad steps, across the spacious front porch, and into the house where I found myself in an eddy alongside Jamie Battle. "I'll show you to your room," he said softly and took my bag. That surprised me, but Bill was busy with his family, so I followed the cousin up the wide central staircase to the second-floor landing.

"Billy thought you'd like this room," Jamie Battle said as we turned down a right-angled hall into the east wing. "It's a little more private and a lot quieter," he added as if he could tell how overwhelmed I was by the Barnes family in full volume.

"Thank you," I said. I modulated my voice to match his softer tones.

The room Jamie Battle opened the door to was large and high-ceilinged. I wondered if all the bedrooms were like this at Beaulieu. Maybe I'd see at least one other of them while I was visiting if my hopes for the weekend with Billy Barnes were realized.

"Lovely." I walked to the three tall open windows. Below was a beautiful rose garden in soothing pastels. I said the obvious, "What beautiful roses!"

Jamie stepped next to me and turned his hazel eyes my way. The color brought up memories: my first boyfriend had had hazel eyes. I wanted to tell Jamie Battle that but decided it was best not to go there on so short an acquaintance. You never can tell what folks think about gay people.

"Thank you," he said. "My grandmother tends it, although she does ask me to do the heavy work. I like the colors." He leaned out of the window a little. A breeze rushed through the room, ruffling his shirt. It was open three buttons, just like Bill Barnes's on the trip down. In a glimpse, I saw a well-developed, less tan chest, black curly hair covering it, and one tight, small brown nipple. I looked up into Jamie Battle's observant eyes, swallowed hard, and made some quick conversation.

"You live here then. Did I meet your grandmother?" Jamie Battle's smile became guarded.

"Yes," he confirmed. "I live here." He hesitated. "Billy didn't tell you?"

"Tell me what?"

"I'm your host. Beaulieu is my place."

The surprise must have shown. Jamie Battle considered my face and then diplomatically turned back to the garden below us. "Nana's probably resting from the heat. But she'll be down to supper, I expect." The rhythm of his voice changed, a cadence I couldn't quite place. We stood next to each other for a minute, staring at the roses.

"Well, then," he finally said with a sigh as regretful as I felt. "I'll leave you in peace. Supper is at eight, dinner at noon, and breakfast any time you want. It's buffet. Fridays we always dress, and we have the garden party Monday of course. Oh, did Billy—"

"Yes," I answered, interrupting. "I brought a suit." In truth, I had brought several.

He looked me up and down slowly. "I was going to offer you one of mine. We're about the same size," he said.

We were both just short of six feet tall. I felt something stirring but wasn't exactly sure whether it was in my host or me. Before we could explore it one way or the other, Jamie Battle excused himself and exited the room. I was left alone with regret and the beginning of an inkling why.

I heard Bill Barnes's loud voice accost Jamie Battle in the hallway with soft murmurs in reply. In another two seconds, Bill was striding into my room. He closed the door behind him with a wink. I became conscious we were alone, at least for the moment, and there was a bed in the room.

"The rose bedroom!" he proclaimed. "I told Jamie Battle you'd like it." He joined me at the window, leaning against the frames, ignoring the garden, no breeze entering now. "How do you like him?" he asked.

"Why didn't you tell me Beaulieu belongs to your cousin? You called it your home."

"It is. Our family home. Anyway, would it have made a difference?"

I pondered that briefly before saying no.

"Well then, how do you like the master of Beaulieu?"

Master made me flinch, but Bill Barnes's cherry lips and pale-blue eyes motivated me to move on.

"He's nice. Very nice. Doesn't look much like the rest of y'all." I hurried to explain myself. "I mean, you're all so blond and he's—"

"Not," Bill finished for me. "There's a story there," he said after a few moments of uncharacteristically biting his tongue. "But I best let Jamie Battle tell it. Would you like a shower before you dress?"

My heart leaped, hoping that was some kind of sexual invitation, but Bill made no move to disrobe. I unbuttoned my shirt, watching him watch me. *Maybe now*, I said to myself, but Bill just sort of snapped to attention, said he'd see me in a little while, and left. I continued taking my clothes off, feeling regretful for the second time in fifteen minutes.

*

Cocktails were served at 6:00 p.m. on the back lawn. We were surrounded by ancient-looking willows swaying gently side to side like hoopskirts in the occasional breeze. I noticed an older woman, bent slightly with age, standing on her own in a far corner. She was pale but with African hair and features. I couldn't imagine who she might be until Jamie Battle joined her and took her arm. I saw then immediately. The story Bill Barnes alluded to had begun to tell itself.

They walked slowly toward me at the old woman's pace. "Mister Henry Williams," Jamie Battle said once they'd reached me. "I'd like to introduce you to my grandmother, Mrs. Annabelle Watts."

She smiled and extended a slender hand, brown with liver spots. "Pleased to meet you, Mister Williams," she said in a soft, soothing voice much like her grandson's. Her eyes were a warm brown, and the smile creases around them told me she had a happy life, or at least she was optimistic.

"As am I, Mrs. Watts," I said, bowing over her hand, feeling quite the southern gentleman. Before my lips could touch down, she withdrew her hand from mine gracefully and asked about my family, which, Black or white, is what Southerners do.

I explained I was from Nashville, that my parents were both living, and I had two sisters and a brother, all married and spread from Austin to Atlanta.

"It's hard, isn't it, not to be with family. I do miss my own people," she said, telling me, if I didn't know already, she was not a Barnes.

"Where are they, Mrs. Watts?" I asked politely.

"Do you know Arcola?" I said I didn't. "It's down in Washington County. Not far really..." Her voice trailed off. "But I couldn't say no when my grandson invited me to live with him. I have my own house." She waited for my reaction.

"Of course, you cherish your independence."

"That too," she said and gave me an analyzing look.

Just then, a Black servant dressed in black livery appeared at Jamie Battle's side and murmured something into his ear. He turned from us to his relatives gathered on the lawn beyond. "Supper's ready, everyone!" he called in a loud, strong voice different from the one he had used since my arrival. He smiled at me. I wondered what that particular look meant. *I'm not what you think I am?*

Supper was in a pale-green wallpapered room with illumination sconces along the walls and a long, well-preserved oak table down its center. Jamie Battle had me sit next to his grandmother, who was on his left. Bill Barnes was on his right, a disruption of the otherwise male, female, male, female seating arrangement. That made me wonder if the cousins were more than just relatives. Maybe that's why Bill Barnes flirted with me but didn't follow through.

During a fine meal of beef bourguignon, hearty red wine, and ambrosia that reminded me of my mother's, I chatted comfortably with Mrs. Watts and, at a much higher volume, with my neighbor on the left, one of the several cousins. Bill Barnes and Jamie Battle kept up a steady conversation in whispers, confirming my suspicions.

Mrs. Watts reminded me of my own grandmother, soft-spoken but with words that had a toughness belying their delivery. She cross-examined me with the finesse of a seasoned attorney.

"Where abouts did you say you were from?"

"Nashville, ma'am."

"Oh," she said and returned her attention to her plate. After a few more bites, she asked, "And what does your daddy do?"

"He runs a store. Auto parts," I added.

She looked at me differently on hearing that, her head back, shoulders tilted. "Do tell. My husband had a store too. Groceries and sundries. Whatever people needed." She looked away a moment. "He passed."

"I'm so sorry."

"Three years ago. That's when my grandson had my house built here. Didn't want me to live alone." We both looked at Jamie Battle, and he raised his eyebrows at us. Mrs. Watts turned back to me. "He's a good boy." She considered her words a moment. "You seem like a nice young man."

"I hope I am."

"You are," she said decisively. "Now, would you please pass me the mashed potatoes?"

We went on to discuss my livelihood, living arrangements, and political views. None of my answers seemed to change her opinion that I was a nice young man, at least as far as I could tell.

After supper, our host excused himself as he stood up. "I have to escort Nana home," he explained to me.

Mrs. Watts took my hand. "A pleasure to meet you, Mister Williams. How long are you staying, did you say?"

"Just the weekend," I replied, feeling unaccountably sad to admit it.

She smiled. "Perhaps you'll come visit me before you go. Come for dinner tomorrow. The two of you," she said, glancing with meaning toward her grandson. I looked at him as well.

"We will," he promised without returning my look.

Mrs. Watts smiled Jamie's smile at me before she slipped her arm through his and they slowly departed the dining room, calling good night to everyone and being wished good night in return.

"Now you know," Bill Barnes's jaunty voice said at my elbow. "Come have a whiskey with me." His hand latched onto my arm and pulled me away with him into the flow of Barneses leaving the dining room. I wasn't too pleased with how he grabbed me and tugged me after him.

In the family parlor, he and I saluted each other and took a sip from heavily etched glasses. "He is my cousin," Bill said as if I'd told him I didn't believe it. "Uncle Stephen's boy." I waited while he chugged his drink as if he had to do that before he could go on. "His mother was Black," he confided after he swallowed. Not Aunt Whoever, just "his mother." And Black, as if that summed her up.

"And that means Jamie Battle is Black."

"Some," Bill acknowledged, sipping on his drink.

"Some?" I took a sip from my drink before I went on. Bill Barnes watched me like a bird of prey. "Where are his parents?" I asked at last.

"They died."

Bill Barnes poured more Jack Daniel's into my glass and refilled his with Maker's Mark. "Stephen was the oldest son, so Jamie inherited," he said. "Lucky for us he didn't want to sell." He leaned his head back and emptied half of the new glassful.

"Did you visit much when his parents were alive?"

"Oh, all the time. Jamie Battle and I grew up together."

"Interesting."

"What?"

"That you never mentioned him before."

"Well, I wasn't ashamed of him, if that's what you mean."

"Why would you be? Because he's Black? Like you said, you grew up with him. Anyway," I said, after a deep breath. "He lives here alone?"

"Yes, suh," Bill said with an already imprecise enunciation. "Jamie Battle Barnes lives in this big ol' house all alone. His grandmother has her own place."

"So she told me. I'm going there tomorrow for supper."

Bill Barnes looked alert all of a sudden. "She invited you?"

"Yes."

He took another big swallow of bourbon. "I've never been inside the place myself."

You're not a nice young man, I thought to myself. *No, not a nice young man at all.*

Just then we were joined by Bill Barnes's unmarried sister and their mother. I assumed this would be the beginning of the usual interrogatory—seeing if I were qualified as a prospective husband—but they just chatted amiably with Bill Barnes and me before leaving for other conversations. Bill poured himself another large drink.

When Jamie Battle entered the room, Barneses ebbed and flowed around him, saying how well his grandmother looked. He thanked everyone politely while working his way across the room to us. Bill Barnes poured him a double shot of Maker's.

"Your grandma is looking hale and hearty, cousin," Bill offered along with the drink. "Her arthritis not acting up?"

"Some," Jamie said. "But not as bad as last spring. Thank you for asking." He turned to me. "Billy says you enjoy a swim."

I agreed I did.

"Maybe we can all go down to the river tomorrow morning while it's still cool," Jamie suggested. "Did you bring your trunks, Billy?"

"Yes, sir, and I made sure Henry Williams brought his too. He's most enticing in them," Bill Barnes answered, winking at me. My face turned radish red. "Aw, now, son. No need to be embarrassed. All those hours at the gym aren't just for your health, are they?"

*

The next morning, after breakfast, Bill Barnes followed me upstairs into my room and closed the door behind us again. My heart jumped for a second time in spite of myself. "How do you like Jamie Battle?" he asked again after sprawling across my bed, already tidied up by unseen hands.

"I told you I like him fine," I replied, remaining standing. Maybe he didn't remember. I went to the windows, not really seeing anything outside.

"What's wrong, son?" Bill asked.

I looked him in the eye.

"Oh, Henry! You thought I asked you down here for myself? You know I'm not gay."

I decided to be stubborn. "Bill Barnes, you don't have a girlfriend. Haven't had one the whole time I've known you."

Bill returned my glare. "Henry Williams, if I were gay, you would have known by now." He sounded serious. "Anyway." He rose quickly from the bed. "Get your swimsuit on. You brought the black one? You looked so sexy at Mary McClain's pool party."

There he goes again, I said to myself but confirmed out loud I had brought the black trunks, per his instructions, and moved to get out of my clothes. Let him see what he was missing.

Bill didn't leave until I was down to my underwear. "No, sir, I would not have let all that get away," he said, wolf-whistling before he left the room.

*

A small group of us walked down the dusty drive and crossed the barely paved country road into the cypress trees along the river. Past the trees, there was a narrow beach and a boat dock without a boat. We set our things on a convenient picnic table and all began to shed our clothes. I watched wistfully as Bill Barnes's sculpted body emerged from his T-shirt and shorts. He was wearing a Speedo in a shade of blue that matched his eyes perfectly.

Jamie Battle took the longest stripping down, and everyone seemed to watch. The mounds of his body curved more naturally than his cousin's, and his thighs were leaner than Bill's tree trunks but still nicely muscled. His forearms, face, and neck were darker than the rest of him. Maybe he was more than just a gentleman farmer. Behind me, I heard Bill Barnes chuckle and turned to see him watching me. He heehawed at my expression and ran for the river. The rest of us followed, and water sports began.

Afterward, lying on our towels, Jamie Battle on my left, I stole looks at his body and the arc of his lime-green trunks.

"He's beautiful, isn't he?" Bill Barnes whispered into my ear from my right side like the serpent to Eve.

I was afraid to answer but whether because Jamie Battle would hear or the cousins, I wasn't sure.

"His mama and daddy were too. He looks some like both of them," Bill said, his hot breath making me hotter.

"Really?" I said, surprised into turning my face so close to his we could have kissed. "I don't see much Barnes in him at all."

"Look closer," Bill advised, showing me the tip of his tongue between swollen lips like he was daring me to do it. "It's there all right."

I avoided making a fool of myself with Bill and looked at Jamie Battle. He smiled at me as if he'd been listening, and I smiled back reflexively. I still didn't see any Barnes in him. I turned again to Bill, but he was on his back now, eyes closed, body open for inspection, and I indulged until Bill cleared his throat, interrupting my fantasies. I looked up from his body to his face. One eye was open; it gave me a wink.

After we were dry, no one bothered putting their clothes back on for the short trip back to Beaulieu. The day was too hot already to care what we looked like. I walked with Bill until he pushed me forward into Jamie Battle, making me land against his nearly naked body with a smack.

"I'm sorry," I said, thinking how solid he was and how cool his skin felt compared to the air around us.

"No problem, Henry," he said, smiling over his shoulder at me. I peeled myself off him and moved to his side. We fell into step.

He brought up dinner at his grandmother's. "Will you be ready by eleven thirty? My grandmother always eats at noon when the whistle blows." He laughed like he'd made a joke. "There isn't really a whistle. Not here at least. But in Arcola, one always blew exactly at noon. Left over from slavery days," he said, his voice suddenly grim.

"I'll be ready," I promised. "How many of us will there be?"

"You, me, and my grandmother."

Was he thinking what I was thinking, and how did he feel about it? For that matter how did I feel about it? I answered myself quickly—partly pleased and partly not. The partly not wasn't something I was proud of.

I took Beaulieu in again as we walked on to its front door. Grand houses like it were supposedly part of our southern legacy. Jamie Battle owned a place where slaves had done the work and borne the massa's children. People like Mrs. Watts and Jamie Battle were descendants of that. No wonder Mrs. Watts didn't want to live in the main house. I was surprised Jamie Battle could. But it was beautiful, and beauty is mighty tempting. That aphorism *extemporaire* drew my mind to Bill Barnes, an example I was beginning to rue. Maybe I should have gone to Nashville after all.

At 11:28, my hand was on the doorknob when someone knocked on the door. I opened it, and Jamie Battle and I were suddenly face to face, his lips almost as close to mine as Bill's had been at the river. They were as bee-stung as Bill's, which was something Barnes about him.

"That's a lovely suit, Henry," he drawled softly, coolly looking down my body as if in my room we were in a different world. I felt the control in him, the deciding. It hadn't been there before. "Shall we go?" he asked after a few moments of looking from me to the windows to the bed and back at me.

Mrs. Watts's house was red brick, modest in comparison to Beaulieu but perfectly fine, all on one floor, with a full front porch, a parlor for receiving, a dining room, kitchen, and a fourth room behind a closed door, which I assumed shielded her bedroom.

"My grandson had this place built especially for me," she said proudly after we were seated in the parlor. "My little house in Arcola wasn't anything as nice." She sounded wistful as she said it.

I looked at a covey of family photos on the upright piano, the faces becoming paler as the clothes became more modern. I particularly noticed one of a youngish couple, the woman dark-haired and olive-skinned—almost as dark as Jamie Battle with his tan, the man Barnes-blond and more handsome than any of them. Mrs. Watts followed my eye.

"That was my daughter Beatrice and her husband, James Battle Barnes," she said, making an effort to get up. Her grandson hurriedly brought the photo to her, and she silently traced the features of her daughter with a loving forefinger.

"She was beautiful," I said when, with a sad smile, she handed the portrait to me.

"Jamie looks so much like his mother," Mrs. Watts said. "Although he has his father's kindness." I was surprised to hear *kindness* used about a Barnes. They were all perfectly nice, but *kind* was not a descriptive I would have chosen for any of them—except, perhaps, Jamie. I looked at the photo of James Battle Barnes a second time. His son looked more like him than at first glance in the shape of the head maybe and certainly in the jawline.

We helped Mrs. Watts serve coleslaw, black-eyed peas, cheese fritters, and ham.

"Would you care for more sweet tea?" she asked.

I said I would although it had more sugar than I preferred.

"Leave room for cobbler," Jamie advised with a loving look at his grandmother as I took a second helping of black-eyed peas.

The cobbler was peach, my mother's favorite. I said yes to a scoop of vanilla ice cream on top. It was a holiday after all. I'd be back in the gym Tuesday to begin countering all these calories.

"Thank you again, Mrs. Watts, for inviting me," I said as Jamie and I were leaving. "Everything was delicious."

"You are most welcome, Mister Williams," she said with her hand comfortably in mine. I hadn't been able to convince her to call me Henry. "I hope we'll have you back with us again real soon." She and Jamie Battle exchanged some silent communication in an extended look before we left.

Afterward, Jamie and I walked back toward Beaulieu, close enough our elbows jostled. "Nana likes you," he said, hands in his trouser pockets. "She doesn't like everyone I introduce her to." I wondered if that meant other gay men or people in general.

"Do you ever get to Memphis?" I asked him after a silence full of unspoken sentences.

He gulped like I'd caught him in a lie. "Sometimes."

"Well, next time I hope you'll be my guest for supper. I don't live too far from Bill's. We could meet there. The three of us could go," I added, amused at my reluctance to include Bill now.

"Oh, I don't stay with Billy," Jamie said, brushing ever-present flies out of his face and not elaborating.

We walked almost to Beaulieu's front porch before Jamie Battle spoke again. "I'd love to see you in Memphis, Henry," he said to the air around us.

"Let's plan on it then."

We looked at each other for a long equivocal moment, but time passed, and the moment did too.

We climbed the wide front staircase together. At the top Jamie Battle stopped me with the barest touch of his fingertips on my suit coat. "We're going to Cleveland for supper tonight. Would you sit by me? I mean, if you need to sit with Billy, I understand." His brow was wrinkling with seriousness.

"Bill is just my friend," I told him. I didn't say I'd hoped he might be more than that. "I'd be very pleased to sit by you, Jamie." He smiled his thank-you, squared his shoulders, and walked into his home like there was something there he had to face.

Cleveland was a town about twenty miles east of Rosedale. It was larger and much more attractive, and the restaurant Jamie had chosen served surprisingly good Italian food. Mrs. Watts did not join us. I rode with Bill Barnes in the convertible—Jamie Battle's SUV quickly filled without me—but at the restaurant I sat by Jamie Battle as promised.

"My mother was a quarter Italian," Jamie said after he and I had ordered, as if I'd asked a question. I could see the Italian in him. "My great-grandfather was in Italy during World War II and brought back a war bride," he explained. "Where are your people from?"

I'd heard this question often enough at school and in my professional life among the upper middle class. I knew he wasn't talking about the current generations. "Not too interesting, I'm afraid. Scotch-Irish, Welsh, and English. Maybe a little Chickasaw."

"That's interesting about the Chickasaw," Jamie Battle said, looking at my light-brown hair and dark-brown eyes. He let his knee accidentally hit mine before he apologized and moved it away.

"It was a long time ago. Too many greats to remember. And it's probably just a family story anyway." I forced a laugh which Jamie didn't join me in. After a moment, I asked why his grandmother wasn't at dinner with us.

"I was afraid she'd get too tuckered out," he answered. "Today was already mighty tiring for her, and I'm taking her to church tomorrow." He thought a moment. "Would you like to join us?"

I agreed to, wondering how Pentecostal the service would be. I was Methodist myself, at least when I went home to Nashville.

Bill had promised me a round trip in the Audi, but the aunt intervened, insisting on taking a ride "in that thing." Jamie Battle stepped in quickly to ask me to ride back with him and I accepted after Bill's younger sister volunteered to give up her seat up front with him. She and miscellaneous family members filled the back two rows, laughing and talking raucously with one another.

Jamie was intent on the road and drove fast through the dark over the narrow country byways, making me check my seatbelt. We arrived at Beaulieu well ahead of the convertible. His family trooped inside, calling to us to hurry now. When I made to follow them, Jamie held my arm. His eyes were shining in the porchlight some servant must have turned on.

"Would you like to take a walk?" he asked.

I replied a walk would be just the thing after a heavy dinner.

He led me across the road, through the cypress, back to the little beach, and onto the dock. For a little while, we just stared down at the dark water drifting by, but then Jamie gave me the same deciding look he'd had in my bedroom, took his shoes and socks off, and sat down on the edge of the dock. I sat next to him. We let our bare feet dangle in the slow flow of the Mississippi. Low waves rippled by in the light of a nearly full moon. Our toes accidentally touched. Then he was leaning, his head aiming for mine. The moonlight showed me his eyes were closed. Mine were wide open.

His lips were softer than I expected, and his hand was strong and gentle at the same time on my shoulder.

After the kiss, Jamie pulled away from me and exhaled. "I've wanted to do that ever since I first saw you," he said with a smile I was beginning to look forward to seeing.

I decided to return the compliment. My lips had just reached his when a flashlight shone in our faces and meandered down our bodies.

"Henry? Jamie Battle? That you?"

Jamie Battle shielded his eyes with one hand.

"Shut that damn thing off, Billy," he said, sounding irritated for the first time since I'd met him. The flashlight quickly went dark.

"Sorry, boys. Thought you mighta got lost. Coming in or y'all gonna stay out here all night?" he asked slyly.

It was a suggestion I realized in an instant I could happily take, but Jamie Battle muttered, "I suppose we better go in, Henry," so I dried my feet with my socks and put them and my shoes back on. Jamie Battle stuffed his socks in his shoes and carried them across the road to Beaulieu. Bill Barnes led the way with the flashlight.

At the porch Jamie Battle sat down to put his socks and shoes back on. "You go on in, Billy," he said.

"You comin, Henry?"

I sat down beside Jamie. "Not just yet." Jamie Battle smiled, and I was glad of my decision.

"I'm sorry we were interrupted," he said.

"Maybe later?"

He smiled again. "Maybe later."

Inside the house, music was playing in the family parlor—light jazz, a little bluesy. Bill Barnes poured three glasses. "Maker's for you, Jamie," he said, handing him one. "And Jack for the gentleman from Tennessee." I stopped short of saying I wasn't a gentleman. I knew some fictions had to be maintained.

"To you," Bill said, toasting us together with a leering grin. The three of us tipped our glasses back in unison, all seeming to need a drink. By the time parents, sisters, one sister's husband, an uncle and aunt, and several cousins had gone up to bed, Jamie Battle, Bill Barnes, and I had knocked back several more.

"Guess I'll go on up too," I said after the last cousin had left. I hoped Jamie Battle heard the regret in my voice.

"Nah. The night is young, boys," Bill said, slurring his words. We had one more with him before he fell asleep. Then, Jamie and I hauled him upstairs, his arms over our shoulders, and deposited him on his double bed with a *whomp.*

"Should we take his clothes off?" I whispered to Jamie Battle, thinking of all the times I'd wanted to.

"I reckon so," he answered. He worked on Bill's shirt while I removed his shoes and socks. I let Jamie unzip his pants, but I pulled them down Bill's thick legs, feeling the muscles as I went. He was a sight, sprawled on the bed in only his underwear. We left him snoring.

In the hall outside his cousin's room, Jamie and I hesitated. After several awkward moments, he gave me a quick kiss, a quicker squeeze, and said, "Good night." I watched him walk off in the opposite direction from mine. I guessed "maybe later" didn't mean tonight.

Alone in the Rose Bedroom, I undressed slowly in the dark and lay on top of the yielding mattress, considering the day and listening to frogs plead for rain. A low breeze swept over me through the open windows like Jamie Battle's fingers on the dock. I thought of him while I drifted off to sleep, but with a start, I woke back up. My door was opening. A dark figure stepped into the room, shutting the door quietly behind it. I watched it walk toward the bed.

"Jamie?" I asked expectantly.

"Nah, son. It's Bill Barnes." He settled onto the bed beside me. "Thought I'd try this gay thing out," he said, reaching for my body.

"Bill—" I started to say, before his mouth covered mine and reduced my words to a mumble.

"You surely do feel good, Henry," Bill Barnes said, shifting his body quickly to on top of mine. "Did you bring condoms?"

"Oh, get off me," I said and rolled him onto the floor.

Just then, my door opened a second time and another figure entered the room. "Henry, you awake?" It was Jamie Battle.

"Turn the light on, cousin," Bill said, which Jamie Battle did. Bill Barnes was on his ass, his back against the bed. "Let's have us a threesome. Never did that with two guys before."

Jamie rushed out of the door immediately. I vaulted over Bill and ran after him in my underwear. I caught him by the arm just as he was going into his room.

"Jamie!" I said too loudly.

He scowled and put a finger to his lips.

"That wasn't my idea," I told him, whispering emphatically. "Bill, I mean. He came in just before you did. Honest."

Jamie didn't answer, but he didn't pull away either. After a long look between us, he ushered me into his room with one hand behind my back and shut the door after us with the other one. The next moment his hands were all over me, grabbing my chest, gripping my back, sliding down to my ass, and holding on. They felt rough, calloused by work, but good like the boys of summer at my grandparents' house. He kissed down my neck and across my chest. His lips counted my abs.

When he took me whole into his mouth, I gasped. "Jamie…" I said, leaving a verbal ellipsis.

When he deemed me ready, he stood up, undid his robe, and let it drop onto the floor behind him.

We took the few steps to his bed hand in hand and lay down, side by side. Jamie's hands traced the contours of my body as if he were mapping them for future reference. I touched his cheek and felt down his body, taking him in hand. He made low sounds, which might have been words. Without words, he turned me onto my other side and scooted close behind me. I was ready.

The next morning, I woke to him smiling at me. His arms were still around me, but now we were face to face.

He looked over my shoulder at the time.

"We better get ready for church," he said. "Do you want to shower first?"

"Why don't we shower together?" I suggested. I borrowed a robe, and we managed to avoid any scandal to and from the bathroom.

Surprisingly, most of the other Barneses joined us for Sunday services except Bill, who as yet hadn't been seen. I rode with Jamie Battle and his grandmother to the simple, high-steepled building Bill Barnes and I had passed in Rosedale on our way to Beaulieu. Grace Episcopal, the sign read. There wouldn't be any hand-raising or speaking in tongues after all. I swore at myself for thinking in stereotypes again.

During the service, I could not stop appreciating how handsome Jamie Battle was in his light-blue linen suit, crisp white shirt, and multicolored tie. His black hair, so rumpled and astray last night, was sleekly combed and gleaming with gel. From time to time, Mrs. Watts peeked around her handsome grandson at me. Each time, she smiled and settled back out of view.

After services, we had breakfast in a café crowded with dressed-up men and women who knew Jamie Battle and had to greet him. He was open and backslapping with them, black or white. A few of them were well-built, apparently single men, which made me wonder. Jamie definitely was not inexperienced in bed but then neither was I.

At Beaulieu, we were greeted from the porch by barking dogs and Bill Barnes, sipping black coffee. "I was so drunk last night," he said to me. "I don't remember a thing."

Jamie and I grinned at each other, and Bill Barnes frowned.

Everyone changed into more comfortable clothes, and some of the younger of us walked back across the road for another swim. This time, I watched Jamie Battle's body openly, and the cousins noticed and whispered among themselves. While Jamie swam with them and I watched, Bill joined me on my towel, landing next to me with a *thud*.

"Had a good night then?" he asked, winking and leering at the same time. I pulled away. He gave me an innocent look. "What did I say?" he asked.

*

Back at the house, while the others rested or read or drank, Jamie Battle took me on a tour of some of his fields. It was his land, his house, and his life—although his father's family always seemed welcome to stay a while and reap some of the benefits.

"Do you see much of them?" I asked while he gazed happily at a healthy expanse of cotton.

"More than you probably think," he answered. He looked me in the face. "They are good people, Henry." Then, he changed the subject to cotton futures, and we went on to another field. I asked who did the work; he couldn't possibly manage by himself.

"Mainly my farmhands," he said. "But I know how to plow and till." I was glad he didn't grin at the word *plow*. Suddenly eager, he asked, "Would you like to take a ride on a tractor?"

I said I would. Jamie clapped his hands in delight and trotted to a shed nearby, asking me to wait. In seconds, an engine burst into life inside the dark, and in seconds more, Jamie was backing out on a small green John Deere.

"Watch yourself," he warned as the tractor huffed and puffed backward toward me. I stepped aside as Jamie turned it toward the field. "Hop on," he said and pointed to where I could stand behind him. "Hold onto my shoulders," was his next instruction. I gripped them as gladly as I had the night before. "Ready?" he asked.

I nodded. *Ready for anything*, I told only myself.

He positioned the tractor wheels precisely between the rows of soybeans, set the harrow down, and began to weed, gradually working his way across the field. I only know this because Jamie explained what he was doing as we trundled through the first rows.

The tractor jostled along, vibrating enough to make my brain rattle. The smell of gasoline and oil accompanied us. As the weeds fell under the machine, I could feel Jamie begin to sweat.

"Why don't you rest a while?" I suggested.

He shut the engine off and looked around at me.

"You ready for a Coke-cola?" he asked.

"I'm ready for anything," I replied, out loud this time.

Jamie Battle's eyes widened, and his mouth opened in a horse laugh I wouldn't have expected from him. But then, there was a lot I didn't know to expect from him.

"Well, come on then!" he said, restarted the tractor, and headed down one last row.

At the end of it, he cut the motor and jumped off. I took his hand and stepped down more cautiously. Then, we ran for the trees parallel to the field and settled on the ground under a particularly large oak. His kisses were the sweetest ones I'd ever had.

Back at the house, only one of the cousins greeted us. "Everyone's gone to Rosedale or swimming," she said. She was in a bikini herself. "Y'all want to walk down with me?"

"Thank you, Livy," Jamie Battle said. "But I think we're ready for a nap." He looked at me for acquiescence. I nodded. "Mind now," he told her. "It's getting hot out there."

"Oh, don't I know it! Well, y'all have fun!" She gave us a wink. The Barnes family was the winkingest bunch I ever saw.

Jamie and I went upstairs and actually did lie down to nap. I thought it was a euphemism. We agreed to make a declaration of some sort by sleeping together in his room. We were just drifting off when a knock came on the door.

"Jamie Battle?" Bill Barnes's voice asked.

"We're napping," he called.

"We?" Bill Barnes said, walking into the room. Jamie yanked the bedspread over us and yelled at Bill Barnes to leave.

"Well, that answers one question," he said, winking at me. "I was wondering where Henry Williams was." He shut the door behind him. "Look at the two of you. A mighty pretty combination, boys." He sat in the chair by the window like he was going to watch.

"What else did you need, Bill?" Jamie Battle asked. He sounded irritated. That made two out of the three of us.

Bill Barnes paid his irritation no mind. "Oh, yes. You got me so distracted I almost forgot. Martha needs to ask you some questions about supper." Martha was the Beaulieu cook.

"I better see to this. It's about the party, I suppose," he said to me. To Bill, he said, "Thank you." Bill stared at us a few moments and then lurched up out of the chair.

"I best be going then," he said, laughing as he swaggered out of the room.

Jamie Battle pulled the spread off us. "Well, that's the cat out of the bag."

"Do you care?"

"Not one bit," he answered solemnly.

I tried to kiss the seriousness off his face, but he pulled away after a series of three.

"You save that for later," he said, pretending to be stern, but he allowed me one more before getting up and getting dressed. I stayed in his bed, thinking. I had never been with a Black man before. I wondered what my family would think. Probably they would disapprove but not say a word about it. My friends in Memphis would say plenty—probably mostly jokes about dick size. I'd have to figure out how to handle that.

Dick size made me think of Bill Barnes who had, I now knew, quite a stupendous one. But how he dealt with his cousin and Mrs. Watts gave me pause. His racism was subtle but obvious when you thought to look. I wondered whether mine was just as obvious. Probably was. Then, why was Jamie putting up with me? Sex, I suppose. But he said he'd visit me in Memphis. Maybe that was just talk.

This is getting me nowhere, I told myself, so I got up, put my clothes back on, and went down to the rose garden. Mrs. Watts was there, big straw hat on, snipping away at the flowers.

"Well, good morning, Mister Williams!" she called to me.

"Good morning, Mrs. Watts. Can I help you any?"

She arched an eyebrow at me. "Have you ever deadheaded roses?"

"No," I admitted. "But I'd be glad to learn."

"Come on then. Here, take these clippers." She looked at my hands. "You need gloves." She looked distressed. "Mine won't fit you. These roses will get you."

"I'll be fine."

She shrugged. "Oh well. See this dead blossom?" I nodded yes. "Go down to the first five-leaf branch and clip it one-quarter inch above." She waited for questions. I had none as yet. "You try."

I clipped the spent rose according to her instructions and waited.

"Well, go on! Plenty left to do. You surely need a hat in this sun. Here. Try mine." It was covered with bright bows and manmade blossoms. I could tell it would be too small for me, but I put it on anyway.

"How do I look?"

"Mighty pretty," a male voice said behind us. Mrs. Watts and I turned to see her grandson with his hands on his hips and a big ol' grin across his face.

"You hush up, Jamie Battle!" his grandmother admonished. "Henry Williams is helping me. Go on now."

Jamie tried to stop laughing, to little avail. The chuckles kept coming sporadically. "I just came out to invite you to dinner, Nana."

"I wouldn't be fit to be seen but thank you just the same. Henry Williams and I will eat at my place." She turned to me. "Well, go on. You've a passel of work to do before you get any dinner from me."

"Yes ma'am. But take your hat back. It's too hot out here for you."

She bent her head for me, and I put the bonnet back on for her. I could see her daughter and grandson in her—and my granny. After she impatiently indicated the waiting roses with a fluttering of her hand, I returned to deadheading under her encouragement and direction.

*

Monday morning, the day of the garden party, I woke up beside Jamie Battle again. He was still sleeping, his chest rising and falling with his breath. His ribcage showed its edges, and his flaccid brown cock sprawled across his groin. I reached out for it, feeling it swell.

"And good morning to you too," he said, stretching and rubbing his eyes with his knuckles. He pulled me into a kiss and an embrace. "It's going to be a busy day," he said, rubbing down my back to my ass and squeezing it familiarly.

"We should get up then," I told him, as he turned me around to spoon with him.

"Yes, we should," he agreed. "Eventually," he added, before putting on another condom.

Afterward, as I walked down the hall to my room, various members of the Barnes family greeted me as if it were the most natural thing in the world to see me strolling from Jamie Battle's room to mine in one of his robes. My own family would have been scandalized for more than one reason.

Bill Barnes came into my room while I was buttoning my dress shirt. "You like him then?" he asked before I could remind him to knock.

"I do," I answered, knotting a rep tie in a full Windsor.

He sat on my unused bed and then leaned across it, one arm akimbo. "I knew you would," he said, not looking very pleased about it.

"Is that why you invited me down here?" I asked, stuffing my shirttails inside my slacks.

"Not really," he answered, leaving it at that. He looked around the room, trying not to say something, I could tell. Finally, he lay back on the bed, hands behind his head. "I wasn't that drunk, you know," he said in a neutral tone.

"I suspected not," I told him, sitting next to him to pull on my socks and tie my shoes.

"I guess I blew it," he said, looking up at the ceiling like God might tell him otherwise. "I should have made my move earlier, in Memphis," he concluded.

"You weren't gay in Memphis," I reminded him, standing up.

He shifted to a sitting position, shiny tan shoes hitting the Persian rug. "I never should have said that," he told me. "I'm sorry I did, truly sorry." He shook his head. "I should never have brought you to Beaulieu," he mumbled, sounding bitter for the first time since I'd known him. "I know the kind of man Jamie Battle likes. What was I thinking?"

"Well, I'm glad you did," I said, tousling and then recombing his hair with my fingers. "Come on," I told him and yanked his unwilling body to its feet. "Let's see about this here garden party." I gave him a quick kiss on the cheek. He smiled ruefully.

"I guess you'll be back at Beaulieu pretty soon," he estimated.

"I certainly hope so," I said and pushed him toward the door. He laughed and opened it, letting me continue pushing him down the hall. By the time we reached the stairs, we were friends again and descended chatting as if nothing had changed between us in the last few days.

The French doors and their screens from the family parlor to the backyard were open wide, bugs be damned. People I didn't know greeted Bill Barnes and stared at me, smiling and curious, as we made our way through the house. Bill introduced me repeatedly as his *friend*, underlining, in my mind at least, what we might have been had we stayed in Memphis. But then we were through the gauntlet and finally outside. Jamie Battle came to join us. He looked so handsome in his tan suit, pale-blue shirt, and green-patterned tie full of tiny pink roses. I dropped my hand from Bill's shoulder.

"Congratulations, cousin," Bill Barnes said sardonically.

Jamie smiled knowingly at him and took my hand.

"Let me introduce some folks to you, Henry," he said, his face sunny. I felt happy, too, mighty happy indeed. It was Labor Day at a sumptuous garden party outside a stately southern mansion, tables piled high with food and drink, people chattering excitedly in a drawling southern way, laughter rising and falling in waves across the lawn. Ladies and gentlemen in every shade of black, brown, and white wore gigantic hats, frilly dresses, and crisp summer suits. I waved at Mrs. Watts, seated with a coterie of other older women, mainly Black. The South had risen again at Beaulieu but probably not quite as some folks had predicted.

Jamie Battle looked about to burst with joy. I accepted a drink of something or other from a servant dressed in white, and we walked hand in hand to meet his friends and neighbors.

They were certainly observing us. What did they see? Two men holding hands? Someone white with someone Black? It didn't matter. I was ready. The party was on.

October

Disaster Day

You don't see many guys like him in a Native American bar unless they're looking for red meat. Too big, too blond, and too white.

"Can I buy you a drink?" I asked, coming up alongside him. He looked startled like a deer in deep brush when he notices your gun.

"Uh, I guess so," he said, ducking his head. His hair was short but curly, the kind you like to catch your fingers in.

"Okaaay, what'll it be then?" I asked, after a few seconds had ticked by. Even in the dim light of the bar, I could tell he was blushing. Good. I like embarrassing white guys. Still, it was kind of funny, him being so big and all.

"A beer is fine." He gulped like he was already drinking one. I waited some more, tapping my fingers on the bar. "Anything," he said, stuttering a little.

I looked down at his tight shirt, tight body, and tight pants. "Anything?" I asked, wondering if he understood me.

He straightened up and looked me square in the eye, so I guess he did.

"Frank," I said, not putting my hand out to shake.

"Randy," he answered.

"Sure hope you are," I said into his ear, giving it a lick.

He jumped away and looked around the bar. I didn't. Everybody in the place knew I was queer, and nobody cared.

"Still want that beer?" I asked, keeping my face close to his.

"Sure," he muttered, his mouth grim like I was bad medicine he had to take.

"A pale ale and an Eight Ball," I told the bartender. Sarge didn't ask which brand or ask for money. He probably figured the white guy would pay.

"Here you go," Sarge said when he sat our beers down in front of us.

"Which one is mine?" the white guy asked, looking nervous. Hell, this guy wanted sex so badly I could smell it. One beer and we're out of here was my bet.

I held the stout up for him to taste. He made a face. I handed him the pale ale.

"That's good," he said, after he swallowed some. "Thank you."

Figures, I thought. *Paleface, pale ale.* I laughed.

"What's so funny?" he asked.

"Bottoms up!" I said, winking at him and clinking his glass with mine. He smiled uncertainly and took a big gulp. No, sir, it wouldn't take long.

"Haven't seen you around. Are you just passing through?" I asked. Passing through would be good. No complications.

"No," he said, looking eager. "I live here now." He didn't say what part of town or where he was from originally, but it didn't matter. I didn't expect us to become Facebook friends.

"How do you like Eureka so far?" I asked him, making conversation while we finished our beer.

"It's okay," he answered. Not exactly a smooth talker. Still, his body looked like it could talk just fine. Time to find out. I chugged the rest of my Eight Ball.

"Why don't you drink the rest of that beer," I suggested, sliding my thigh in between his. He chugged it so fast he nearly choked. I patted his broad back, feeling muscles on top of muscles. "Let's go," I said when he stopped coughing.

On the way out, I slapped his ass, just to let the boys know I'd landed him. There were hoots and laughter behind us.

"Don't do that," he said, frowning enough to make his face not look so pretty. I put my hands up in surrender mode.

"Okay. Sorry," I said, trying not to smirk.

He looked me over like he was deciding something. "It's not far," he said eventually. "We can walk." He started loping off. We both had long legs. Our strides matched.

We left downtown and headed into the residential streets. Except for the occasional dog bark, it was quiet like only a small town in the middle of nowhere can be. The sky above us was full of stars. I loved nights like this on the rez, sleeping outside during the summer, looking up at all the constellations they told us about in school, thinking of the elders' stories. Different names, different explanations.

"This is it," he said outside a three-story Victorian.

"Do you own this?" I asked, prepared to be impressed.

He chuckled, which I liked much better than his nervous laughter. "No," he said. "I rent an apartment." He opened the door. "That's my landlady's apartment." He nodded toward a door to our right. I tiptoed up the stairs after him.

His place turned out to be the whole second floor, so whatever he did, he was making plenty of money. If it was meth, I didn't want to know. He didn't do his cooking in the flat, at least. Unfortunately, I know the signs. The place was nice, decorated in earth colors, with paintings on the wall, a comfortable sofa and chairs, and an expensive-looking electronics system, including an enormous flat screen. He sure must like TV.

"You want another beer?" he asked. I decided I could wait if he could.

"Sure," I said. "Got any Lost Coast?" That was the local brew.

"No," he answered. "Next time."

Whoa, I thought. We hadn't even made it to bed yet, and this guy was planning our wedding.

"Make yourself comfortable," he said, leaving me on my own in his living room.

I looked at the paintings on the wall while I waited.

"You like art?" he asked behind me.

"Some," I said, taking a can of Coors. Coors tastes like piss, but I said thanks anyway. "Have you been to Morris Graves yet?"

"Who's that?" he asked.

"The art museum," I said. I almost added whom the museum was named for but held my tongue. One more beer, one fuck, and I was gone.

"Maybe you'll show me some time," he said. There he went again, planning ahead. Now, *I* was getting nervous.

"Maybe." I wanted badly to change the subject. "Hey, what do you do for a living?"

He squirmed and looked away.

"It's okay. None of my business. Well, do you want to do this thing?" I asked, putting my beer down. He didn't answer so I stood up and pulled my shirt off. That would give him something to mull over.

"I'm a highway patrolman," he said quietly. I sat my Native American ass back down on the sofa really fast.

"You're a cop?" I asked, my mouth hanging open. He gave me a hard stare, looking suspicious. I put my hands up. "Doesn't matter. I just didn't picture you as an officer of the law."

"How did you picture me?" he asked all flirty and looking mighty cute again.

"Naked," I told him.

He laughed, so I moved closer, held his head with one hand behind it, and pulled his face toward mine. His short hair was thick and soft. So were his lips. My other hand went inside his shirt, and the first moved to his crotch.

"Where's the bedroom?" I asked, slapping his ass when he got up.

He didn't protest that time.

I liked watching him get out of his clothes, his big white body appearing slowly like he still wasn't sure about what we were going to do. That might have made me reconsider, but I was already naked and lying on his bed.

The mattress was nice and firm, and I was starting to get tired. The ride back to the rez would be full of drunks. Probably run me and my bike off the road. Maybe I ought to stay over after all. *I bet I can convince him,* I told myself.

He was finally naked. He had a little paunch but not bad.

"I signed up for a gym," he said, sounding defensive. I hadn't said a word.

"Don't worry about it, baby," I whispered. "Come here." He walked to the bed. I sat up, ran my hands up his legs. "You feel fine." I tumbled us onto the bed.

I hadn't really done much to him before he was twisting and groaning. I reached for where I'd strategically placed a condom on the little table next to the bed. He looked nervous again.

"You ever do this before, buddy?" He was definitely acting like a virgin.

"Sure. Plenty of times," he said, sounding tough.

I didn't believe him of course, but there was no way I was leaving at that point in the night. "Hold on and relax. I'll be gentle," I told him. He started to object, but I just started with the basics, and he shut up fast.

I moved from *A* to *B* to *C* pretty slowly, but he began moaning and bucking right away. "Easy, baby," I cooed. "We have the rest of the night." Better let him know I was planning on staying, one way or the other.

"I can't help it, Frank," he said. It sounded weird, hearing my name come out of this white guy's mouth. I decided not to stay after all. I leaned into him, speeding up, telling him what I thought of him.

"Motherfucker. Asshole. White shit."

He frowned up at me.

"What?" I asked, putting the fuck on pause.

"Why did you say that?"

"Say what?" I asked like I didn't know. He repeated my monologue for me. I rolled over on my back and looked up at the ceiling. I was so tired. I turned onto my side and faced him. "Okay, I'm sorry. You want to try again?"

He said no.

"You want me to leave?" I asked, praying to the Great Spirit.

He said no again.

"What *do* you want then?" I asked him, trying not to sound sarcastic.

He took me in his arms and slid close. He felt good; I didn't pull away. He massaged my back. That felt even better. Then, all of a sudden, somebody's snoring woke me up. It was mine.

"Sorry," I said. He was on his side, head propped up with one bent arm. He must have been staring at me while I was sleeping. That was freaky.

"Don't worry about it," he said, smiling, like listening to me snore was the perfect ending to a lovely evening. "Go back to sleep, Frank." He turned away from me and let me hold him in spooning position.

"You sure you don't want to try again?" I asked him.

"Go to sleep," he repeated, and pretty soon it was him snoring.

*

The next morning, as soon as it was light, I meant to get up, get dressed, and leave as quickly and quietly as I could, but instead, I spent several minutes watching him sleep. He looked like an angel—well, okay, like the white version of one, at least. Before I could stop myself, I was running my hand across his wide shoulders and down his thick arms, feeling blond fuzz along the way. It woke him up. He looked at me, all tousled and groggy and sexy.

"I have to go," I said, trying to make it sound like have a nice life.

"No," he mumbled, holding onto my shoulders with those thick arms.

"I have to go," I said more insistently, wrenching away and getting pissed. He sat up and watched me get dressed.

"Do you want a shower?" he asked. I shook my head no. "How about my number?"

I arched an eyebrow. "Sure," I said, zipping my jeans, although I had no intention of calling him. I tried not to look when he got up and bent over, stepping back into his underwear, or when he turned around. Either view might have shaken my resolve somewhat.

"Do you want some breakfast?" he asked. He handed me the scrap of paper like it was the menu.

I shook my head. If I opened my mouth, I knew a yes would fall out.

"Not even coffee?" he said, sort of whining. The whine made it easier to say no.

"We're having a powwow Monday," I told him. "I have a lot to do back on the reservation." Both facts were true.

"You live on a reservation?" he asked like it was something terrible.

"Yep, born there, grew up there," I said, putting my socks and shoes on. "Thanks." I stuck my hand out. Might as well be polite about it. He grabbed me in a huge bear hug which nearly broke me in half.

"Wish I could come," he said like I'd invited him. "But I gotta work. It's Columbus Day, and I'm the new guy."

I pulled away from him. "More like Disaster Day," I muttered.

He didn't get it.

"That's what Columbus was for us Native Americans." I frowned the message home. "A disaster. Well, see ya." I walked out of the bedroom.

He followed me like a tall puppy. "Call me, okay?" he said, looking very young and very cute. I wanted so much to kiss him, but then I'd probably stay for coffee, and then we'd have breakfast, and then I'd want to take him back to bed, which would be short run good and long run very bad.

"Sure," I answered, closing the door after me.

On the street outside his building, I took the scrap of paper with his number out of my back pocket and looked up at his windows. Randy was watching, still just in his underwear. He waved. I waved back and then ripped his number into four pieces and dropped them on the sidewalk before I walked away.

I rode the bike hard back to Hoopa, thinking about the look on Randy's face, but once I got back to the rez, I forgot about him pretty quickly. I was new on the tribal council, and Disaster Day was the first thing the old guys had put me in charge of. I'm sure they were hoping I'd screw up. See, they'd say, a college education don't mean shit. Plus, I worked in the white man's world as a ranger at Redwood National Park. Some people thought we should keep ourselves separate. Great idea. Too bad there aren't more jobs on the reservation, bro.

The elders told me not to make Disaster Day too political. That was impossible, I said. Commemorating the white invasion of Native country had to be political. What did they want, a party? They nodded their heads yes, collectively smirking at me.

It was too late to back out, so I decided I'd give them a party all right.

Monday morning, things were going pretty well. The women were cooking up a storm, and the AmeriCorps kids were busy putting up banners and picnic tables in the lot between the casino and the Humboldt County Deputy Sheriff's office, which was closed. BJ, the Hoopa guy who ran it, was one of the Jump Dancers. He said if we needed anybody, he could call for reinforcements. That made me laugh. If we Native Americans had had reinforcements, maybe there would never have been a Columbus Day.

At 10:00 a.m. on the dot, I started off the festivities with a speech. I gave a little history of Columbus, Cortez, Pizarro, the Pilgrims, wagon trains, gold strikes, and European diseases. I could see people nodding off, so I cut it short and introduced the dancers.

I was taking my turn with the drums when I noticed the other drummers were looking at something behind me. It was something all right—Randy, in his highway patrol uniform, which he filled out really well.

"Joe," I said to one of the guys waiting for his turn on the drum. "Will you take over for me?" He sat down as fast as I stood up and started pounding and singing off-key as loudly as he could.

Randy looked at my bare chest and deerskin skirt. He stared so long it was like he was counting the shells in my necklaces. I led him away from the noise.

"Can I help you, Officer Hammond?" I asked him, having noticed his name badge.

"Some speech," was all he said, folding his arms across his deep chest and spreading his khaki legs apart a little. His tall boots looked mighty hot. Oh, man. I was about to have a very embarrassing moment.

"What are you doing here?" I asked, trying to sound gruffer than I felt.

"Officer Carpenter asked me to be his backup today. Just checking in," he answered, looking like he hated me. Damn, why didn't BJ warn me? "Look." He lowered his voice. "I thought we had a good time." I kept my mouth shut. "I saw you tear up my number. Why'd you do that?"

"Did you listen to my speech?" I asked him, squirming a little.

Randy didn't seem to notice; he was that mad at me. "Sure, you hate white people. Then, why the hell did you pick me up in the bar?" I could feel his hot breath on my face. "Why'd you come home with me?"

I was almost as angry as he was. "Payback," I said. "Native Americans have been fucked over by white men for centuries. Now, it's my turn."

"Fine," Randy said, standing up straight and looking at me like I was a tick. "I've done what Office Carpenter wanted. Call me if there's any trouble."

He trotted away. Everything about me, even my brain, wanted to yell "wait," but Evelyn Redwood came up to me just then.

"It's time for the Jump Dance," she said.

I had to make the introductions, including Officer BJ Carpenter.

*

Tuesday at work, I had just finished a talk to twenty tourists about North Coast flora and fauna when the same Officer Hammond entered the meeting room, wearing his fitted uniform and a noncommittal expression. I ushered the tourists out of the room toward the souvenir sales area and confronted him.

"What are you doing here?" I asked, trying to ignore the cleft in his chin.

"Somebody called about a bear in the parking lot," he said.

"Bear in the parking lot? Nobody…" I realized he was kidding.

He smiled. "I was just passing by and thought I'd drop in." He didn't seem mad at me anymore, and truthfully, I was glad to see him—or at least part of me was.

"And how did you know I work here?" I asked.

"Well, BJ told me," he said. Hmm. Maybe, if he had a thing for Native Americans, Randy had found out those initials didn't just mean Bryan James.

"What do you want?" I asked, trying not to remember Randy naked or picture BJ kneeling in front of him.

"What do you think?" he said, loud enough for the tourists to hear.

I pushed him inside my office and shut the door behind us. "Can't you get the message?" I asked, trying to be stern.

"Can't you?" he answered, grabbing my arm. My mouth fell open, ready to tell him to get his hands off me, but he said in a soft voice, "Come on. Let's go out again. You can curse at me if you want, tie me up…"

"Spank you, use whips and chains on you?" I asked. *The tourists better not be able to read lips,* I thought. They were all staring through the glass wall of my "private" space.

"Whatever you want," he said, giving me stare for glare. I blinked first.

"Sit down," I told him, settling heavily into my own chair. "I'm not a sadist." I put my entwined fingers under my chin, watching him while I thought. He did look awfully sexy in his uniform, and then there was that image of him naked. It just would not go away. I sighed and took a deep breath. "I don't date white guys."

"You just fuck them," Randy said bitterly. I could understand that. I was bitter, too—for different reasons.

"Something like that," I said, through my teeth. This time I didn't blink. Who cared what this guy thought?

Randy shook his head, looked away, looked back. "Okay, no date. You want to meet at that bar again?" He spread his legs, sending the invitation visually as well as verbally.

"Why me?" I asked, resisting the urge to pull down my pants and his, tourists be damned. "You have a fetish or something?"

"No," he said, sounding offended. "I just thought you were nice. And handsome."

"Nice?" I said in surprise. I could handle handsome, but nice wasn't a virtue I cultivated.

"Yeah, nice," he repeated, standing. He placed his hands on my desk, displaying the heavy musculature of his arms, and leaned toward me. "Come on," he wheedled like a kid asking for ice cream.

"Okay. Teepee Room, this Saturday, 10:00 p.m." I said in a rush, knowing I was making a mistake. "One beer; then we fuck at your place. I won't stay over."

"Okay. Deal," he said.

"Deal," I said, shaking his hand, remembering how good it felt, all rough and calloused. He pulled out of my grip and started to leave. I began shuffling papers on my desk, pondering whether I should cancel our nondate before he walked out of my office.

"Hey, how did Disaster Day go?" he asked, holding the door open.

"Fine. No disasters." He waited until I chuckled before he laughed at my little joke. "We paid the bills and made a little money for the history museum," I said grudgingly, looking up. He was at the door, his ass telling me not to change my mind.

"You guys have a history museum?"

"Yeah, us guys have a history museum."

"I'd like to see it," he said, looking so young and hopeful.

"You should, next time you're passing through the rez," I told him. "It's open Monday through Friday ten to two, Saturdays ten to five." I felt bad but didn't look up again until I heard the door shut.

Saturday, I spent way too much time getting ready. *It's not a date,* I kept telling myself. I could show up in dirty clothes, hair not combed, stinking like shit, and it wouldn't matter. *Sure, it wouldn't,* a little voice said sarcastically. My spirit animal. I called him Fred.

I thought about Randy's big, white, solid body while I shaved and showered for the second time that day, ironed a nice checkered shirt, and selected my best leather jacket and tightest jeans. I looked at myself in the mirror. I was six feet tall, black-haired, brown-eyed, with a mustache and soul patch, a natural tan and a warrior's body—courtesy of the twenty-four-hour gym in Eureka. I was Native American, 100 percent, a registered member of the Hoopa Valley Tribe. Natinook-wa. That was our real name. *Hoopa* was a Yurok word. The Federal government didn't care. I didn't either. This was going to be just sex. I squared my shoulders, held my chin high, and slammed the door of my double-wide on the way out. I was in no mood to be messed with.

When I walked into the Teepee, heads turned but then they always did when someone came in the door. The place was dark, which I figured was to hide how dirty it always was, but the light at the entrance was like a spotlight. One of the other Native Americans whistled. I waved at him and scanned the bar for Randy. He was in a corner, looking like he'd been sitting there for an hour. Four brown bottles were lined up in front of him. Dead Indians, some people called them. Those people are assholes. "Am I late?" I asked, looking at my phone. It said five minutes till ten.

"Nah," he answered. "I was early. Got nervous, sitting at home. Thought I might as well have a beer while I waited."

"Looks like you've had several," I said. I didn't need another drunk. Had plenty of those on the rez and in college. Maybe I should head back to Hoopa. *To what,* Fred asked.

"Let me buy you one," Randy said, trying to stand up. I caught him before he fell and started us walking toward the door. "What are you doing? Come on. Let's have a drink," he said, slurring every other word. I ignored him.

"Get on," I told him after I'd started the bike. He hopped right on, giggling. "Just hang on. I won't go fast." I felt like revving the motor and doing a wheelie.

He held on all right—with one hand. The other tried to undo my belt and unbutton my pants. "Stop that," I yelled over my shoulder. I increased our speed and went through a couple of red lights. At his place, I helped him off the bike and then redid my jeans and belt.

My urge was to dump him on the lawn, but I decided to do the honorable thing: get him into bed and then leave. "Give me your key," I told him. He began to fumble around in his jeans, without success. I put my hand in his pocket, and his eyes lit up. I found his keys all right.

"Whoo-hoo!" he yelled and leaned in for a kiss. I dodged, opened the door, and pulled him inside. I put a finger to my lips and pointed at his landlady's door. He winced and whispered, "Okay, okay."

As we climbed up to his place, Randy leaned heavily against me, crushing me into the railing. Once we were inside his flat, he started taking the rest of his clothes off right away. He didn't notice I wasn't until he was down to his underwear.

"What's the matter?" he asked, leaving the white briefs halfway down his creamy thighs.

"Let's get you into bed," I answered, pulling the Hanes back up for him.

"I like that idea," he said, giggling again.

In the bedroom, I settled him into a chair while I pulled the bedcovers back. Behind me, I could hear him rustling around, and then his arms were around me, clamping me tight. He was now definitely naked.

"Did you ever think of growing your hair longer?" he asked, hiccupping once or twice in my right ear.

I broke his hold and moved behind him to ease him into bed, ignoring his question. He was definitely a red queen. I pushed him, and he landed with a plop, spread his legs wide, and held up his arms. "Ready!" he sang cheerfully. It was hard to not to accept the invitation. I took a condom out of my jeans.

"Move over," I told him.

He started yelling after just a few minutes. "Please, Frank! Oh, God! Oh, God!" If the landlady hadn't heard him before, she must have heard him then.

After I finished, he kept his arms and legs tightly wrapped around me, like C-clamps. I could feel his heart beating against mine. My breathing slowed and merged into his. The next thing I remember the room was dark and we were lying side by side under his blankets. I could have left, but Randy was holding my hand. I could have broken his grip, I think, but I didn't want to.

"You have to go. I know," his voice said in the dark. He released my hand.

"Not really," I answered, taking his hand back.

The next morning, over caffeine and kisses, Randy gave me believable assurances he wasn't an alcoholic. "I was nervous," he said. "I really like you."

That makes me *nervous,* I said to myself. But after too many additional words—and kisses—I took Randy's info again and headed back to Hoopa on the Harley. A couple of my friends were having coffee outside the Cup of Joe, staring at one of the creeks that ran through town on its way to the Trinity River. I decided to have a third cup with them.

"Hey, brother!" Wayne said. I've known him since we were babies, had sex with him first when we were twelve. At seventeen, I was his best man.

Wayne and I shook hands and bumped chests.

"Hey, dude," the other guy said. "You still fucking that white guy?" News travels fast on the rez.

"Come on, Dan," Wayne said. Danny was more his friend than mine. He had come back to the rez just the year before.

"Just asking. They sure fucked us over. Might as well fuck 'em back when we got the chance, right, Frankie?" I ignored the question and went inside to buy my coffee. When I got back, Danny had left.

"Where'd he go?" I asked.

"I told him to leave," Wayne said. "Don't let him get to you. He's still screwed up."

"I know," I agreed. Being half Native American and half Black might do that to you: two reasons to hate white people, instead of one.

Wayne and I sat a while, watching the creek run, drinking coffee, saying nothing. Wayne was usually comfortable with silences, but I could tell something was on his mind.

"What is it?" I asked.

"Maybe it's none of my business," he started with, "but we been friends a long time, Frank. This white guy. You seen him twice now, right?"

I nodded my head yes.

"This the first time you stayed over?"

I shook my head no.

Wayne mouthed the word "oh" and settled back in his fold-up lawn chair. I leaned across mine to reconnect our eyes.

"What?" I asked.

"He's white," was all Wayne said, returning my stare. I collapsed into my lawn chair.

"I know," I said forlornly.

"You like him though?"

"I think so. I don't know. Yeah. I like him," I said, feeling as confused as I sounded.

"Good," Wayne said.

I looked up, startled by his approval.

He took another sip of coffee and looked blissfully off into the morning air.

"Good?" I asked.

"Yeah. You been alone too long. It's good to be with someone." He smiled into the distance again. It had been nearly ten years for him and Shauna.

"Even if the someone is white?" I asked.

He looked at me earnestly. "Hate eats you up, Frank," he said. I figured we were both thinking of Danny at that point. He smiled again and tapped his paper cup against mine. "Here's to love, brother!"

"It's not love, Wayne," I said.

He shrugged and tapped my cup again.

I took a drink even though it wasn't love.

We listened to the creek again and to our thoughts. Mine were about Randy, about all the white guys I'd fucked and hated, how it wasn't like that this time. Wayne interrupted our silence.

"When you gonna bring him by?" he asked.

"You already saw him. At Disaster Day."

He blinked. "Oh, you mean the Columbus Day powwow," he said, making me wince. "That doesn't count, does it? I mean, it wasn't official."

"Nothing is official now," I said, deciding it was time to go. Wayne grabbed my arm to keep me from leaving.

"All I mean, Frank, is I'd like to meet the guy. You could call it education, show him what life is like on the rez. You always say white people need to get educated about us, right?"

He had me there. "Okay," I said. "I'll invite him."

Wayne smiled like he knew a secret.

I went back to my double-wide and made a date with Randy for the next Saturday. I promised to cook dinner.

It wasn't an easy six days. One minute I'd be looking forward to showing Randy around my home, the next one I'd be pissed. "It would be so much easier if he were

Native," I said out loud on Wednesday in the public restroom at the visitors' center.

A throat in the stalls cleared itself, a toilet flushed, and a stall door opened. It was Gary, one of the mechanics for the park's vehicles. He lived in Orick, just outside the northern end of the park. We had tried to date, but nothing clicked. Too bad. He was cute—and Native American.

"Hey, Gary," I said like I hadn't been talking to myself.

"Hey, Frank," he said like he hadn't heard. "It's been a while. What's up?" He looked pointedly at my crotch.

"Not much," I said, looking back at his.

"You want to get together again sometime?"

"Sure."

"Great," Gary said, licking his lips. "How about Saturday?"

I turned away from him and washed my hands again. "Uh, afraid I can't Saturday. How about tomorrow?"

He came up behind me and reached around. "I can't wait that long either, man. How about tonight after work?"

I agreed and started breathing again.

We left at four, right after the visitors' center closed, and went to his place, a little house he rented on a side street off Highway 101, Orick's main road. He didn't ask me to sit down or offer me a drink. We went right to his disheveled bedroom and took off our clothes.

Gary wore his black, straight hair long. It spread all over the pillow, framing his face. *Like a Native American angel,* I thought. Not like Randy's blond curls. I tried to focus on the slender brown body beneath me but couldn't get Randy's pale muscles out of my head. I couldn't even look Gary in the eye. In my head, I kept seeing Randy's pale-blue ones.

After we finished, I thanked Gary, put my clothes back on, and left for Hoopa. When we saw each other at work the next day, it was as if nothing had happened. I guess nothing much had.

At home, my fingers itched to call Randy but images of Gary and me made me use the remote instead. I couldn't tell you what I watched.

The next day at work I called his mobile.

"Hello?" he answered. I could hear road noises.

"Are you in your car?"

"Yep," he answered. "I'm on duty."

"Should I let you go?"

"Nope. What's up?"

I took a breath. "I'd like to see you before Saturday."

"Wow!" Randy exclaimed like I'd made his day. "I'd like to see you, too, man!" he said enthusiastically. "When?"

"Tonight?" I wished I hadn't made it a question.

"Wow!" he said again. "Great! Want to come by the house?"

"I will, but let's have dinner first," I answered. "I'll pick you up."

"That's okay," he said. "I'll drive. You navigate." His laugh was like flutes accompanying the drumbeats in my chest.

I disconnected, amazed at how happy I felt. *No regrets?* Fred asked. *None*, I assured him, but I could tell he wasn't convinced.

*

Outside Randy's place, I hid the flowers behind my back. When he answered the door, I thrust the bouquet at him, and he smiled like sunshine.

"Come on up," he said. "I'll put these in water. They're beautiful. Thank you." I leaned over to kiss him, landlady be damned. He jerked away but moved quickly back into position. "Thank you," he repeated.

I watched his ass rotate up the stairs. Our reservation was for seven thirty. Maybe we should have sex first. *No, I told myself. Keep it in your pants, dude.* I ignored admitting what waiting meant.

"What's in the bag?" Randy asked, once we were behind his door.

"Change of clothes," I told him, winking. "Where's the vase?" I took the flowers away from him and walked toward the kitchen.

"I don't really have one," he said. "Nobody ever gave me flowers before."

I stopped in my tracks and met him with another kiss as he bumped into me. "They should of," I said, letting my lips linger on his. I opened my eyes and pulled away. Sometimes, it was still a surprise he was white. "Anything will do. Next time, I'll buy a vase too." I heard the *next time*. Oh, well.

While he was driving us to the restaurant, I wondered whether I should have booked a table at some nicer place, like the Brick & Fire or the one in the Hotel Carter, but we were headed for the Lost Coast Brewery now. It would have to do.

"What looks good?" I asked after we were seated and had our menus.

"Well, I'm not really big on fish," Randy answered, scanning the list. I made a mental note to buy steaks for Saturday.

His eyes finally found something on the menu his stomach liked. When the server came back, he announced he'd like a "Hot Brown" and winked at me. That was pretty brave of him—the wink, not the entrée choice. Hot Brown was basically chunks of beef on a sourdough roll.

The waitress turned to me with the expression most whites use on Native Americans like "you're not supposed to be here but since you are." *Oh, well*, I thought, *there goes your tip, honey.*

"I'll have the Eight Ball Stew and a small green salad. Ranch dressing," I told her before she went through the list. "Do you want anything to start, Randy?" I asked.

When Andrea heard that, something clicked in her eyes. *Oh, the brown guy's paying the bill.* From then on, her service was excellent.

"I'll have a salad too," he said. "Same dressing."

After we'd shared a big slice of chocolate cake, I paid with my American Express. Andi, as she told us to call her, had worked her way back up to 15 percent. I'd had two beers and Randy none. "Driving," was his one-word explanation of a Coke to Andi. I felt better about his claim not to be a drunk.

Back at his flat, Randy turned on some elevator music and left the lights low. We kissed and fondled each other halfway out of our clothes until he asked, "Want to go to bed now?"

"Sure," I said, jumping up so fast I made him laugh. He laughed even harder when I pulled him to his feet, all two hundred and twenty pounds, and pushed him toward the bedroom. He started trotting, his big feet thundering across the low-weave carpet. I wondered out loud what the landlady would think about that.

"She's not home," he told me. "Neither are Diane and Jimmy. We're all alone," he said, stripping quickly. "We can make as much noise as we want!"

I made sure he did.

The next morning, he made coffee and breakfast. We jostled for the bathroom sink and showered. I got into my uniform, and he got into his. *It could be like this every morning*, Fred said.

"Anything wrong?" Randy asked. I shook my head. He persisted. "You're frowning."

I gave him a kiss to shut him up and then my mobile, email address, and every social I had. It was official now: the white guy and I were dating.

*

At work, I was adjusting my uniform in the men's room when Gary came in.

"Late night or early morning?" he asked.

"Both," I said.

"Hoopa or Yurok?" he asked, still grinning.

"Neither," I answered.

His grin decreased. "Karok?" he asked.

"White," I told him to forestall any more guesses. We were running out of tribes anyway. The remainder of his grin faded immediately, and he stepped to one of the urinals, unzipped, and started pissing. I left for my office. Neither of us said to have a nice day. But Randy made up for that. He sent several texts and messages during the day; not enough to drive me crazy but plenty. When he called me that night at home, I enjoyed the ninety-minute conversation although to tell the truth, I don't remember what we talked about. Randy says I gave him a complete history of the Hoopa people and the white man's transgressions against us. That sounds like something I would do.

Saturday, he arrived at the door of my trailer fifteen minutes early with twelve red roses and a vase. "Good thinking," I told him. No one had ever given me flowers before—or a vase.

We barbecued outside, creating smoke and attracting attention. I introduced Randy to about half the tribe before the corn and baked potatoes were done and I could singe the steaks. Nobody was surprised my dinner guest was a man, but they did react to him being white. Some were amused, some angry. Maybe it wasn't such a good idea to invite him to Hoopa. On the other hand, it had to happen sometime.

After steaks, a bottle of wine, two condoms, and a great night's sleep, I took Randy to Cup of Joe Sunday morning, trying like hell not to take his hand during the ten-minute walk. Wayne and Danny were back in two of the lawn chairs. I waved, Randy waved, and Wayne waved back. Danny looked away, frowning. Randy and I could have walked back to my place, but after we bought our lattes, I grabbed a chair, and Randy took another beside my friends.

"This is Randy," I told them. "Wayne," I said, pointing at my adolescent fuck buddy, "and Danny."

Wayne said hi and smiled.

Danny said, "Saw you at the Columbus Day powwow." He wasn't smiling.

"Disaster Day," I corrected, daring Danny to say anything else. He didn't but Wayne, Randy, and I talked plenty.

By the time we left, I could tell Wayne approved. That meant something to me. Danny's sour looks and disapproving silence did not.

"Where's the museum?" Randy asked on our way back to my trailer. I steered us in the right direction. It was even open. Mary Jenkins was on duty that day.

"Oh, good!" she said to me. "Frankie, I got to run home a minute. Will you watch the museum for me?"

I agreed I would, happy to help Mary out.

"Hello," she said to Randy on her way out with a smile on her lips and questions in her eyes. When we were alone again, I took the opportunity to give Randy a long hug and longer kiss. I missed his body already.

After I let him go, he began looking at the exhibits. I thought he would spend his time with the half-naked male mannequins in traditional clothing, but he passed them by in favor of the Hoopa basket collection. I explained our basket-weaving to him, what an art it was—practical but still an art. "If you're going to make something, why not make it beautiful?"

"You're beautiful," he said, leaning in to kiss me and hold my shoulder. Mary cleared her throat behind us.

"I'm sorry," she said, ducking her head and scooting back behind the counter.

Randy asked her a question about the baby basket.

"Oh, it had a leather strap," she said, drawing a line with her finger across her forehead where the strap would have rested. "I can't take it out since it's, like, really really old but you..." She proceeded to explain for fifteen minutes how it worked, how it was made, who made it, everyone who had used it and how old the last kid carried in it was now. I was proud of Randy; he didn't fall asleep once.

Back at the double-wide, we sat across the kitchen table from each other and discussed what to do with the rest of Sunday. There wasn't much except the casino and church. Randy said he'd rather take a walk, so I showed him where I grew up—the school, the new hospital, all the dusty roads I had walked and run, the creek Wayne and I swam in, the riverbank where we had various forms of sex. I didn't tell him the last part.

"Some time, I'll have to show you where I grew up," Randy said just as we passed my parents' house. I had no plans to introduce them that day, but all of a sudden there was the house and my mother was outside, waving us in.

"Where was that?" I asked, before I opened the gate to the front yard.

"LA," he answered as Mom came over to us. She gave me a big hug and Randy a doubtful smile.

"Come in! Come in!" she said in her life's-good voice just as my dad came to the front door and unintentionally blocked our way.

"Come in," he echoed more quietly, stepping aside.

Mom served us more coffee. "I didn't mean to invite myself for a meal," I told her when she offered lunch.

"You didn't," she said acerbically. "I invited you. Both of you," she added in case Randy wondered. That made me feel better about her doubtful smile.

Little did I know.

I helped Mom make the sandwiches while Dad and Randy talked about the army. Dad had served in between Vietnam and Iraq. Randy was in the reserves, which I learned by overhearing. There was a lot I didn't know about him yet. Oh well. There was a lot he didn't know about me too.

Mom interrupted my thoughts, which was good because Randy and I were naked in them. "He's white," she whispered.

"Really?" I asked, bugging my eyes out at her.

She took the Swiss cheese out of my hands and slapped slices on the turkey. "How long?" she whispered.

"Two weeks," I whispered back.

"Two weeks?" she said, punching me with her small, bony fist. "And you just now brought him by to meet us?"

I rubbed my arm. "I didn't bring him by. Besides, he's white," I reminded her, trying not to laugh.

"You shouldn't talk like that, Frankie. It's prejudiced," she said primly, slicing the sandwiches in half viciously. I kept my mouth shut. Never make your mom mad, especially when she's Native American and armed with a sharp knife.

Mom looked over at Randy and my dad and watched them talk a minute before calling out, "Lunch is ready!" She put the sandwiches on the yellow Fiestaware plates she reserved for company.

Mom had Randy sit to her right, so she could ask all the usual questions. She must have been satisfied with his answers because, at some point, she smiled at me—and not a scary smile either. She almost looked happy.

When lunch was over, Randy offered to help her clean up, and she smiled at me again. Definitely happy now. None of the daughters-in-law ever volunteered to help with anything.

I sat with my dad on the couch.

"He's a nice man," Dad said softly. "You know he's a patrolman?"

"I know," I answered.

"Your grandfather was an officer of the law too," Dad said. "Tribal police," he explained, with a nod of his chin punctuating the sentence fragment. That was news to me, but I didn't argue. My father had his memories; whether they were accurate was his business.

As we left my parents' house, Mom grabbed my arm to hold me back. Dad was talking Randy's ear off again.

"He's a nice boy," Mom said, echoing Dad's judgment.

"Even if he's white?" I asked, keeping my face straight. She punched me again even harder. "Ouch!" I yelped. "That hurt."

"You deserve it, talking like that. When are you bringing him back? We'll invite your brothers—and those women they married. We can cook a real Native meal for him," she said, looking like she was already planning the menu.

"Soon," I promised her. *Very soon*, I promised myself. I turned to go but she held me by the short sleeve for one more question.

"Did he bring you flowers yet?" she asked.

I said yes, he had.

"Good sign," she said, giving me a little push out the door.

When Randy and I finally reached my place again, I locked the door behind us. He pretended to be surprised, and I wiggled my eyebrows at him. "I thought we could play ride the pony again," I said. "Or maybe mounted police." He laughed and started taking off his shirt. I loved seeing that big chest again.

"First though," I said, taking him into my arms. "Thank you."

"For what?"

"For making me a better man already," I told him. He looked quizzically at me and asked how. I gave him a kiss and promised to explain it someday. Maybe after we had kids. We could adopt and...*whoa, Cochise!* I told myself.

I led Randy into the bedroom. When he was naked again and sprawled across my bed, I looked his big body over, shaking my head.

"You're so white," I said, more to myself than him.

"I could get more sun."

I gave him a look.

"Tanning salon?" he asked, eyebrows raised and wiggling. He was such kid, a big kid but still...

"It doesn't matter," I told him, easing inside where we're all the same color—where color doesn't matter.

I could use some sun, too, I thought as we began. We could take a vacation. LA maybe. I could meet his family. I wondered if his mother were as bad as mine. I smiled. Nobody could be that bad. I noticed Randy smiling up at me. Blond hair, blue eyes. Maybe Columbus wasn't all bad. If he hadn't accidentally discovered the new world, I wouldn't have met this guy.

"What are you thinking about?" Randy asked, holding me off him.

"Funny story."

"About what?"

"Columbus."

"Columbus?"

"Yeah, Columbus," I said and settled back on top of him. He didn't ask any more questions after that.

November

Home on Leave

I was in my old room with posters of famous athletes still on the walls. My trophies lined the bookshelves. The comforter my mother crocheted for me covered my double bed. The same curtains, bought at Sears, framed the window. My teenage and college clothes hung in the closet or lay folded neatly into drawers.

"Maybe you'll be able to wear them again," Mom said behind me. I looked at her in disbelief. I'm an inch taller than high school and weigh forty pounds less than college, thanks to PT and carrying a ninety-pound pack.

"Okay, Mom. I'll try them on."

She smiled at me like only a mom can and smoothed an imaginary bump in the comforter. She had mailed another one to me—in red, white, and blue—during my basic training. It was on my bed back at Fort Benning. I didn't care what the guys said about it. It said home to me, and home was a good place to be, especially at Thanksgiving.

My parents had met me in a new car at Logan. On the drive to Lawrence, they had asked the usual questions about the flight, the food, what I was going to do during my visit and whom I was going to see.

"Mary Jo Gleason is in town," my mother said with an expectant smile. I didn't have any specific plans yet, but one thing was for sure: I didn't plan to hook up with an old girlfriend from high school.

In my room Mom brought it up again—not Mary Jo Gleason but dating women. "Any Georgia peaches?" she asked.

"Plenty, Mom," I answered and started selecting clothes to try on, culling obvious ones for the Saint Vincent de Paul bin.

"I'll leave you to it then," she said and turned toward the door. Over her shoulder she added, "That sweater always looked good on you." I took my high school varsity sweater out of the Saint Vincent pile and hung it back in the closet.

After Mom went downstairs, I stopped sorting old clothes and changed out of my uniform, which I hung in the middle of my sartorial past. I dressed in civvies bought in Georgia and went downstairs to watch football with my dad.

"Go help your mother," he said, giving me a smile and a nod of his head in the right direction. I looked a lot like him from the neck down. From the chin up, I was all Mom.

As soon as I got through the swinging door to the kitchen, my sister, Mary Margaret, yelled, "What? No football?" I gave her a smooch and watched her shell peas. She looks like Mom too—all dark hair and pale skin. I still burn, even after all my assignments to sunny locales. My sister smiled our mother's smile, handed me a knife, and jabbed hers at waiting bunches of carrots. We played sous chef and talked. She didn't ask me about girls.

After a few minutes, I heard the front door open and three loud male voices coming our way. One was Dad's, another was my brother's, and the third I didn't know. Its owner came into the kitchen first, leaned down, and gave my mother a kiss on the cheek.

"Hi, Mrs. D. Thanks for the Turkey Day invite!" the stranger said, all grinning bonhomie. My mother returned his kiss and accepted a hug. "Hey, M and M," he greeted my sister. I thought only my brother Vince and I were allowed to call her that, but since my sister smiled and waved her knife at the big guy, I figured he must be the new boyfriend, new enough for me not to have heard about him yet. But then, I have been away from home a long time and hard to stay in touch with. That happens when your address is Iraq and Afghanistan.

Whatever and whoever he was, he stuck his big right paw out at me. "You must be the Special Forces Ranger. I'm Chris Donelle." French last name, Maine accent. No wonder Mom liked him. She's lived thirty years in Massachusetts and still says *ayeh*.

I shook hands with him. Good grip.

"Good to meet you, Chris. Yep, I'm Nick."

I expected him to let go then, but a look of recognition flashed through his eyes, and he held on tight. I really hoped he wasn't M and M's boyfriend, for her sake.

"Hey, hey! Break it up, boys!" a thunderous voice yelled in my ear. My "little" brother. It didn't take long for him to muscle in between us, all six foot three and two hundred and twenty-plus pounds of him, to give me a bear hug. Contact with a man felt good even if it was just my brother. I wondered how Chris Donelle would feel against my chest. His face was cute, in a boyish way, but beefy was his strong point. "Welcome home, bro!" Vince yelled in my other ear, which drew my thoughts away from nice-looking *Canadien* men with Maine accents.

"Why, thank you, Officer Della Sante," I said to him. "Congratulations on finishing police academy, buddy!"

Vince squeezed me again before letting go. "Good to have you back, Nicky. Good to have you back," he repeated more quietly. I know my family worried the next time they saw me it would be in a body bag. But he returned to smiling. "Yep," he said. "The safety of Lawrence, Mass. depends on me now. Well, Chris too. We were in the academy together."

I turned back to Mr. Six Foot Five. "You came down from Maine to join the police force *here*?"

He shrugged his shoulders, hands out, head cocked. *Très Québécois.* "Got to go where the jobs are. So, you noticed the accent, eh?"

Before I could answer with an ayeh, Mom put her oar in. "Now, Nicky, remember you're half Mainer too." Vince and I knuckle-bumped, and Mary Margaret rolled her eyes.

"Aw, Vicky, don't hold that against him," my dad chimed in. Mom whacked him with her pasta spoon. What would Thanksgiving be without a little pasta on the side? Not much at our house.

"Okay, it's too crowded in here," Mom said, waving the spoon threateningly. "Everybody out unless you're planning on helping." Vince and Dad left immediately. I heard their voices moving from the dining room into the family room.

Chris stayed, not taking his eyes off me. He wasn't exactly subtle. "What you want me to do, Mrs. D?" he asked. My mother surveyed the culinary battlefield.

"Why don't you help Mary Margaret with the fresh peas."

"Or, you could help Nicky with the carrots," M and M interjected before he could make a move toward the pile of green in front of her.

I gave her a questioning look, and she wiggled her eyebrows at me.

"Okay," he said, giving her a wink and opening the knife drawer without having to ask which one it was. He pulled out a parer. I took it away and handed him a utility knife like mine.

"You cook?" he asked like it was an important question.

"Sometimes," I said, trying not to stare at his crotch bulging over the edge of the worktable in the middle of my mother's kitchen. I thought about his body, and something in mine stirred, but I shook it off. I was only home on leave for the long weekend.

"Wash your hands first," Mom reminded him.

"Right," Chris answered. To me, in a low sexy voice, he said, "Save my place."

"No problem," I told him, watching him booty bump Mary Margaret aside at the sink and her bump back. That was how she handled brothers, not boyfriends.

He returned, wiping his big mitts with the hand towel. "M and M," he yelled over his shoulder. "Catch!"

Mary Margaret turned, snagged the towel like the girls' basketball star she once was, and reinserted it through its ring. He came around to my side of the table.

"You must have sisters," I said, pushing half of the remaining carrots his way.

"Four. I'm the only boy."

Too bad for his parents, I thought, *if they're expecting grandchildren with Donnelle as their last name.*

He and I sliced, side by side. He joked his last name was almost Della Sante because he was at the house so much.

"Why didn't you just move in here?" I asked. "You could have had my old room." It was time the Nicholas Della Sante Commemorative Space was used for something other than storage of clothing and memories.

"I told him that," Mom said. "But they wanted their own place." Chris moved slightly away from me while Mom was talking. Him and Vince? I wondered if my baby brother was gay too. Poor Mom and Dad. Two gay sons and a daughter who didn't want children. They wouldn't do any better than the Donelles in the grandparent department.

I made conversation, trying to figure out the lay of the land. "So, are you just out of college?"

"No way, soldier," Chris answered, shifting his hip and thigh closer to mine. The juxtaposition felt good. "I went straight from high school into the Marines. Four years. Semper Fi! How long you been in the army?"

"Six years, almost seven."

"Did you make it to Iraq?"

"Twice."

"Me too," he said quietly. I didn't ask questions. Some guys talk about it; some guys don't.

"I hear you're an officer," he said after the silence.

"A captain," my mom said proudly, which reminded me she was listening.

Chris came to attention, executed a right turn, and saluted me sharply. "Sir!" he shouted into my face. I returned his salute halfheartedly. He made a left turn back to the worktable. "You must have gone to college," he said like he was calculating our age difference.

"I did," I answered, waiting for him to finish his subtraction. "I'm twenty-eight," I said after a minute. Math didn't seem to be his strong point.

He looked me in the eye. "I'm twenty-two. Same age as Vince."

We were quiet after that. Twenty-two and twenty-eight is a big difference, especially if you're the twenty-two. But then he asked nonchalantly, "How long is your leave?"

"Four days," I answered.

"You can do a lot in four days," he said, his broad shoulders accidentally bumping against mine as he leaned across me to gather some wayward carrot slices.

"I plan to," I agreed, adding my slices to his pile. Maybe I wouldn't have to troll the Boston bars after all—that is, so long as he wasn't already Vince's boyfriend.

When Mom declared the turkey done, Dad came in to carve, like always. Vince helped ferry food to the table, razzing his buddy and being razzed back. My little bro didn't read as gay, but I wasn't sure my gaydar worked within the family.

We ate dinner right on time. If my mom said six, she meant it. The men at the table shoveled food in pretty fast, which Mom loved. I ate more than I should have, but I told myself I'd be running it off in the morning.

"Hey, bro," I asked Vince. "Are you up for a run in the a.m.?"

"Sorry. Not tomorrow, Nicky. I got the early shift."

Chris piped up. "I'll run with you, soldier."

"Aren't you guys partners?" I asked.

I watched Vince's eyes to see if he understood my double meaning.

"Nah," my brother answered, taking a break from the mashed potatoes. "They split us up after the academy. Younger guys with older."

"Then you're on, jarhead," I told the marine.

"Nicky!" my mother admonished.

Chris just laughed. "No worries, Mrs. D. I can take it." He gave me another wink. *I bet he can,* I thought to myself.

After dinner I tried to help Mom with the dishes, but she shooed me out of the kitchen and started filling the dishwasher. "Mary Margaret can help with the pots and pans," she said. "You go sit with your father and brother."

"And Chris," my sister added. She gave me a sly look before she started rinsing out the turkey roaster. This is what happens when you come out to your sister. She's always trying to set you up with someone.

I wandered through the dining room, hearing the sounds of Patriot fans ahead. The three other menfolk were lounging in front of the HD, but Chris jumped up before I could take a seat. "Hey, Nick. How about you show me all these trophies I been hearing about?"

Vince laughed at him. "You've seen them."

Chris got a little red. "Yeah, but there were a couple I wanted to ask about."

"He won everything. End of story," my brother said, muting the TV during the commercial.

I understood Chris's motivation perfectly. "Sure," I agreed, turning toward the hall and staircase to the second floor. Chris followed closely behind me, growling a couple of times on the way up. At the landing, I turned to him. "What about my brother?"

"Vince?"

"He's the only brother I have," I replied. Chris looked confused. I decided to be explicit. "Are you and my brother lovers?"

He nearly choked with laughter.

"Okay, okay," I said. "Stupid question."

He kept laughing.

"Shut up, will you?"

"Mmm," he purred. "Is that an order, sir?"

"Yes," I answered. I decided to be more forgiving about the sir business. Maybe he was into being told what to do. I handle that. After all, the army says I *am* a leader of men.

We headed down the hall, toward my room. Chris growled all the way but more *sotto voce*. We entered and gave my room a survey.

"I sleep here sometimes," he said, his voice husky. "When your folks ask me to stay over." He closed the door behind us.

I looked at the doorknob like a cat expecting that looking would make it turn. "They might think that's weird," I said, still staring at the door.

Chris shrugged.

"So, which trophies were you interested in?" I folded my arms across my chest and faced the carefully dusted display.

"This one," he said, growling again and spinning me into his arms. The boy wasn't shy.

"Oof," I said when our chests smacked together. "Meaty."

"You like 'em meaty?" he asked, eyes already half shut and lips heading for mine. They made a surprisingly soft landing.

"At ease, marine," I said, pulling away from him although it felt good. "That's a little too fast for me, especially with my family downstairs."

"Oh, they know," he said.

"Not about me."

He looked doubtful.

"Really," I reiterated. No need to mention my sister. Who was this guy anyway?

His face went all gooey-eyed. "I'd like to see you while you're here," he said like he was asking me out on a second date.

"You will," I said, trying to stay cool. "We're taking a run in the morning, right?"

His face dropped. Clearly, cool was not what he had in mind. "Yeah," he replied. He turned back to the trophy shelves and picked up the one I'd been handed graduation night. "What was this for?"

"Highest GPA," I answered.

"They gave trophies for that?" he asked, looking astonished. He had the full emotional range.

I nodded and he put the loving cup back in its place. Well, not exactly in its place, but I knew my mom would fix that.

I heard my sister's voice outside my room. "You guys decent?"

Chris looked down at his crotch with alarm.

"We're coming!" I yelled back at her.

I heard her snicker down the hall.

*

The next morning the man-boy walked into my room while I was still in bed and half asleep. If I'd had a gun, I might have shot him. I was still that jittery, no matter how many talks I had with myself.

"What the hell?" I said and reached for the clock instead of an army-issue revolver. It read 5:30 a.m.

"I wanted to see what you look like in bed," he answered mock innocently, grinning like the cat who didn't eat the canary.

"Happy?" I asked him, sitting up and exposing my chest. I kept the sheet across my lap. The guy had an immediate effect on me.

"I could be happier," he said, moving his crotch in front of my face.

"We're running, remember?" I said, exiting the opposite side of the bed and standing, facing away from him. I pulled on a dirty undershirt, clean sweatshirt, and baggy sweatpants. He was in baggy shorts and a tight, sleeveless shirt, which showed off his body nicely but didn't seem very practical given it was almost officially winter and already officially freezing in New England.

"Aren't you going to be cold?" I asked him.

He puffed his huge chest out and showed me his guns. "This is nothing. I'm from Maine, remember? I run hot."

"You sure do," I mumbled, bending over my suitcase to find my socks and running shoes, ignoring the urge to do something I'd never done in my parents' house—at least while they were home.

"What did you say?" he asked from behind me.

"Nothing."

"Come on, tell me," he said, sidling up against my bent-over ass. I straightened up like he'd stabbed me.

"Don't do that." My voice shook only a little.

"Okay, okay," he said, backing away, hands up.

I finished dressing without further incident.

"Ready?" I asked.

He snapped to attention, saluted, and barked out, "Yes, sir."

I thought we'd have nothing left to say to each other since we'd spent the entire forty minutes on the icy streets talking—when we weren't laughing—but we continued to chat as we trotted up to my parents' house. The kitchen lights were on.

"Let's go in the back," I suggested.

He winked and leered.

"Mom's up," I told him, and his face dropped.

I gave him a get over it punch, and he nearly fell on the icy sidewalk. I caught all two hundred and forty pounds of him in my arms.

"My hero," he said, looking too young and too cute with his rosy cheeks and big blue eyes staring up at me.

"Come on, jarhead." I set him back on his feet. I started toward the kitchen door. He caught my arm before I took a second step.

"Maybe we should go in the front and sneak up the stairs." He looked serious.

I shook my head, put a finger to my lips, and pried his hand off my bicep.

We opened the kitchen door carefully, hoping to scare my mother. She and M and M were sitting at the breakfast table, drinking steaming cups of something hot. Mom had her back to us. Neither of them jumped when we yelled variations of "ahhhhh!"

"There's coffee on the counter," Mom said calmly without turning around, her slender fingers indicating the direction of caffeine.

Mary Margaret looked from me to Chris and back at me. "Good run, boys?" she drawled.

We answered with a joint *yes* and poured ourselves some black coffee.

"Sit with us," Mom said, pulling out the chair nearest her.

"We stink," Chris unnecessarily informed her and sipped his coffee standing at the counter. I stood alongside him, and Mary Margaret smiled like she thought her matchmaking chores were done, as far we were concerned. "Let's shower," he whispered to me in his not very quiet voice. M and M shot a glance at Mom, but she just kept smiling at the room in general. "Drink up," Chris encouraged, pushing my mug further into my mouth.

"Don't make me choke," I said and shoved his hand away, feeling the coarse black hairs spread across the smooth brown of it, feeling the instant attraction of the other.

"One of you can use our bathroom," Mom called after us as we left the kitchen. Dad must have left for Boston already. He always went to work the day after Thanksgiving, even when he didn't have to.

Chris leaned toward me and whispered, "Not what I had in mind."

"You can use Mom and Dad's," I said, trying not to laugh at his disappointed frown.

In the communal hall bathroom, I saw the door opening behind me in the mirror. Chris appeared with a leer on his face and a tan towel wrapped around his middle parts. "You done already?" I asked, aware of the physical reaction happening to me at sink level.

"Mostly," he said, dropping his towel. I tried not to cut myself in midshave. He moved close, settled against me, and reached under my arms for my chest. It would have been so easy to give in—the door had a lock I hadn't used—but I doubted whether Mom kept the second-floor bathroom stocked with condoms. However, there were other things we could do.

I was giving several of those things serious consideration when my mother yelled, "Breakfast!" outside the door with a lock which wasn't engaged.

"We're almost done, Mom," I yelled.

"Five minutes," was all she said in response, not reacting to the *we*, verbally at least. Chris didn't move away.

"I'm not having sex in my parents' house," I warned him. "Go get dressed." I began shaving the other cheek.

He sat on the toilet seat and sulked. "I don't have any clothes," he said, glowering up at me.

I looked him over, trying not to feel regret I hadn't locked the door and given him his five minutes. "You can probably wear my college clothes."

"I do," he replied, still sulking.

"What?"

"Sometimes. When I stay over," he said.

I frowned.

"Too kinky?" He grinned again.

"Go," I repeated, pulling him up and shoving him toward the door. "Wait!" I yelped before he could open it. I looked outside the door.

"Coast clear?" he asked, smirking at me. He wrapped his towel around his middle and sauntered out.

After breakfast, I walked Chris to his car. "What are you doing tonight?" he asked. Before I could answer, my mother's voice reached us from the porch.

"Come over tonight for leftovers, Chris."

We looked at each other. I could see kismet in Chris's eyes.

"Sure thing! Thanks, Mrs. D," he yelled back at her. "See you later then," he said to me, keeping his arms down with a noticeable effort. I kept my hands stuffed in my pockets.

I spent the day texting friends and borrowing the new car to meet up with them for coffee, lunch, brunch, and more coffee. By dinner, I was ready for a nap, not more to eat and drink.

I had just parked the car in the garage when a dark-blue Mustang pulled up the driveway. Chris hoisted himself out of it in his police uniform.

"Sorry," he apologized. "I just got off duty."

"You look good in a uniform," I told him. *Really good,* I thought to myself.

"I bet you do too," he replied wistfully.

I closed the garage door and walked us inside the house.

*

We fought after dinner over who would clean up the kitchen, boys against girls. The boys' team was Chris and me; my brother and father had headed to the family room as soon as Mom gave the signal that dinner was over. After Mary Margaret cheerfully retreated and Mom gave in, I settled in to scrub food debris into the disposal, and Chris loaded the dishwasher. I had a feeling of déjà vu, us standing side by side at a sink like this. *No,* I told myself firmly. *Don't go there.*

"So, how was your day?" I asked him, trying to make conversation and then realizing that was a question couples asked.

"Nothing special," was all he said. I guessed he didn't like to bring his work home with him. I could understand that. "What about you?" he asked.

"Saw a bunch of old friends," I said and waited for him to ask for details.

He looked behind us at the empty room, gave me a searching look, and asked forthrightly, "You wanna come over to my place?" The scent of him was strong in the room.

"Tonight?"

"Tonight," he confirmed, taking a clean pot out of my hands.

"What about my brother?"

"He'll be cool with it."

I didn't know the configuration of the rooms at their apartment but even the possibility of my little brother listening while the marine and I did the deed did not sound enticing.

"I think I'll pass," I said, turning my attention back to the remaining dishes.

He took my wet hand in his dry one. "Do you like me?" he asked earnestly.

I gulped. "Of course—" I began.

"I mean, do you *like* me?"

"Chris, I'm here on leave. I go back Sunday." He let my hand drop. I knew I'd said what had to be said, but he looked so sad and, unfortunately, so adorable. "Look, okay, I like you," I said. He turned to me with bright eyes and the most beautiful smile I've ever seen on a man.

"Come over tomorrow night then. Your brother has late duty."

I thought it over. One plan I'd made was to get laid one night out of the four I was back home. Gay was okay in the army now but not great, not if you really wanted a career, which I did. I nodded yes. Chris moved in for a celebratory kiss. I fended him off with my hands and headed for the family room.

Saturday was spent visiting relatives with my parents and Mary Margaret. If I'd had time, Mom, I'm sure, would have dragged me up to Maine to see my grandmother and more aunts, uncles, and cousins. The Boston metropolitan area was exhausting enough. I thought about texting Chris and begging off, but a promise is a promise, as my father always told me, and it would still be sex without standing and staring for hours in a Boston bar or two.

When I arrived at the boys' apartment, Chris met me at the door with a finger to his lips. "Your brother's here," he whispered. "He got reassigned to the early shift."

"You didn't think to warn me?" I whispered back.

"Who's there?" Vince called from what must be the living room. I walked toward his voice, getting a smile ready. My brother was sprawled across the couch. A considerably smaller widescreen than my father's was on to the Celtics. "Nicky!" he exclaimed and jumped to his feet. I walked into his embrace.

"Would you like a beer?" Chris asked the room in general.

"I'll have *one* with you guys," Vince emphasized, letting me go. "But we have to make it quick. I need to be in bed by nine. Got the early shift again." He shook his head ruefully.

Chris exited for the kitchen, wherever that was, and returned cradling three bottles in two hands. Vince and I took a Sam Adams from him. We unscrewed simultaneously.

"To the marines!" I toasted, trying to make the best of it.

"To the army," they answered. *Clink, clink, clink, clinks* all around.

Chris took long pulls on his beer while Vince and I chatted. It looked as if he was going to hold Vince to a quick one. He finished his and asked, "Anybody want another?" Mine was still half full, but I said I'd take another. He trotted off to the refrigerator.

Vince called after him, "None for me, remember!"

Chris returned with two bottles, handed one to me, and stood by Vince as if to hurry him along. My brother obligingly chugged the rest of his beer, stood up, and said, "Good night then. See you tomorrow, Nicky." He hugged me again before shambling down the hallway in his flip-flops, T-shirt, and boxers.

Chris and I did not stay up long after Vince. We gave it maybe a half an hour until my brother was done with the bathroom and behind the closed door of his bedroom.

We crept down the hall past Vince's room. I could hear snoring already. "He brings women home," Chris whispered as if he had to justify what we were doing. Inside his room he turned on the light and looked me over. "I wish you had your uniform on."

"You're into uniforms?" I whispered back.

"A little," he said, taking off his shirt and shorts in record time. I stripped down a little more slowly. "So hot," he whispered when I was down to my BVDs.

"Why are we still whispering?" I asked.

He pointed at the opposite wall.

"Vince?" I mouthed.

He nodded and yanked me close.

The battle began.

Chris established a beachhead on my ass, holding on tightly while he made a prolonged frontal assault on my lips. My fingers feinted around his obliques to his butt and dug in. We were at an impasse until he began lip and teeth skirmishes on my face and neck, followed by a heavy tongue barrage. I tried a surprise assault on his chest, claiming meaty handfuls of territory, but his mouth and hands counterattacked in the same territory on me.

"Maybe we should flip a coin," I said.

"Huh?" he mumbled, not even looking up. He was biting now.

"Never mind," I whispered. I dropped to my knees. Someone had to raise the white flag. After a few minutes, we changed positions. Chris wasn't much good, but when he looked up for approval, I tousled his hair and smiled anyway. He started kneading my ass and growling again.

He looked up with that look, the one that says it's time. I gulped nervously. He stood and, in a clean lift and jerk, had me in his arms.

"Chris!" I yelped.

"Shhh. Your brother," he said in a husky *sotto voce.*

He carried me bride-style to the bed and gently deposited me on the king-size expanse. I almost expected rose petals on turned-down sheets, the way he was handling me.

Then, without any further preliminaries, he climbed on top of me and pushed my legs apart with his knees. "You okay, baby?" he asked. I nodded nervously. No retreat now. He had breached my defenses.

Afterward, he looked down at me, hair all in his face. "Whew!" was all he said before diving back into my neck. In the morning I noticed the hickey in the bathroom mirror. I tried washing the bruise away, pretending it was just dirt.

"I'm sorry," Chris said unconvincingly when I pointed it out to him. He looked proud like he'd meant to leave his mark.

"Hmph. Well, I guess I can borrow some makeup from M and M," I said.

He wrapped his big arms around me like I was captured territory, which I suppose I was. "Aw, come on, baby. Don't be mad. Your brother's gone," he said in a low, cajoling voice and started nuzzling my neck. No way I was ready for another hickey. I put the flat of my hands against his chest.

"Okay," I said. "But this time we flip."

"Flip?" he asked, his eyes darting left and right like he was looking for an exit. "I dunno. I hear it really hurts."

I didn't bother to ask whether he was a virgin. "It does," I confirmed. "But then it feels really good. You might like it."

"Maybe," he answered, very doubtfully. "Let me think about it."

"Don't think too long," I said. "I'm leaving tomorrow morning."

"I could visit you," he said, looking an earnest teenager again.

"In Georgia?" I didn't know if I liked the sound of that.

"Sure. Why not?"

I could think of a lot of why nots but didn't say anything. I had made my request, and he had made his. I dressed and left. Chris didn't try to stop me. As I passed by Vince's room, the door was open, displaying a bed in disarray and a room full of debris. I wondered when he'd left and how much he'd heard. My guess was plenty.

At my parents, Dad was shoveling new snow. He handed the shovel to me. "Reinforcements," he said. He didn't ask where I'd spent the night.

Mom didn't require any explanation either. She came out on the porch and announced to us both we could go to the eleven o'clock mass like it was no problem I'd come home late from an overnight with an unknown participant. She smiled at me, shivered, and rushed back inside.

Mary Margaret helped me disguise the hickey after my shower and didn't ask any questions either although I could see she wanted to.

Dad and I dressed in somber dark suits, my mother in a stiff-looking navy dress, which was probably from Talbott's, and M and M in a daringly red pantsuit and set off for Saint Michael's. I drove, with Dad in the front and Mom and Mary Margaret in the back. At first no one spoke. I didn't know if it was because I hadn't come home the night before or because it was my last day of leave. But as the church came into view, everyone began talking all at once.

"When are you coming back, son?" my father asked, looking so sad I nearly cried.

"You're seeing Chris—and Vince—before you go, right?" was my sister's question, clearly tacking on Vince's name as an afterthought.

"We're meeting them for brunch," my mother answered.

That took care of one question. I left my father's hanging.

At mass and after, over coffee and cake in the parish hall, I saw dozens, if not hundreds, of people I knew by name or at least by sight. Nearly every one of them thanked me for my service. I never knew what to say to that.

We ate brunch at Gilfoy's. If that place ever permanently closed, my parents would starve on Sunday afternoons. Vince and Chris were waiting for us in a family-sized booth. Mary Margaret slid along the maroon faux leather to meet my brother in the middle. My mother and father followed her. That left space for me next to Chris. I began to get suspicious.

After I sat, he asked me, "When do you leave?"

"Tomorrow morning," I answered, taking my eyes off the menu to look into his eyes. They were demanding specifics. "Ten-oh-seven, Delta flight one-one-two."

"I'll take you."

I started to decline his offer, but my father said, "Great! Thanks, Chris," of course. It would mean he wouldn't have to take time off work after all. My mother started to say something, but M and M gave her a look. Vince continued to study his menu.

*

I said goodbye to my family the night before, but they were all up early to say goodbye again very early Monday morning. Chris stood in the open door, holding my bags. When I reached my sister in the gauntlet, she whispered in my ear, "Don't screw this up."

I tried to keep my face noncommittal and followed Chris out the door. Before I got in his car, I waved to all four of my family members standing in the cold. It might be a long time before I got to see them again. It might be never.

The two of us were mostly silent on the way, except for Chris's gruff confirmation of my departure flight time and airline. "You can just drop me off there," I said, pointing to the curb outside terminal *A*.

"I've been thinking," he said, putting the car in park. I watched the time and parking police nervously. "About, you know…"

"Chris…" I began. A parking officer knocked on the windshield. Chris gave her the thumbs-up. I opened the passenger door.

"I'll park," he suggested. I shook my head. He popped the trunk.

"I'll call you," I said as he lifted my bags out, and I took them from him.

"Really?" he asked.

I nodded and let him hug me. He got back in the car. As he pulled away, he put his left arm out of the window and waved. I had bags in my hands so didn't wave back.

I watched his car longer than I meant to. When it disappeared, I started walking toward the automatic door. Would I call him? I probably had to. What would I say? I had no idea.

The doors to terminal *A* opened, and I walked through. My cell phone rang. I dropped my bags and removed it from my pocket.

"Yes?" I answered.

The doors closed behind me.

December

Eight Nights

A package was waiting for me Monday morning, wrapped in blue paper and white ribbon. There was a card attached. The computer-generated printing read *Dear Steven, Happy Hanukkah.* I'm not Jewish but my name is Steven, and it was my desk, so I untied the ribbon and pried apart the blue paper and gold tissue. Inside was a simple black rubber ring two inches across. What kind of joke was this? A cock ring? Who would give me a cock ring? After staring at it a while, though, I wondered if I should try it on. I stretched it tentatively. Voices approaching made me hide the thing in my desk drawer as fast as I could.

Later, during a bathroom break, I slid it on in the privacy of a stall. A perfect fit. My brain said *weird*, but my cock seemed to like it. It swelled, ready for action, so I let my right hand have its way with me. Afterward, I eased the thing off and went back to work, not that I accomplished much. I spent most of the morning researching Hanukkah. Eight nights, miracle of the oil, symbolic of the survival of the Jewish people, gift giving each day. Got it.

I pondered what kind of Jewish admirer would give me a cock ring for the first night and what would he give me tomorrow. Images of cute Jewish men at Hendley Cavanaugh paraded through my thoughts. During an ostensible coffee break, I made an eleven o'clock tour of their company locations and looked meaningfully at each of them, but no one looked meaningfully back.

At six, the cock ring and I left for the evening. I wore it until I went to bed. My hand got very tired.

The second day another package said hello when I arrived. It was a little larger and softer but was also wrapped in blue and white with a small card on top. *Happy Hanukkah* it repeated, adding *Wear me today.* I opened and closed the tissue quickly. I had seen a jock strap inside, and it looked used. I scanned our office bay for hidden cameras, waited five minutes, and then thought *why not?*

I took the package to the men's room. Back in the same stall, I held the jock up for a second look. It was white, or had been, and, yes, there were yellow stains on the crotch. Thinking about sharing cock space with another man made me horny. I rushed out of my slacks and boxers and slid the jock up my legs. The cup was tight around my cock and balls. The straps bit into my ass. The waistband was my size. Hmm.

That night, I introduced my first two gifts to each other. They played together nicely.

Wednesday, I arrived a half hour earlier than usual, but the package still beat me to my desk. This one was bigger yet, pliant but semi-hard. So was I. I ripped into it. A black leather vest. Kinky. And expensive. Was I being bought? Yes, I answered, and took my jacket off. The vest felt a little tight over my undershirt, dress shirt, and tie.

That night in the privacy of my own ten by ten studio apartment (plus the kitchenette), I dressed up in all three presents and stared at the full-length hanging mirror that came with the lease. One look proved you *could* take the Midwest out of the boy.

The desk was bare at 7:00 a.m. on the fourth day. I waited, listening for footfalls on the carpet. I thought I heard some but when I tiptoed into the hallway to look no one was there.

The rest of the morning, I tried not to leave my desk. I would catch this guy or burst my bladder, whichever happened first. Unfortunately, I had a lunch date. I thought about canceling, but Scott was a nice guy and the closest thing to a friend I had at HC. At the deli we always went to, I told him about the Hanukkah presents.

"Wild," he said after swallowing a bite of brisket on rye. "Are you Jewish?"

I scoffed. "Do I look Jewish?"

"You can't always tell," he answered, staring at me over his sandwich. I had never noticed how slanted his eyes were or how aquamarine. They kept hold of mine while he chewed. I imagined him biting me—just a nibble here and there. *Kinky, Steven.* But he'd never shown any interest in me. Was he even gay? I hadn't been able to decide.

"Well, anyway," I said, breaking the hold his eyes had on me. "I'm Presbyterian."

Scott looked amused, but then he almost always did. He had this cute little smile on his face every time I saw him. He dropped the uneaten portion of his sandwich onto his plate and pushed back from the table. "Let's take a walk before we go back," he said and stood up, even though I hadn't finished my Coke. That was the only thing I didn't like about him. He had to decide everything. But when he stood up, I did too.

Back at the office, there was a package on my desk, but it was just FedEx. Probably an author. Some of them still used print. My boss came out of her office as I read the shipping label.

"Who's that from?"

"It doesn't say."

Amy clapped her hands in mock excitement. "Oooh! Mystery!"

I pulled the tear strip and peeked inside. A glimpse of blue wrapping paper paralyzed my hands.

"It looks like a present. Maybe it's for me," she said. Authors and agents sent her thank-yous all the time.

"It was addressed to me," I muttered.

"Oh, well, what do you think it is? It's not your birthday, is it?" She looked a little panicked.

"No, it's not until March." I stalled, opening the FedEx packaging only incrementally, trying to think of an escape clause.

"Oh, let me do it," Amy huffed. She grabbed the FedEx mailer and ripped the present out of it. "Oooh, pretty paper. The card says *Happy Hanukkah. Use this.* Use this? What does that mean?" She folded her arms across her ample chest. "I didn't know you were Jewish."

I grabbed the package back. "I'm not."

"Well, *I am.* Maybe it's for me after all," she said. Then I had to explain—without too many details—why it most likely wasn't. She started laughing, covering her mouth with her hands. "Stevie has an admirer. What else did he get you?"

"How do you know it's a he?"

"Duh." She rolled her brown eyes behind her glasses. "It must have been good since your face is so red. But far be it for me to pry into the private affairs of my employee," she said in a phony toney accent before punching my shoulder. "Oops! Don't file a grievance or anything."

I waited until she was back in her office and on the phone before I headed to the men's room. The stall was like my clubhouse now.

Present number four was an anal douche. Shit! I was glad Amy wasn't in the stall with me. If she thought my face was red before, she'd think it was about to explode now.

I fanned myself and looked the apparatus over. It was chrome and very elegant looking, not the usual plastic and rubber thingy. This douche said *I spent some money on you.* It also said *I want to stick something up your ass.* That made my sphincter lurch. I rewrapped the douche for later consideration.

That night, back on East Seventy-eighth Street, I got naked, hooked the douche up in the shower, stuck the nozzle up my ass, and turned the faucet on. Fuck! Too hot. After a little adjustment, I filled 'er up and was ready to go.

Friday, I got to work at my usual time. I was confident there would be a fifth present and had a hunch my mystery gift giver would be making himself known to me pretty soon now. After the douche, his intentions were clear.

The fifth package was twelve inches long, slender, and hard. I had a bad feeling as I read the card. After *Happy Hanukkah,* it greeted me with *Practice with this after douching.* Uh oh. I removed the tape.

Damn! I had never seen one this big. When I set it on my desk, it loomed even larger, leaning toward me, supported by its two balls. It was perky *and* huge. But it was the lubricant enclosed that had me really worried; the dildo wasn't meant to be merely decorative. I needed counseling, so I punched in Scott's extension number, figuring I'd have to leave a message at this early hour.

"Scott Roth," a non-recorded voice said.

"Oh, good. You're in already. Could you go to lunch with me today, please?" I asked, hating the whine I heard in my voice.

"Anything wrong, Steve?" he asked in a reassuring baritone.

"I'm not sure," I answered.

"Okaaay. See you in the reception area at ten till."

I agreed and hung up. Good ol' Scott. Just what I needed: someone normal.

He had the same brisket sandwich he always had and the same iced tea. When I ordered a cocktail, he raised his eyebrows and gave me a questioning look.

"I need a drink," I told his eyebrows and his eyes. He shrugged.

"Okay. So, what's up?" he asked.

My head made a circuit of the crowded, noisy restaurant. I leaned in close. "I got a dildo today."

"The fifth night," he said meditatively.

I leaned closer. "Does it have anything to do with Hanukkah?"

Scott's laughs were like barks, deep darks rumbling up from his chest. Speaking of his chest, it was looking mighty good that day. Had he been working out? I noticed his face was hairy.

"Are you growing a beard?" I asked.

"No," he said as the waiter handed him his iced tea and me my mojito. After the waiter left, he asked, "Are you afraid of it?"

"The beard? No, it looks great." He stared at me with those eyes. I jumped a little in my seat. "Oh! The dildo!" I exclaimed—too loudly. Nearby diners raised their eyes from their plates. Scott's looked amused. "A little," I admitted, knocking back a good slug of the mojito.

"I can see why, after the douche. Did you use it?" he asked and took a sip of tea.

"I did. I mean, I've used everything else."

"Hmm," Scott said, like he was looking at photos. Our sandwiches appeared, and he stopped asking questions. I didn't blame him for not wanting any more lunch conversation about douches and dildos. We updated each other on the continuing melodramas of his department (accounting) and mine (editorial). Once he'd finished, Scott paid the bill and wouldn't take my money. "Keep it in your pants," he said, giving me a wink.

Out on Broadway we walked in tandem for a block, like we always did. We were about the same height and had equal strides. All of a sudden, he stopped and took my bicep in a shockingly strong grip. He *had* been working out.

"Look, Steve. You don't have to do anything you don't want to," he said to me seriously. His eyes were fierce, and his mouth was grim. It was like he was protecting me. Did I need protection?

"Where do you think this going?" I asked. He was making me nervous.

"It doesn't have to go anywhere," he answered in a reassuring voice. "It doesn't have to go any further than it's gone already."

He seemed so definite. I wished I could be. "How can I stop it?"

"Don't open the presents. Stop using them. You probably won't get anything over the weekend anyway," he said, stuffing his hands in his pockets. His pants were tighter than usual.

"Are those new slacks?" I asked.

He looked down at his legs. "No. Why?"

"They look really good on you."

"Thanks," he said, the little smile back at the corners of his mouth. "Anyway," he prompted, "the weekend."

"Right," I said. "Why wouldn't I get more presents? Aren't there three more nights?"

He observed me with his head tilted back a little. "Sounds like you want it. Them," he corrected himself.

I looked away. "Maybe." What I didn't want was having to decide on Fifth Avenue in front of Saint Patrick's Cathedral. It just seemed wrong.

Scott started us walking again while I ruminated. Open; use. Open; use. Both were up to me. What the hell, I decided. It was just a dildo, not a marriage license.

Scott interrupted my musings. "You're thinking again," he said. I'd almost forgotten he was there. "Maybe you should just go with how you feel. Hey, speaking of that, do you feel like a movie tonight?" My little heart leaped. Scott hadn't suggested we get together outside of work before. On the other hand, there was the dildo and my instructions.

"I think I'm going to be busy tonight."

He looked askance at me, a strange light in his eyes. "You're going to use it, aren't you?"

I gulped a couple of times. "I think so. But what about Saturday? I mean, for a movie," I added quickly. I didn't want to lose my chance with him, in case he was gay and all.

"Saturday's good," he said. "Let me look over what's playing, and I'll call you this afternoon." He steered us back into the office.

I sat at my desk, considering my date with Scott. Was it a date? I hoped so. Amy asked me why I was smiling. Who wouldn't be? I had two dates in one week, one of them human. Call me popular!

It wasn't until I was on the subway home that I wondered when I'd told Scott one of the presents was a douche.

At home I went through my new routine: douche thoroughly and don my gay apparel. I turned up the radiator and lay on my sofa bed with the dildo and the lube. My sphincter tightened. *Don't wimp, Steve—and get a towel.*

Ass on the towel and legs in the air, I lubed myself and the dildo so thoroughly I worried I wouldn't have enough to last the weekend. The note said *practice*, which I took to mean more than once.

My cock and I both got tired of thinking, though, and I didn't want all that lube to go to waste so I poked the beige head inside me. Did beige mean he was Caucasian? The sudden pain distracted me. *What the fuck! This thing is wide! Is he this thick? And don't tell me he's packing twelve inches! Is that why he got me this size and told me to practice?* I thought about my mystery man's theoretical cock size while I eased the dildo in further and, before I'd run through all the permutations, the dildo's balls feet hit my gooch.

Okay, it was in. Now what? Never having used a dildo, I wasn't sure but, logically, fucking should follow insertion. I pulled the faux cock out of me and pushed it all the way back in. That was stimulating so I accelerated the ol' pull and push, gripping the balls feet. In sex and life, it's good to have something to hold onto.

I got into it, rolling over onto my stomach and raising myself into doggy position. I tried to picture my Hanukkah Harry inside me, all twelve inches, and started to pant and curse. Pretty soon I was saying *fuck me, fuck me* like I was in a porn movie. My own cock was about to burst, and all of a sudden it did. A real gusher. I reclined on my side, breathing hard, with a foot-long still up my ass, trying to imagine HH coming inside me. Somehow, he wouldn't come into focus, but I kept trying all evening, visualizing various men from the office doing the deed. Aaron Sampson was quite the six foot four stud. In my mind he came like a locomotive. David Geilert was adorable naked. Unfortunately, we fought for the bottom.

Scott was my favorite fantasy man, however, what with his wolf eyes and new muscles. He definitely huffed and puffed and blew my house down. *Please God*, I prayed, *let him be gay and not just a bro!*

Day Six dawned. Even though it had been a late night, I woke up early, like a kid at Christmas, wondering if I'd get anything. My aching asshole reminded me I'd gotten plenty. I played with myself a little, remembering. A little became a lot. I was nearing the finish line when someone buzzed to get in downstairs. Fuck! Probably crazy Charlene, locked out again.

"Charlene?" I asked the intercom.

"Yes," she said, giggling.

I buzzed her in, but she kept buzzing back so I put on my used jockstrap and a pair of baggy shorts to hide my erection and ran downstairs. No Charlene but there was a blue-and-white package in the foyer. My guy had been here! I wanted to run after him, but New York streets are filthy and I was shoeless. I figured I'd already lost him anyway, so I scooped up my present and double-timed back up the stairs and into my apartment, closed the door, and ran the deadbolt. I felt the package up. It was round and bumpy. Round and bumpy? And that described what exactly?

A dog collar was the answer. *Interesting. Let's review, Steven. Cock ring, jockstrap, vest, douche, dildo, dog collar.* I looked at the card.

Happy Hanukkah. Be a good boy tonight.

Did he know I was going out? And how did he know my address? That was creepy—restraining order creepy. I sat down on the bed like I'd been pushed. Like I had asked Scott, where was this headed? I better think this through. I decided to make a latte. Coffee always helps me process.

I set the mug on the kitchen counter next to the dog collar. It was human sized. I unsnapped it and laid it out flat across the faux Formica. I ran my fingers down the line of pointy metal studs and debated while I took another sip of coffee. *Oh, why not?* I put it on. The leather was cool and tight against my neck. It felt strange—but strange hot. I went to my mirror. *Woof. I look good all messed up. I should never comb my hair again. Okay, Stevie, let's do this.* On went the cock ring inside the jock. I inserted my arms into the leather vest and looked in the mirror again. *Double woof, dog boy.*

I started masturbating but stopped with a sigh. Hanukkah Harry might not accept such behavior as being good. With another sigh I removed my gifts and pulled on slacks, a sweater, and a jacket. I ran errands to get out of the house and out of reach of my toys. I only came back to shower and dress for my movie with Scott. I considered using the douche—just in case—but decided if anything happened between me and Scott that would definitely *not* be being good. Anyway, Scott Roth's homosexuality was as yet unconfirmed.

At 5:45 I left again to take the subway south to meet Scott at the Astor Plaza station at 6:30 like he told me to. He looked terrific in black and tight. He definitely was more muscular. How had I missed this development? We knuckle-bumped and I followed him to a theater in the East Village. Afterward, I followed him to dinner nearby. I waited until he had ordered our pierogis before I told him.

"A dog collar," I said, apparently again too loudly since the straight couple at the next table looked disconcerted. I lowered my voice. "It was downstairs, in my building."

Scott whistled through his teeth. "Wow. How'd he know the address?"

"Exactly."

"What did you do with it?" he asked. His voice was overly eager but who wouldn't get off on the porn value of my situation?

"I opened it." I mean, what did he think I did with it?

"In the foyer?"

How did he know there was a foyer? There's always a foyer, I told myself. "No, upstairs. In my apartment."

"When?"

Another odd question. "As soon as I got in the door."

He nodded and asked, "Did it fit?" What was this, an interview for the *Times*?

"Perfectly. Size sixteen."

Scott seemed to make a mental note, like he wanted to remember my shirt size for my birthday or something.

Oh, well, let him. Accounting made a lot more money than editorial.

"How did it feel?" he asked, his eyes narrowing.

I remembered how cool and tight the leather was around my neck, how hard and sharp the studs were against my fingers. "Good."

"Good?" he asked, sounding underwhelmed.

"Really good. Really hot," I said, leaning forward to whisper. That answer seemed more satisfactory, although it looked like he had more questions, but I wanted to know more about him since we were on, at minimum, a sort of date so I changed the subject to New Rochelle (where he'd grown up), K-college schooling, and dietary preferences beyond brisket and pierogis. As he gave his answers, I saw I'd probably done a good job in my fantasy of estimating how Scott would look naked. His chest and biceps bulged out of his tight black short-sleeved shirt and, when he got up to use the men's room, his crotch and ass were also bulgy. I began thinking very bad thoughts. I resolved after dinner to go directly home but, after he paid, Scott suggested we have a drink and started walking immediately west. I trotted to catch up. A half block past Broadway on West Fourth we came upon a sex shop—videos, vibrators, and various.

"Can we go in here?" I asked.

"Sure," he agreed, smirking. "What? Not getting enough toys from your mystery man?"

"I may need more lube."

Scott's smirk got bigger.

Inside, I didn't know where to begin, but Scott pointed to the left. "Lube's over there," he said. He was right. Lube, lube, lube, all kinds of lube. "This one's good." He handed me an enormous container. It was the same brand as my little one. "Sounds like you need the giant economy size." He gave me a wink. Damn. If he wasn't gay, neither was my mystery man.

I paid the nice lady at the counter and we were at the Broadway line before I realized he didn't mean drinks as in nearby. I couldn't imagine my lube and I out on the town on a Saturday night. I should get home and practice anyway.

"Maybe we shouldn't," I said.

Scott faced me slowly. He didn't look happy. "Why not?" I held up the plastic bag and he snorted. "Where we're going that will be a feature."

"Where *are* we going?" I asked as I followed him down the subway entrance steps.

"Chelsea," was his one-word reply over his shoulder as his feet sounded a staccato rhythm down the staircase. I watched his body with renewed interest. *Be good, Steve,* I reminded myself, pumping down the stairs after him. We got our MetroCards out just as a Broadway Local pulled in.

"Perfect timing," Scott said, with lots of teeth. *Woof, woof,* I thought to myself.

Scott held onto a strap so I did the same, although there were seats. We passed Twenty-third Street and got off at Twenty-eighth, starting across town. "Where are we going?" I asked again.

"The Eagle," he replied gruffly. Homosexuality confirmed! The Eagle was a famous leather bar. Scott was dressed for it, but I wasn't.

"I left my vest at home," I joked.

"Too bad," he said, giving me a look that took my clothes off. *Be good,* I whispered. *Be good.* "Does it fit?" he asked. More with the fitting.

"Yes. Kind of tight though."

"You should wear it open." It sounded more like a command than a suggestion.

The Eagle was packed, including the sidewalk, but Scott just took hold of my hand and ploughed his way in. People noted my lack of leather with disapproval. I felt *déclassé* until the same people started saying hello to Scott.

"Do you come here a lot?" I asked, but the question was lost in the hub and bub. I asked it again when we reached the bar.

"Sometimes. I like Wednesdays."

"Why?"

"Jockstrap night," he said, moving us to a space along the wall he created with his body and his eyes. He fitted me in next to him. I could feel his warm breath on my face. His lips were so close. It was getting harder and harder to be good.

We drank our beer, talked to some of his friends, had another beer, and then Scott asked me home with him.

"I live close," he added. I thought of how Scott's lips might feel on mine and how good his arm felt around my back, but I also thought of Hanukkah and that stalled my libido. Harry seemed to know I was going out. I looked around the bar. He could be here.

"No," I said quickly before I could say yes.

Strangely, Scott didn't look disappointed. If anything, he seemed pleased. "Oh, right. You have to be a good boy tonight." And then he gave me the sexiest look. It made me shiver. He grinned lopsidedly. "I shouldn't tease you. Another night maybe. If your mystery guy doesn't work out." He gave my butt a squeeze, which made me reconsider my resolve. Scott let me go. "Come on, we'll get you a Lyft back to East Seventy-eighth Street."

"How do you know where I live?" I asked in surprise.

He looked startled for the first time since I'd known him but recovered his cool. "You told me."

"I did?"

"Yes, you did," he said definitely. He punched digits into his phone and announced, "Jason will be here in five. Hope he's not cute."

While Jason—who was not cute—waited, Scott and I stared regrets at each other. He leaned in for a quick kiss and I let him. There was no sustained contact and no tongue, so I figured it didn't qualify as being that bad.

Scott shut the car door for me. I watched him go back inside the Eagle. He was a little bowlegged, which was sexy. Suddenly, everything about Scott was sexy. Somebody would be a lucky dog tonight. At home I put everything on and didn't even try to imagine the dildo wasn't Scott.

The next morning my phone woke me, telling me it was almost eleven. It was Scott, calling me on FaceTime.

"Hey," his voice said, all soft and breathy like he was lying next to me. He looked terrific.

"Hey back at you," I said, smoothing my hair.

"Don't worry," he said. "You look good all messed up." My heart did flip-flops. "So?" he asked, after a few moments of me staring lovingly at him on my iPhone.

"So?" I responded.

"What did you get?"

I jumped out of bed with the phone. "I don't know. I just woke up."

"Oh, dude, I'm sorry. I'll call back. By the way you look great in the jock," he said. I moved the phone back into head and shoulders territory.

"No, that's okay. Hang on. I'll look." I slipped my jeans on and left Scott on the bed. I nearly tripped over the package when I opened the door. I carried it back to Scott, feeling for information along the way.

"It was right outside my door!" I said, holding Scott with my head against my shoulder while I tried to open the package.

"Man!"

"I know."

"What is it?"

I put Scott face up on the bed and tossed blue and white left and right. "It's a leash. Like, a dog leash." I showed it to him.

"Well, at least it coordinates with the dog collar."

"This is no joke, Scott."

"You're right. It isn't," he said solemnly. "Is this freaking you out too much?" I loved it when he got solicitous.

I tried to reassure him and myself. "Hey, after the dildo and the dog collar, it shouldn't, right? The thing is, it means something."

"It *all* means something, Steve."

"I know but a leash? I never thought of that as a gift for humans."

"I know some guys who do," Scott said, laughing deep and real. I loved watching his face, feral eyes crinkling, big white teeth showing between thick red lips. I shook myself and made my lips say something.

"The Eagle, right?"

"There and other places," he said, all mysterious. His *non sequitur* changed the subject. "Your dog's a golden retriever, right?" Huh? Oh, of course he would have seen the photo of my parents and my dog back home in Indiana. It was on my desk at work.

"Right," I agreed, wondering where we were going with this.

"What's his name?"

"Boy."

"Boy?"

I hated telling this story; it made me sound so stupid. "Boy the Second really. When we got Boy the First, my dad said *here boy* so I thought that was the puppy's name." Scott laughed. Such a nice laugh. I thought about all the laughs we'd had last night and about his invitation. Why hadn't I said yes? Damn. A cock in the ass is worth two in the—what?—mail?

"Want to meet for brunch?" he asked in the middle of my self-recrimination.

"Sure!" I said before I could ask myself whether a second date constituted being good. "Shall I come to Chelsea?"

"No," Scott said quickly. "I'll come to you. What's the address?"

"You mean you don't remember?"

"Huh?"

"I told you, right?"

He laughed a little weirdly. "Right."

At one, I buzzed him in and waited on the landing. "You're almost there," I yelled down to him when I saw his dark hair come into view. He looked up, grinning and looking better than a body has a right to. When he reached my landing and stood next to me, he seemed taller than usual.

"You grew."

"Boots," he replied. I looked at his feet. Big clod-stomping boots, my grandfather would say. Engineer boots, Scott corrected him.

On their way down Scott's body, my eyes noticed how good his leather vest looked on him and how enticing the bulge at his crotch was. I lingered along his meaty thighs and calves. After the boots I made my eyes go directly back to Scott's eyes, with no stops along the way. He wiggled his eyebrows and looked around, that little smile on his face. I realized we were still in the hall. "I'm sorry! Come in," I said. "I'll show you my toys."

Spreading them out for him, I started to get aroused. "We better go," I said quickly, standing up.

Scott looked at the bulge in *my* crotch. "I'd sure like to see you in all this," he said in a voice like a growl.

"Scott..."

"Okay, okay. I know you. Help me up." He reached up an arm. I pulled him to his feet, his hard-on landing next to mine. "You sure?" he asked in a low hiss. I wasn't, but I pushed him away anyway.

"Let's eat," I said nervously.

That night I played with myself and my toys for hours. At first, I tried not to think of Scott. I really did. That proved impossible. Butt up, butt down, butt on the side, it was all Scott. I had to take two pills to get to sleep, which meant I woke up late on Monday morning with a grogginess two cups of caffeine didn't eradicate. I sent Amy a text. She sent back an *!* and a *?*. It was ten o'clock when I ran into the office. Everyone stopped what they were doing and watched me approach my desk. I didn't care.

I couldn't believe it. My desk was empty except for a little card. Wasn't this supposed to be the big one? I ignored everyone and tore open the envelope. The card still read *Happy Hanukkah* on the front. Yeah, yeah. I read the message inside.

You remind me of your dog. Same hair color. Come to this address tonight at nine o'clock to get your final Hanukkah present. Wear everything. Bring the leash. Don't forget to douche.

Harry was certainly bossy.

I called Scott and he met me downstairs for coffee. I showed him the card.

"Are you going?" he asked, thick black eyebrows arching.

"I don't know."

"After all this? Don't you want to know who he is?" He sounded exasperated.

"I'm sort of interested in someone else now."

"Do I know him?" He looked jealous. That made me feel all warm inside.

"Yes."

"And you're not going to tell me who he is?" he guessed.

"Absolutely not."

He thought a moment. "You should go," he said in that irritatingly decisive way he had. But I agreed. I would like to know who the guy was. This might be my only chance. After all, this was the last night of Hanukkah.

"Want to have lunch today?" Scott asked.

"No," I told him. "I have an errand to run."

I left work early and took a cab home with my package. I douched extra, extra carefully and took a long shower. Once I was clean inside and out, I put on the cock ring, dirty jock, a clean white T-shirt, and the vest. I slid into ripped jeans and threaded a wide black leather belt through its loops. Then, I pulled on my new engineer boots. I'd bought them at lunch, inspired by Scott's pair. I clicked the dog collar into place around my neck and grabbed my leather jacket.

I took a look at myself in the mirror before I left and thought maybe I'd just stay home. *Go,* my mind yelled so I grabbed the leash and did as I was told.

The Pakistani Lyft driver stopped in front of the address in Chelsea and gave me a final wink in the mirror. He had flirted with me all the way downtown. I declined his offer of contact information regretfully.

Up the stoop and at the door, I checked the apartment number. No name. I buzzed and was buzzed in, no intercom words spoken. That was disconcerting, but I squared my shoulders and walked through the building entrance into the foyer before the buzzing stopped. I took a breath, exhaled deeply, and took another breath before heading up the stairs to Apartment 207.

The door opened before I knocked. I saw a man about my height, dressed in a black leather harness, skintight leather pants, and engineer boots. He was slender but well-muscled. Except for the harness, his torso was bare. His shoulder muscles were tattooed, like epaulets. He wore a biker's cap and dark sunglasses. His skin was pale, pale olive. He was Scott.

"Scott! Shit, man. What the fuck?"

He looked me up and down, ignoring my outburst, and asked in a voice without inflection, "Did you bring the leash?" I held it up in confirmation, unable to speak. My arm was shaking. I knew my voice would quake and quiver even more.

Scott attached the leash to my collar, pulled me into the apartment, and led me to the bedroom where he removed my vest, shirt, boots, and jeans. One finger traced the outline of my erection in his jockstrap.

"My dog's big," he said, looking pleased for the first time. His fingers reached inside the jock and felt for the cock ring. "Good boy," he said, with the smallest of smiles.

I shivered in anticipation.

"I have another present for you," he said. There was no smile now. "It's the eighth night, remember?" I nodded. "Remember?" he snapped.

"Yes, sir," I barked.

"Stay," he said, showing me the flat of his hand before crossing the bedroom to the bureau. He returned with another blue-and-white package. I opened it as quickly as I could, after he gave me the command. Inside the box was a mask, a dog mask. I so did not want to hear what came next.

"Put it on," Scott commanded.

I slipped it over my head, afraid I wouldn't be able to see or breathe but more afraid to disobey. To my relief the eyeholes were large, and the snout had holes for air. I took my first breath inside the mask.

Scott checked it for fit and my comfort. When he was satisfied all was well, he told me to get down on all fours. "You douched, right?" he asked, with a threat in his voice. I started to answer but he jerked on the leash, choking me quiet. "You're a dog now!" he told me emphatically. I barked twice for yes. Scott stroked my back. "Good boy," he said before he inserted the dildo. I clenched in fear. "Relax," he said sternly. I did my best.

Scott slid the dildo all the way in. "You've been practicing," he said, sounding proud. I knew my smile wouldn't show through the mask.

He prodded me several times and then pulled the dildo out. "You're clean," he said. "Good dog," he repeated, patting my head. Behind me, I heard him unzip his leather pants and slide them down his thighs, tear open a package, and put the condom on. I yelped when his fingers inserted lube inside me.

"Quiet!" he said sharply, jerking my head back with the leash. I tried not to make another sound. "Yes," he groaned as he pushed inside me. He was big but, happily, less so than the dildo. He grunted as he began. I yipped in pleasure. I understood now. It had taken eight days—and nights—but I finally understood.

"Happy Hanukkah," he said, licking my ear.

I barked in happiness. What a miracle.

Acknowledgements

Thank you to my first readers for making these stories better: my partner Wayne Goodman, the Algonqueens, and 18th Street Writers.

Thank you to Rob Rosen, editor, author, and friend, for believing in my work and publishing it.

Thank you to Mrs. Sheets, my fourth-grade teacher, who first taught me to be inspired by visuals and to write.

Thank you to Wayne and my friends Gar McVey-Russell and Genanne Walsh for a diversity reading.

A different version of "Eight Days" appeared as "Eight Nights" in *Best Gay Erotica of the Year, Volume 4*, edited by Rob Rosen (Cleis Press, 2018).

About the Author

Richard May's short fiction has been published in his collections *Inhuman Beings: Monsters, Myths, and Science Fiction* and *Ginger Snaps: Photos & Stories* (with photographer David Sweet) and numerous anthologies and literary periodicals. Rick also organizes two book readings at San Francisco bookstores, the Word Week annual literary festival, and the online book club Reading Queer Authors Lost to AIDS. His ancestors are Scottish (on both sides), Choctaw, Shawnee, German, and English. He hopes to honor all of them in his life and work. He lives in San Francisco.

Email: richard.may1313@gmail.com

Facebook: www.facebook.com/richardmaywriter

Twitter: @richardmaywritr

Also Available from NineStar Press

Connect with NineStar Press

www.ninestarpress.com

www.facebook.com/ninestarpress

www.facebook.com/groups/NineStarNiche

www.twitter.com/ninestarpress